ERNEST HAYCOX

ACTION BY NIGHT

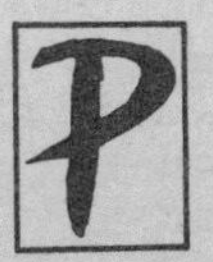

PINNACLE BOOKS
WINDSOR PUBLISHING CORP.

PINNACLE BOOKS

are published by

Windsor Publishing Corp.
475 Park Avenue South
New York, NY 10016

First Pinnacle Books printing: September, 1991

Printed in the United States of America

ACTION SPEAKS LOUDER . . .

"Maybe I didn't make myself plain to you," Tracy Coleman said slowly.

He flung the table aside and sent it crashing to the floor. George Pairvent rose and kicked away the chair; his hand went to his gun.

Coleman came at him. He twisted Pairvent's arm, pinning it back until he yelled and the gun dropped. Coleman knocked it aside with his foot, and dealt Pairvent a blow that sent him reeling against the bunks.

He stepped back. "Have I made myself plain this time?"

ERNEST HAYCOX
IS THE KING OF THE WEST!

Over twenty-five million copies of Ernest Haycox's rip-roaring western adventures have been sold worldwide! For the very finest in straight-shooting western excitement, look for the Pinnacle brand!

RIDERS WEST (17-123-1, $2.95)
by Ernest Haycox
Neel St. Cloud's army of professional gunslicks were fixing to turn Dan Bellew's peaceful town into an outlaw strip. With one blazing gun against a hundred, Bellew found himself fighting for his valley's life—and for his own!

MAN IN THE SADDLE (17-124-X, $2.95)
by Ernest Haycox
The combine drove Owen Merritt from his land, branding him a coward and a killer while forcing him into hiding. But they had made one drastic, fatal mistake: they had forgotten to kill him!

SADDLE AND RIDE (17-085-5, $2.95)
by Ernest Haycox
Clay Morgan had hated cattleman Ben Herendeen since boyhood. Now, with all of Morgan's friends either riding with Big Ben and his murderous vigilantes or running from them, Clay was fixing to put an end to the lifelong blood feud — one way or the other!

"MOVES STEADILY, RELENTLESSLY FORWARD WITH GRIM POWER."
—*THE NEW YORK TIMES*

Available wherever paperbacks are sold, or order direct from the Publisher. Send cover price plus 50¢ per copy for mailing and handling to Pinnacle Books, Dept. 17-504, 475 Park Avenue South, New York, N.Y. 10016. Residents of New York, New Jersey and Pennsylvania must include sales tax. DO NOT SEND CASH.

Contents

1

MOUTH OF THE CANYON

He traveled steadily northward over a land of grass that ran ever onward and faded at last into a farther flatness his eyes could not see; and distance and openness and emptiness were all around him. He crossed rivers turned to dust by the heat of summer and fall and he slept where starlight found him, in buffalo-rutted depressions, in willow coverts where the mourning dove hovered, in endless acres of spice-strong sage whose dry branches rustled before little winds; and sometimes through the night came the wild and far-out murmur of an antelope band running free.

He first saw the mountains as a darkness behind the horizon's haze, three hundred miles away. They grew before him, bold and black and high, and one day the trail which had carried him all the way from Texas entered a canyon and suddenly near sundown he looked behind and saw that the fair and open plain was gone.

The jaws of the mountains had closed upon him and the mountains were around him, rough and old and massively somber from their million centuries of survival. A river ran in its canyon beside the road, and in the canyon was a wind freighted with the coolness of high peaks, with the raw sharp smell of the mountains themselves; and twilight's shadows broke and swirled like fog on the giant knees of the mountains and the echoes of the river ran back through a hollow stillness to re-echo on the sounding boards of unseen canyon walls.

In all this there was a strangeness that stopped him and sent its thready feeling into those places a man keeps his ancient instincts, and his guard rose at once so that he was like a dog bristling at things not known, yet very real. The pressure of the mountain country, its secrecy, its hint of dark-hidden glens, its massive indifference, was upon him. The horizons were gone and the safety of the open land was gone and only the stars above remained familiar. He sat still, keening the smells which were new and the sounds which were different and watching shadows that had a thickness and a motion like nothing in his experience—and then he smiled a small, tight smile and rode on.

A steady growing sound was before him. Half an hour onward he turned a bend and found that the canyon stopped sharp against the barrier of a cliff two hundred feet high. Centered in the cliff was a clear break perhaps forty feet wide out of which came the river with a white turbulence that sparkled through the dark; and into that same break ran the road, upward-climbing. There was a small meadow here, and a roadhouse and a barn and a corral and a man standing in the house's doorway. Above that doorway, on the second floor, was a window at which a woman's face momentarily showed, framed by lamplight. He looked up at her and saw the half-expectant smile on her face just before she drew back.

The man in the doorway said: "If you're lookin' for supper, get down."

Tracy Coleman remained in the saddle. A lamp moved through the lower part of the house so that the man in the doorway was silhouetted, his tub-like fatness, his huge bald head, his round and smooth and sly face. "This Gateway?" asked Coleman.

"Gateway," said the man. "And this," he added, tapping his chest, "is Luke Wall. You're lookin' at the Four-Bit House. A meal is four bits. Lodgin' is four bits. It is a fancy of mine. When I came here, climbin' out of that river like a man would climb out of hell's own fiery pit, I had four bits in my pocket."

He was a talker and talkers were usually fools. But Coleman reserved his judgment, for Luke Wall's conversation was like a screen thrown quickly around other things. As he spoke idly on his eyes searched Coleman.

"Out of that river?" murmured Coleman. "From where?"

"From the same place those fellows started from," said Luke Wall, and pointed into the meadow. Turning, Coleman saw a row of white headboards in the darkness, marking graves side by side. "They came down the river, too. Water's life most anywhere except here. This water is death if it gets at you and it is always tryin' to get at you. I'm the only man that ever ran the Cloud River gorge and lived. Me and my four-bit piece. I was crossin' from Dan Stuart's range to the Horsehead side and the current got me. I'm a thousand years older than I look."

"Horsehead," said Coleman in his same soft and murmuring voice. "How far's that?"

"A day by the road," said Luke Wall. Then a woman called from the house, "Supper's ready," and Luke Wall ceased talking and turned in the doorway to show a big Roman nose and heavy lips against a moon-shaped face.

Down on the plain fall's warm air would be still clinging to the earth; but here a mountain-damp wind blew steadily from the gorge. Stepping from the saddle Coleman noted the three horses already at the rack—a big roan, a little roan with a white star in its forehead, and a buckskin; by habit he put their descriptions in the back of his head. He took his own horse around to a watering trough at the corner of the roadhouse and gave it a short drink and loosened the cinches, meanwhile feeling the presence of some other man or person in the shadows to the rear of the house. That made two people who seemed anxious to see but not be seen. It was part of some kind of story. Coleman took his horse back to the race and stepped into the roadhouse.

Luke Wall sat with one other man at a table in the center of the room; the other man lifted a rust-colored head and placed pale-blue eyes on Coleman with a brief interest. An elderly woman came in with a coffee pot and put it on the table and went away; there was a fireplace at the end of the room and a bright fire burning. Coleman sat down to eat.

The red-haired young man said: "You got the room fixed up, Luke?"

The roadhouse keeper's face was yellow, his eyes round and thick-lidded. He nodded. "But if she's going on through to War Bonnet she won't want to stay overnight here, Ben."

"Maybe—maybe not. When she comes off the stage show her to a room. Then I'll go up and talk to her."

"Show her to the room yourself."

"Never met her before," said Ben.

Luke Wall made a motion with his chin; he was an indifferent spirit buried comfortably within broad layers of flesh. Boots scraped by the front of the house and for a moment Coleman saw a man pause near enough the doorway to be touched by the out-reaching lamplight. His face came around, ruddy and self-content; he took his measure of the three within the room and strolled casually on. Two of the horses, Coleman heard, moved away with him.

The red-headed Ben, his back turned to the doorway, had not seen the man but he heard the horses depart. The expression of trouble was replaced by a wise grin.

"You got odd company around here, Luke."

"So," said Luke Wall.

There was the sound of other horses wheeling rapidly into the meadow and the lifted shout of a driver. "Hup, Queen—hup, Babe!" Excitement made a bright thin shift over Ben's features. "Stage, Luke," he murmured, but did not move. Coleman, having finished his supper, rose and walked through the door. The big roan and the small roan with the star were gone. He flattened his back to the roadhouse wall and pushed up his hat; he rolled a cigarette, watching the sweaty bodices of the stage's four horses turn black when they came into the beam of the house light. The driver jumped down and flung open the stagecoach door. He said, "Thirty minutes for supper," and walked into the roadhouse.

A woman glanced out from the coach door and turned a pair of thoroughly cool eyes on Coleman. He had a cigarette in his fingers at the moment; he dropped it and moved forward, offering his hand. He took part of her weight as she swung lightly down and he heard her brief "Thank you," as he stepped back. She was a dark woman in a dust-gray dress which held her tightly at waist and breast. She wore a small hat with a half veil on a mass of gloss-black hair dropping in a long fall behind her head; her face was small and exact, her features clear. The strong light shining against her made her close her eyes and at the moment Coleman noted the ripe and self-possessed curve of her mouth. She opened her eyes on him; she gave him a straight glance and walked toward Luke Wall who now came from the stage house.

"You'd probably be Valencia Wilder," he said.

Her voice was round and soft and reserved. She could, Coleman thought, handle men as she pleased. "Yes," she said.

"Maybe," suggested Wall, "you might like to fresh-up before eatin'. The room at the top of the stairs."

She nodded and passed Wall. But her mind was not finished with Coleman; when she reached the doorway she turned her head and gave him a deliberate glance and moved into the room, leaving behind her a fragrance and the memory of her skirts' faint rustling. Coleman saw the red-headed Ben standing inside, stiff and still. Ben said nothing to the girl; he followed her with his eyes as she went up the stairs and passed from sight.

Coleman reached for his tobacco and put a cigarette together. He lighted it and he stood with the burning match cupped at his face, fine short wrinkles coming around his eyes. He dropped the match and put his foot on it, drew a long breath of smoke and moved on to his horse. He leaned against the horse and smoked his cigarette half through, remembering how this girl had appeared as she stepped from the coach. The color of her eyes was the color of blue velvet almost black; there was a lot of knowledge in those eyes.

He led the horse to the trough, and on to the corral, removing saddle and bridle. The sound of the river never let up; it was a sledgehammer heartbeat in the chill, damp dark. One streak of motion disturbed the shadows beyond the corral. He looked steadily that way until he saw two people walk slowly side by side along the margin of the river, and he heard the quick soft laughter of a woman. He came back to the roadhouse's front room laid his saddle on a rack and hung up the bridle. The red-headed Ben had disappeared. Luke Wall was in the yard unhitching the stage horses and the driver, who had already bolted his supper, sat back in his chair and gave out a great belch.

Ben Solvay started up the stairs as soon as Valencia Wilder closed the door of her room. He knocked on the door, heard her voice and entered. He left the door open so that she would not be afraid. He removed his hat and he met her eyes and tried to conceal his embarrassment. "I'm Ben Solvay," he said.

He admired her for her self-possessed silence as she studied him. He had expected a plain woman plainly dressed, ill at ease because of the strangeness of the thing they were doing; but she was neat and to his eyes she was beautiful and nothing appeared to trouble her. Even as he found himself gratefully shocked, he knew everything was wrong. The black, still wisdom in her eyes greatly disturbed him.

"I had you pictured differently in my mind," she said. "But I am not disappointed. I was to have met you in War Bonnet. This isn't War Bonnet, is it?"

"Thought I'd ride down and catch you here. War Bonnet's got more people in it—and maybe they'd wonder why

I had to introduce myself to you one day and get married to you the next."

"You're thoughtful. I got that impression from your letters. You can shut the door now."

He closed the door and put his back to it and he remained silent while she appraised him, her head slightly to one side, her glance seeming both sympathetic and critical.

"In none of your letters," she murmured, "did you ever really say how it was you came to know about me."

His partial smile somewhat relieved the flat determination of his plain, square face. All of his character was there for her to see. The honesty she had commented on, the steadiness, the dry practicalness—these were visible to her. He was not a man with secrets beneath him. "Friend of mine came through this country during the summer and told me a story about a fellow who had come to Fort Loring from Arizona to start a ranch and make some money. He made some money and sent back to Arizona for the girl he figured to marry. She came up but the day before she got to Loring he was killed. So she buried him. You were the girl."

He watched her to see if his talk brought back grief to her, but all he saw was the unchanged interest of her eyes. She said: "Was it pity that made you write?"

"It was something my friend said about you. You buried your man and you stood at his grave and didn't cry. But you said this country had cheated you so you'd stay and take your pay from it somehow. I thought about that for a couple months. It stuck in my mind—the kind of a girl you must be. So I wrote."

"I often wondered why you didn't make the trip down to Loring to see me, instead of writing."

She discovered then the most characteristic side of Ben Solvay, his painstaking consideration of all things. "There was no use of my coming down there to take this first man out of your mind. You buried something with him a second man couldn't get. So the second man had to offer something different. Well, you said you'd stay in this country and lick it. That stuck with me. You were a lone woman gamblin' on prospects. So I wrote and offered you my prospects. A letter was best for that. It could say everything straighter than I could talk it to you."

"You were honest. You said all the worst things first."

"I put the prospects as clear as I could. I told you what I've got and what life up here would be like for you. There's only a few women in the Basin. Lonesome country. You'll never starve and you'll never know meanness from me. One thing I can't provide—which is the thing the other man meant to you."

She started to speak, looked at him carefully a moment, and said nothing. Ben Solvay ventured an incomplete smile. "I know my limits. I'm meant to do the ordinary things that have got to be done. You can give me what a man must have if he's to live like a human being. I can give you a way of staying in the country. Maybe that will be enough." Then he added an afterthought which rather startled her with its directness. "And maybe it won't be. This is the turning-back point. You've seen me. It can end right here if you wish."

The suggestion challenged her. "People get old, turning back, and they get nowhere. I want something to show for my life." Once more she placed on him her perceiving glance. "You are disappointed in me."

"I expected less," he said, quite honestly. "I expected somebody plain and practical, somebody used to the straight calico, which is all I've got. You came from better than that. I can tell those things. The bargain would be good for me but bad for you."

"You're wondering what I was and how I came this far from Arizona?"

"You came to marry a man," he said.

She opened her mouth to answer him; and again she stayed the answer and studied him, and at last said: "The past is past. If you have not changed you're mind . . ."

He dipped his head, staring at the floor, and he began to show extra color. He wished her to see no uncertainty in him and he owned a steady man's religious belief in keeping a bargain. This bargain was with a woman and therefore all the more binding; yet he had his uneasy doubts concerning her and, hard-pressed, he came upon a reasonable excuse for delay. "I will not permit you to make up your mind until you have had a long look at me. Ride on to War Bonnet and put up at the Alma House. I'll see you every day for a week. By then you'll know for certain."

She had never lost her sure command of the scene, and now she said quietly: "I understand."

He flushed, now ashamed of his doubts. "You can have no idea what the sight of a woman as beautiful as you are does to a man like me. But if I took advantage of you—a week is short enough time for you to see what you're getting into."

"Take me to supper," she said.

The stage driver stood impatiently and sourly at the doorway when they came down the stairs, and he said: "Don't expect me to wait."

Ben Solvay, having gone through a scene which left him in a poor frame of mind, let go at the driver with his irritated voice. "You'll wait, Jim."

The driver grumbled and left the room. Solvay moved after him, more and more uncomfortable, leaving Valencia Wilder alone with her meal. She stood up to the table and poured herself a cup of coffee and walked to the fireplace as she drank it. Luke Wall made a racket with the fresh horses in the yard and Coleman came into the room, dipping his head at the door. He moved casually on until he was near her. He took off his hat and laid it on the table; he rolled up a smoke. "Going on to War Bonnet?"

"Yes."

He lighted the cigarette, he stared at the bright leap of the fire. Valencia Wilder moved by him to place the empty coffee cup on the table. She stood at the table's end, her back to him; he watched her shoulders lift. She seemed to be looking at the door when she spoke: "That smoke smells good."

He turned and walked to her, looking down at the heavy

shine of the light on her hair. Outside, Luke Wall cursed the horses as he hitched them and the river laid its never-ending drumming over the meadow. "Long ride ahead of you," Coleman said.

"Yes."

She turned her head to him, a shadowed unsmiling repression on her face; her lips stirred and turned still. "Here," he said and held the cigarette to her mouth. She took a slow, indrawn breath of smoke and expelled it. She kept her glance on him. She said in a half voice: "Thanks," and moved to the doorway.

He followed, he watched Ben Solvay hand her into the coach. As the driver swung around the meadow her face showed at the little window of the coach door; she smiled at Solvay and afterwards her glance lifted and came to Coleman, the smile dying. The stage rolled on toward the canyon's mouth.

There were the sound of the river and the sound of the stage; then as the stage left the yard and at once entered the jaws of the gorge the sound of the river absorbed it. Tracy Coleman listened carefully to that change, for the ways of the earth were close to him and each day held its newness and each night its fresh mystery. Ben Solvay stood solemn in the doorway's lamplight. Luke Wall came up from the barn and paused. These three men were silent, ignoring each other, and somewhere a new sound struggled out of the canyon's guttering racket and in another few moments a pair of riders trotted from the canyon, wheeling before the roadhouse.

One man wide and heavy on the saddle, past middle age and showing gray hairs below his hat brim. The house light reached his face and glittered against frosty blue eyes; his voice grabbed Luke Wall and roughly used the tavernkeeper.

"My daughter been here?"

Wall was slow with his answer, as though he were framing it beforehand in his head. The other rider was small and restless; he waited and he listened and his glance roved the yard with steady suspicion. Wall said: "Lately, Dan. But she rode on, sayin' she might be back to put up overnight."

"Anybody else been through here?"

"The stage," said Wall.

The big man looked at the redhead. He said: "What you doing here, Solvay?" Then he turned his eyes to Coleman and, not knowing him, studied him. The small rider, still controlled by his suspicions, left his saddle and strolled along the horse rack, watching the ground. "Three, four, five horses been standin' here."

Wall murmured: "You arguin' with what I said, Tap?"

The little rider straightened around. He didn't answer; he looked up at the big man and the big man answered for him. "Get out of the nettle patch, Luke."

"Take what I tell you or don't ask questions," said Wall.

The big man said: "Whose horse in the corral?"

Tracy Coleman spoke. "Mine."

"I didn't get your name."

"I didn't give it," answered Coleman. He saw the affront plow deep into the other's temper. The big man had the earmarks of a cattle owner all about him, with such a man's accustomed sense of power and unchallenged authority. His broad face showed a vein-netted redness, his broad mouth lay trap-tight as he considered Coleman's implied rebuke. Presently he gave out a grudging admission.

"Your privilege." Then he added a warning. "If I ever see you on my range I'll ask you again and I'll get an answer."

"That may come," said Coleman, straight and idle against the wall. Over at the edge of the meadow the shapes of the two people he had earlier noticed moved discreetly through the blackness and presently disappeared in or behind the barn. A little later one shape came on from the barn, leading a horse, and moved in vaguest outline toward the jaws of the gorge, disappearing.

"Drew Trumbo been down here, Luke?" asked the big man.

Luke Wall shrugged his shoulders. "That wouldn't be my affair, Stuart."

The big man pulled his horse around, said, "Come on," to the little rider with him, and rode toward the gorge. Ben Solvay said: "I'll ride with you," and stepped to the saddle, following. Coleman listened to the sound of these various travelers fade away. Damp wind flowed from the gorge and the mountains were a vast heaving outline against the pale-black sky. One star fell and the light of its millions of years made a scratch on the heavens and died. He said: "Who's the big fellow?"

"Dan Stuart," answered Wall and stepped into the house.

Coleman strolled toward the corral and paused there, watching the dense up-and-down streak of darkness which was the mouth of the gorge. His horse came to the edge of the corral and put its nose through, reaching for him. He went around the corral to the barn and came to a small door, standing open. He stepped through the doorway and took a match from his pocket and struck it on a thumbnail. The bright burst of light fell on the still shape of a woman standing before him.

He killed the light at once, but he had the clearest memory of her face and its alert, half-smiling expression. Her hair was a deep-toned yellow and he remembered how straight she had been standing. He said: "Better stay here a bit. Those fellows might double back and take a second look."

The near melody of laughter was in her voice. "Did they ask for me?"

"The big man did."

"Did he ask about anyone else?"

"The name of Drew Trumbo was mentioned."

There was a horse somewhere in the barn, grinding on its bit. The rank smell of the barn was sweetened with the odor of fresh hay. The girl walked over the packed-dirt floor and her voice held its softly amused tone. "Why would they double back?"

"The oldest trick in the book. Maybe the big man

wouldn't but he had a fellow with him with a sour-milk disposition. That fellow, I judge, is a bloodhound."

"Tap," she murmured, her voice less amused. He swung about, catching the short, sharp tattoo of a horse above the river tone; and saw a single rider come before the stage house, dismount and step inside. The girl's shoulder came beside him. "That's Tap," she murmured. She was tall for a girl, the edge of her shoulder touching him below his shoulder point. "Where," she said, "did you learn about doubling back?"

"I have done it—and it's been done to me."

"If you're on the run," she said, with some doubt and some reserve, "you're in the right country."

Tap came from the roadhouse, got into the saddle and turned back to the gorge. Luke Wall appeared at the house's doorway, a huge block against the light. "I think Tap's gone," said Coleman, "but if I were you I'd still wait a little."

"You went out of your way—but thanks."

"Most of my troubles," he told her, "have come from going out of my way." He left the barn and, keeping well away from the lanes of house light, returned to the roadhouse. Luke Wall watched him come forward, his face Chinese-blank; he stepped aside to let Coleman into the house. Luke Wall's idle voice came after him. "Man that gets tangled in the affairs of the Basin people never is a lucky man. Take Room Three."

Coleman found the room and immediately went to bed. Just before falling asleep he heard the girl's voice downstairs. She was talking to Wall and she was laughing.

2

CAMPFIRE ON THE DESERT

Daylight came across the sky in changing sheets of color. Out on the desert, which was hidden from him by the knees of the hills, sunlight would already be turning the gray soil warm but here in the canyon the shadows hung on and the air was thin and raw and bracing, containing the rich rank odors of the mountains. He lugged his gear to the corral and saddled his horse; he stood by, making up his morning smoke. The horse, fresh with the desire to go, put a cold nose against him and pushed him aside, whereupon Coleman stepped to the saddle, let the horse have its morning buck, and turned to the gorge.

As soon as he entered it twilight settled about him and dampness moved against him, and the roar of the water was a tumult around him. The road lifted gradually from the river and the canyon walls grew higher, now presenting a straight alley, now bending. Below him the river battered against its rocks with a furious energy which had, through the tens of thousands of years, worn this canyon away.

A set of fresh tracks preceded him and these, he judged, marked the girl's trail. He had heard her leave the roadhouse considerably before daylight. Of her he thought a moment or so, visualizing her face and her smile and closely remembering the sound of her voice. Then he put all that from his head, for this was a strange country to him and therefore bore strict watching. All up from Texas he had thus studied the land, so that now he could draw a map upon the ground of each river and creek he had crossed, each hill and pass, each town and roadhouse; he could describe the quality of grass along the trail, the conditions of summer water and winter shelter, the brands of the various trail herds seen. There was this map in his head, filling out day by day. The world was a natural world of weather and grass and beef and of this world he was an attentive scholar. Somewhere far east was another world, in this year of 1878, of which he heard vague rumors; in that world men lived crowded together, worked according to the clock and surrendered their freedom to authority placed above them; and all that made a terrible picture of little souls sweating in an endless treadmill.

At noon the road ran precariously between river and canyon rim, with a thousand feet of space either way. During middle-afternoon he reached a summit and passed through rough hills of pine; near sunset he confronted a rolling plain surrounded on all sides by the black rim of mountains. This was the Basin, a yellow sea of grass cupped high in the hills. The grass plain itself was broken by low ridges, so that he could not command a full view across it. Here and there in the distance he saw cattle and here and there men riding on fall roundup. Far to the left he observed again the slash of the river. Beyond the river was more yellow grazing country backed by timbered mountains.

He cooked bacon and coffee and sat at the edge of timber while sunlight laid golden windrows across the forward land and sank beyond the western escarpments. Twilight lingered longer than seemed natural to a flatlands man. Proceeding through this twilight and on into the dark he sighted the tawny core of a campfire. An hour's riding brought him within a hundred yards of it and here he stopped and sent out his call. "Hello, camp."

He received no immediate answer. Shapes of men sat backed against the firelight and one shape slowly rose and slowly turned. A chuck wagon stood near the fire, half a dozen horses were on picket close by. Farther out on the plain lay the bulk of other horses. A voice came to him at last, noncommittal and grudging: "Come in."

He rode in, even then with a guard lifted against the rank and hostile quality of that voice. Four men lay close to the fire, now turning to look upon him, and one other man stood above the fire. On that long lank one he placed his attention, on the loose and dusty clothes hanging to a scarecrow frame, on the thin neck and the narrow wedge of a face with its little flat ears and its dust-reddened eyes. He surveyed Coleman with a dry and scheming expression, with steady suspicion. He said, with ungracious hospitality: "Light. Beans left in the pot."

"Had supper," said Coleman. He dropped to the ground and he built a smoke and seemed thoroughly preoccupied by it, but was not. He was seeing the crew, the young boy with the matted hair, the older one with the faded, leaf-brown cheeks, the one whose brilliantly green eyes sparkled above half a beard, the chunky-shouldered man smoking a pipe. This last one idly poked a sage stem into the fire and solemnly ignored Coleman. There wasn't any sweetness in the outfit; it didn't hang together. There wasn't any story-teller to soften up rankling dispositions at the end of a hard day, there wasn't any easiness or fun. They sat still, self-wrapped in private thoughts, alert to trouble, sullen toward him.

"What range am I on?" Coleman asked.

It was the old one with the brown-parched skin who finally said: "Horsehead."

Coleman licked his cigarette and lighted it. The sour man standing at the fire would be the foreman. He threw the match into the flame and relaxed on an elbow. "Pretty stars," he murmured. "This a Horsehead crew?"

The foreman shifted his long feet and spoke at last. "Horsehead crew and no job open if that's whut you're after."

"Maybe I wouldn't like it here anyway," murmured Coleman. "Country's colder than Texas. Kind of crowded in by mountains."

The young boy with the head of tangled hair showed a youth's sudden intolerance of criticism. "Whut the hell keeps you here if you don't like it?"

"That," said Coleman, still soft, "is scarcely your business, son."

The boy showed his teeth in callow contempt. "Big mouth," he said.

He was directly next to Coleman, seated on his blanket three feet away. Coleman bent, drew his arm across his chest and swept it over the distance. His open palm chopped the boy's open mouth with a full-length swing that sent the other backward, stunned and yelling; in another moment the youngster rolled like a cat, sprang up and retreated toward the fire. He stepped into the fire and ducked sidewise, spreading his legs apart. His long hair hung down over his eyes and anger shook his arm when he pointed it at Coleman. "I'll blow your guts—"

Coleman used his voice as he had used his hand. "You're a fool standin' against that light, boy. Shut up."

The boy stood still. He let his arm fall slowly against his side. He kept his feet apart and then he drew a hand over his mouth. He stood futile in the light, a mass of humiliation, with insufficient bottom to go through with what he had started. Nobody else had taken up the quarrel. The lank foreman continued to watch. The man with the beefy shoulders slightly turned, showing a face whose left side had been plowed by a bullet. That one, Coleman judged, had danger in him.

A rider moved rapidly in from the night, his voice coming on. "Pairvent." He brought his horse to a standstill within the round circle of the fire and said again, "George." The horse fiddled in the dust and circled around; when the rider faced the light again Coleman recognized him as the man who had been at Gateway, spooking in the night. Coleman remembered the name Dan Stuart had used. Drew Trumbo—that was his name.

Pairvent, the foreman, went around the fire until he stood near Trumbo. Trumbo said: "We're cleaned up on Stuart's and my range. You through here?"

"All through."

"Tomorrow the main roundup will finish Gunderson's west side, near town. Then we're through. The owners will be meetin' in War Bonnet. Be there around nine o'clock in the mornin'."

He had, on first approach, cast one incurious glance at the group; and now cast another and discovered Coleman. His face showed a break of recognition and for a moment he seemed inclined to speak to Coleman. Then he thought better of it and moved out upon the prairie. Beyond the firelight he halted, calling back. "One more thing, George." Pairvent followed him, these two parleying in the dark. The heavy-shouldered puncher again began to stab the fire with his sage stem and the young lad slowly came back to his blankets and saddle, gathered them and moved around to the far side of the blaze. Drew Trumbo set his horse into quick motion, scudding away. Pairvent returned slowly into the light, his glance reaching for Coleman. He stopped near Coleman, looking down. Suspicion was a pinpoint of light in his recessed eyes.

"Pairvent?" murmured Coleman. "George Pairvent of Horsehead?"

Distrust freshened in Pairvent and he backed away until he had the fire on his left elbow. He stood still, his gathered muscles straining his bony body. "That's right," he said, rustling the words in his throat.

Coleman lifted a hand to the breast pocket of his coat and pulled out a letter. He rocked forward and extended the letter the full length of his arm. "Yours," he said.

Pairvent shoved a guarded question at him. "Where you from?"

"Texas."

The string-shaped foreman seized the letter. He drew away watching Coleman as he opened it; and even then he grudged the necessity of taking his eyes from Coleman, reading and looking up and reading again. The chunky puncher with the sage stem watched this with a growing interest. He smelled something, and the others smelled something; they were all alert.

Pairvent folded the letter together and held it over the flame. Coleman said at once: "That will change nothing. I'll keep it."

Pairvent dropped the letter on the ground. The corners of his mouth formed deep angles. "Ray," he said to the chunky puncher with the sage stem, "take the outfit back home at daylight." He circled the chuck wagon and got his horse from picket and rode again to the fire. He sat on the saddle, long looking at Coleman. Then he said: "We'll see," and swung about, galloping away.

The chunky Ray tossed the sage stem into the fire. He had a broad face and a chin built for battle; he was a big-lipped, deliberate man with his eyes so near shut that he seemed to be smiling. He looked over at Coleman, evidently full of speculation. He yawned and used his boot to shove the dying coals of the fire together. "Like poker with the deuces wild," he murmured.

Nobody answered him; he sat crouched over, staring at the fire and deeply involved in his thoughts. Coleman rose and unsaddled his horse and led it out on the grass, driving down a picket pin. He came back, made up his bed from the saddle and the saddle blanket, and settled to rest. The stars were fully showing, the air was sharp and strong-scented. Near sleep he saw Ray still dreaming before the fire.

At daybreak the Horsehead crew turned west to the river while Coleman lined out northward toward War Bonnet over a beautiful land of rolling grass separated by ridges into independent valleys. He passed over one valley, rose through scented crests of pine, and entered another valley, until at last he saw before him the great wall of mountains which closed in the Basin. The river curved at the foot of the wall; and here, beside the river and against the mountain's sharp slopes, lay War Bonnet, the east-facing windows of its two dozen buildings aflash with morning's strong sunlight.

He saw only a few people abroad on the street as he passed stable and saloon and store and blacksmith shop and headed into a rack before the narrow front of a restaurant. He had eaten breakfast at the Horsehead chuck wagon; now after two hours' riding he was hungry again, and so entered the restaurant and sat up to a second breakfast and permitted himself to idle over his coffee—a man taller than the average rider, heavier of bone and more solid in chest and arm. Constant riding had trimmed him lean; exposure to rain and sun and cold and dust had built within him a reserve of vitality—and the vitality showed. On his body were the marks of his trade in the shape of broken bones, and here and there a white scar from some encounter or another with cattle or horses or men. Never in his life had he known real shelter or comfort, never had he felt complete security; and therefore in him lived a philosophy of accepting the little moments of rest and pleasure whenever they came, against the greater times of trouble, against nights when there would be no sleep, against the sudden climaxes which, though unseen ahead of him, were nevertheless stationed along his career as inevitably as the days on a calendar. Uncertainty was a star shining over him, guiding him into strange ways, and because of that uncertainty he had learned never to make long plans, never to harbor fear of the future and never to sleep with a memory of the past.

He finished his coffee and bought a tinder-dry cigar; and stood in the restaurant's doorway with the fragrance of the cigar cloudy around his face. He had a head of black hair and a pair of eyes half between violet and powder-gray over-hung by black brows. His nose was long and his mouth heavy and his skin, with all its weathering, was fair and unwrinkled. He stood and walked as though there were no hurry or strain in him and when he smiled he seemed careless and unthinking; otherwise, in repose, his face had a faint melancholy shadow upon it.

Loitering there, he saw riders move out of the yonder yellow grass and come fast inward, singly, in pairs, in groups; and presently the town took on life. He recognized Dan Stuart and Tap as they arrived and later noticed Drew Trumbo come in alone. All these men were owners or foremen. Coleman could sort them out as precisely as he could sort out brands of cattle at a loading pen; an owner always had an air. Most of them pulled in by the saloon and entered for a drink, afterwards walking on to the hotel. Somewhat later Coleman observed George Pairvent come to the saloon's doorway and stand there. Coleman put away in his head the fact that Pairvent did not join the owners of the hotel.

It was then a little after nine o'clock and sunlight and street dust made a silk-silver haze against the day. Ben Solvay came from a back quarter of town and racked before the hotel. He stood a moment on the street, smoking a cigarette thoughtfully; he saw Coleman and his eyes briefly acknowledged Coleman. Casting away his cigarette with a definite gesture, as though his mind had been made up, he entered the Alma Hotel. Coleman had not finished his cigar. He dropped it and ground it beneath a foot and moved upon the Alma. As he reached its doors he heard another horse run fast in from the desert and turned to see Dan Stuart's daughter step from her horse before it had entirely stopped.

Coleman, directly before her, lifted his hat. Her glance came to him, showing slight surprise. "You're here," she murmured, and gave him a thoughtful inspection. The spirit of this girl was light and quick and the edge of a smile stood at the corners of her mouth even when she was grave. She said, "You're taller than you seemed last night," and walked on to the store. Coleman noticed how carefully George Pairvent watched this scene from the saloon. He remembered that as he entered the Alma.

The cattlemen were in the dining room beyond the lobby, somebody's voice laying its heavy weight upon the group. Coleman noticed Valencia Wilder in a corner chair, as composed as she had been at Gateway. Ben Solvay stood before her with his hat in his hand, soberly talking. Even as Solvay talked her glance came away from him and met Coleman's eyes; after he reached the dining room's doorway she still watched him.

Coleman saw that it was Dan Stuart who was standing at the end of the dining room and flinging his naturally aggressive voice toward the rest of the group. There were a dozen men here, bunched up in two groups at opposite sides of the room, like the division of a standing vote—side equally against side. He would have speculated on this had not Dan Stuart, seeing him, thrown out a warning.

"You're in the wrong place," he said. "This is a cattlemen's meetin'."

"I'm in the right place," said Coleman.

"Representin' what outfit?"

"Horsehead," answered Coleman.

Change came over the room like sundown's cool wind. Dan Stuart shook his head with an irritated impatience. Tap stared. He made a pushing gesture at Coleman with his hand; he started toward Coleman. Drew Trumbo, handsome in his flushed way, covertly watched.

Stuart said: "George Pairvent represents Horsehead."

"A question occurs naturally to me," remarked Coleman. "If he does, what's he doin' at the saloon instead of here?"

"That's something else," said Stuart and closed his big jaws like a trap.

"Maybe," agreed Coleman and took from his pocket the same letter he had earlier shown Pairvent. "And it also may be he once represented Horsehead. He no longer does."

He opened the letter, feeling weight behind him; he looked about and saw Ben Solvay at the doorway and in the lobby he noticed Stuart's daughter, and other men now collecting. They were all listening. "I'll just read this," he said.

To George Pairvent and the Basin:—

It has come to my attention the last three years that

my ranch on Horsehead lacks management. I further feel, from information now and then coming down the trail, that Horsehead has acquired a poor reputation.

Being an old man, I cannot personally come up to set things aright. Nor have I sons to send. I am therefore putting Horsehead in the hands of the best of my foremen, Tracy Coleman, to do with it as he wishes and in whatever manner he wishes. From this notice forward Tracy Coleman may be considered to be the owner.

To all my old friends in the Basin, and particularly to Frank DeLeon if he's still alive, my best howdy. And to all of them, so long. The riding was fun and the world was fine. Now I'm an old dog crawling into a thicket to die.

BEN-TIM HOWLETT

"Why," said somebody, "old Ben-Tim remembers me," and looking up Coleman saw an older man run a hand across a pure-white set of mustaches. "We were the first in the country, Ben-Tim and me. But Ben-Tim always liked Texas best. So he went back."

This was the only remark, this touched recollection of an old-timer who was apparently Frank DeLeon. Otherwise the cool current ran strong against Tracy Coleman. He felt it push at him; he felt his aloneness. He folded the letter and returned it to his pocket. "I'm representing Horsehead."

Dan Stuart shook his head. "Go back and tell Ben-Tim he let Horsehead go too long. Tell him the Basin respects a man's rights to a piece of range so long as he uses that range for beef, no longer. Tell him he ran it from a distance too long and that now he's got nothing to put on that grass, while other men here with plenty of beef are cryin' for grass. It was free range when he came here and it is still free range today. But free range is only for the man that can show good use of it. Tell him he's no longer got it. And he can't give you somethin' he hasn't got. The Basin will split that grass among the men here. Go back and tell him that."

"How," asked Tracy Coleman, "do you propose to split it?"

He thought then he knew what put these men into their two separate groups; the question fell into a silence and the silence remained, and he saw Dan Stuart look slowly around him and he saw Drew Trumbo's face take on an odd expression, and the coldness which had flowed so steadily against him seemed now to swirl among them all. They had decided to break up Horsehead, but each man was scheming for Horsehead.

"That," said Dan Stuart, "comes later. You're in the wrong game. Ride on."

Coleman put both hands in his pockets and looked above the group, beyond them to a window. Out through the window he saw white clouds bright in the sunshine, and the ragged pine crests of the hills. Each day brought its troubles and a man seldom had a warning; sometimes he had to make an answer on the fall of the moment and to hold to that answer until the sky fell in.

"It was a long ride up the trail," he said, "and it would be a longer ride back. I came to take over Horsehead, and that I will do. As long as one Horsehead cow walks on that grass it remains Horsehead grass. If there is no cow to eat it I will turn my horse upon it. If I lose my horse I'll stand on that grass with my own two legs and claim it."

Dan Stuart, unaccustomed to resistance, shouted back. "The moment you set foot on Horsehead we will regard you as an outlaw, to be treated as such!" Then, because he was a man with a powerful temper and a will that would not be crossed, he permitted himself a further, unguarded statement. "You'll be joinin' the rest of the outlaws already there."

The cavalry-mustached Frank DeLeon said immediately: "I'd let that remark die, Dan."

Dan Stuart may have regretted the remark, but he growled, "Let it stand. Stay off Horsehead, Coleman. Otherwise the shape of a tree and the shape of a rope starts walkin' with you."

Coleman did a strange thing. He smiled, and the smile roughened his face and mildness went out of him. "It would be better if you shot me down than to let me leave the hotel. If you open a war on me there'll be fewer of us here at the next meetin'. I will be at Horsehead Ranch by noon today. That man among you who sets the dogs on me—that man I will personally hunt down and destroy, unless he gets at me first. I do not believe in beginnin' trouble but if there is to be trouble I do not believe in mercy." He turned and walked from the room.

3

ON HORSEHEAD

Crossing through a lobby half-filled with townsmen and riders, Coleman noticed Dan Stuart's daughter, all the liveliness gone from her. One man loitered in the doorway, so engrossed that he made no attempt to step aside. Coleman paused, waiting; the man made no move, and suddenly Coleman thrust him aside with his arm and left the lobby.

Pairvent was still near the saloon. Coleman turned along the loose boardwalk and came upon him. Pairvent never took his suspecting eyes away; now, as on the night before, he drew his thin muscles together and made himself ready for the trouble he never ceased to expect.

"Last night," Coleman said, "you left camp on the run. You figured to get yourself some help. Who'd you think would help you? You've got no friends in that owners' crowd."

Pairvent's answer was a dry rustle. "You think so?"

The ranch owners and their foremen came from the Alma, drifting to the horse racks, moving toward the saloon. Pairvent's glance went to these men, searching them with a hard care; and as he stood there, lank and strained like an animal undecided on attack or flight, he seemed to keen the very air of town for an answer. Stuart and Tap left

War Bonnet in a run that raised little rolls of dust behind and other men walked by Coleman into the saloon. Drew Trumbo crossed the street afoot, cast a quick glance at Pairvent, and went down a small alley.

All during the last hour Coleman had turned the problem of Pairvent through his mind; and it was that quick glance between the men—as revealing as speech—which made answer for him. He knew then what he must do. "Go back to Horsehead," he said to Pairvent. "I want to talk to you."

Pairvent, suspicious of every living thing, stared long at Coleman; and at last he gave a curt nod and walked into the saloon. Coleman turned back to his horse before the Alma. Ben Solvay waited there for him, and said: "Like to see you for just a moment," and beckoned him into the hotel.

The crowd had left the lobby. Valencia Wilder still sat in the corner chair, quiet and small, but disturbing the air of the room by her presence. She watched Coleman come up and as he stood above her he noticed again the smoothness of her body within her dress, the richness of her lips, the odd and still light of knowledge in her eyes.

"This," said Ben Solvay, "is Valencia Wilder. And this man's name is Coleman."

Coleman removed his hat before her. He met the steady onset of her glance while Solvay went on with his dry, practical conversation. "I heard you were takin' over Horsehead. It is a nice house down there and an old Mexican woman who keeps care of it—brought up long time ago by Ben-Tim Howlett." He paused a moment, collecting his words carefully. "We expect to be married, but not for a week or so. This hotel is no particular place for a woman to stay. Tonight bein' payday the town will be full of drunks. Horsehead is a fine place and the Mexican woman makes it proper enough. Maybe you'd take Miss Wilder to Horsehead and let her put up there as long as may be. It will relieve my mind."

Coleman studied Ben Solvay until the latter showed a

trace of embarrassment. Coleman was smiling. "My friend," he said, "you must sleep sound at night."

The mind of Ben Solvay was entirely practical. "Sure," he said, "but what's that got to do with this?"

It was impossible for him to know if Valencia Wilder had been earlier aware of Solvay's idea. She continued to watch him and she was silently saying something to him, her eyes widening into a full glance.

"My pleasure," Coleman said, directly to her, "if it seems suitable to you."

"I'll get a buckboard," Solvay murmured, and immediately left the hotel.

Coleman took the time to build a cigarette. His lips were thick at the centers and when he swiped the cigarette with his tongue his teeth struck a white flash against the tan of his skin. His cheekbones made flat weights high on his face. He lighted the cigarette and looked at her. "His idea?"

"Perhaps so." She watched his eyes throughout a continuing silence, and then for the first time her directness wavered and she dropped her glance. "Let's not start that way," she murmured.

Solvay returned and took up her small leather trunk from the floor and lugged it through the doorway. Rising, Valencia Wilder made a little gesture with her hands. She moved across the lobby before him and, near the door, turned around. "You're alone—and the rest of the country's against you."

"I am usually alone," he said.

"People," she said, "will try to get at you and break you. I know about that. They have tried it against me. People are dogs. I hope you fight them."

The features of the girl lighted with spirit. He was surprised at her strong talk but he liked her better for what he had seen; she stood for something. He took her arm and escorted her to the buckboard and gave her a hand up. Ben Solvay climbed to the seat, said, "See you on Horsehead," and put the team down the street at a trot.

Other riders made their departure, leaving War Bonnet

half-empty. Coleman stepped to his saddle and turned out on the trail of the buckboard. Pairvent was no longer before the saloon but as Coleman put the street behind him he looked about and saw Horsehead's ex-foreman step from a shed on the rear side of town, toward which Drew Trumbo had earlier gone. Little pieces of information like this, patiently accumulated, at last made up a story. The buckboard traveled southwest under bright sunlight, following two ruts which formed the road. The ranchers who had left town now were fading into the grasslands in all directions before Coleman. Deeper south he saw the blur of cattle trailing away.

Ann Stuart was in Mary van Hogh's dressmaking shop when Trumbo cut down the alley; she saw him, and later noticed Pairvent drift in the same direction. She had been talking to Mary van Hogh about a dress and as she talked she had her troubled guess as to what would be happening. The politics of the Basin were an old story to her, made up of jealousy and greed and intrigue; and in this her father played the greater part. She had not thought Trumbo would follow their pattern.

Later she observed Pairvent return from the rear of town. She made her excuses to Mary van Hogh, left the shop and threaded the alley to the back end of Morphy's abandoned store. A board wall ran to either side of the store's rear yard and thus formed a shelter; in a little while Trumbo came into the boarded compound.

"I thought you might come," he said.

He had a good smile and he had a way of showing how much he liked these casual meetings. It warmed her throughout to see the appreciation in his eyes and for a moment she forgot about Pairvent. Drew came before her, looking down with his wish in his eyes, making her desirable by the things he expressed in his glance. Long lonely and knowing almost nothing of sympathy or affection from others, she waited for these moments and treasured them; and of late had been permitting herself half hopes.

"I wish," he said, "I could ride up to your front door like a gentleman."

"My father would furnish the reception." She shrugged her shoulders. "I wish there was some way of making him gentler on people, hating less." She had another thought. "Is there any particular reason, any personal reason, why he dislikes you?"

"Maybe I just settled too close to his range. What he sees he wants—and maybe he wants my small outfit. Let it pass."

"Nothing like that passes. Somebody's got to fix it. I haven't had much luck."

He gave her a keener glance. "Don't you and your father get along all right?"

She had a great deal of pride and she had never spoken of her relations with her father to any other soul. She would not now. "Private affairs are private, Drew."

He laughed the rebuke aside. "When and where will we meet again?"

"On Star Cross Ridge some morning, I suppose. Drew, why are you meeting Pairvent?"

The question caught him off balance and he had no ready answer. He looked at her with a completely expressionless face. He said slowly, "Did I meet him?" Then he knew this was the wrong answer and corrected it. "George has got his troubles, the Basin tryin' to cut Horsehead from under him. Comes to me for advice now and then."

"Keep out of sagebrush politics and just plug along with your own ranch. Don't ever get tied up with the owners. The Basin changes almost everybody. You must not let it change you. You stay an honest man."

"Honest," he said, and laughed again. "Honest and poor."

"Better that way," she answered and watched the personal, wanting expression come to his face again. He had only once tried to kiss her and she had not let him, being sure neither of herself nor of him. Since that time he had held his distance but she knew he would someday try again, and she wondered, when that time came, what she would do.

He had a streak of humor, sharp and sometimes self-ridiculing, which pleased her. He said suddenly: "What dark thoughts are runnin' through your head now?"

She smiled back. "Whether to have the next dress blue or brown. See you soon." She turned out of the alley, reached her horse and went out of town at a full gallop. Departing horsemen made dots on the desert. Nearer, idly jogging along the Gateway road, she saw the new man, Tracy Coleman; her thoughts went to him easily and at once.

Riding southwest over the plain, Coleman thought of Ben-Tim Howlett's final instructions and advice, delivered from the porch of the Texas ranch house. "My time to die," Ben-Tim had said, "has come and I want my ledgers clean before I go. If I'd ever had a son, Tracy, I'd been pleased to have had him like you. And if my son was a-standin' in your shoes this minute I'd be thinkin' of the worst chore I could give him. It's the tough things that are good for men, not the easy ones. So I'm sendin' you up to the Basin. Somethin's wrong there. Horsehead is your ranch—if you can hold it."

He recalled how Ben-Tim's weather-etched face had turned reminiscent. "I was the first cattleman in that country and I took the best chunk of range. I held it against the worst pirates you ever saw. Some are still there and now they're thinkin' Ben-Tim's old and has got no right to grass he don't walk on. An absentee owner is always fair game for the neighbors. If Frank DeLeon is still alive, give him my love. But watch Dan Stuart. He always wanted to be king and he'll skin you and dry your hide if he can. Maybe you can make it, maybe not. Still, you're like me. The fun of it is the tryin' and the cryin' and the laughin'. That's all the fun there is, I think."

Ben-Tim, sitting so old and tired in his chair, hadn't shaken hands. He had added: "I recall when you first came to work for me, as wild a lad as ever I saw. You have settled considerable but still you're smellin' the breeze. There is somethin' you want. I don't guess you know what it is, but if you are ever to be a steady man you will have to go out and find it. Otherwise you will be the sour and restless kind." Then old Ben-Tim had turned his eyes away and his voice had grown rough. "Well, son, go find it. Good-by."

Ben-Tim had been as much of a father as he had known and that parting had been tough; for they both knew they would not see each other again.

The prairie's steady, grass-yellow undulations were before him, broken by low hills to east and south. Around ten in the morning the prairie came upon the river at a low bluff and the trail dropped to water running shallow over a gravel bar. The river was mountain-cold, its undertow deceptive. After he crossed over he stopped a moment, hearing the low thrum of the current below him as it passed into a deeper canyon and began its tumultuous run for Gateway, twenty miles away and five thousand feet lower. This ford, he guessed, was the only practical crossing in the heart of the Basin. Below and above it the mountains formed deep canyons.

As he climbed the farther bluff he saw the buckboard wheeling southwest toward a pine ridge ten miles away, and here he had a first good look at the fair, rolling grass of Horsehead Range, cupped in the great hills; and the memory of Ben-Tim's face, mirroring the fun and the danger of his eighty years, came vividly to Tracy Coleman. His own beliefs and desires were the same. Life was freedom and action, and even its bitterest moments were great. A man was made to sweat and cry and laugh; otherwise he grew small and his spirit shriveled and the vital juice went out of him, leaving him a shadow upon the greatness of the earth.

The buckboard vanished inside a grove of pines which ran down from the southwestern ridge. The road gradually carried him into this grove and he saw Horsehead's ranch quarters lying in the mottled shade and sunlight of the pines—the long low house, the bunkhouse and corrals and sheds spread around it. Back of these quarters the trees of the ridge rose away rank upon rank and the day's warm air brought a strong resin smell into the yard. One man stood by the bunkhouse, watching the yard—the lank kid whom he had slapped to the ground the previous night. Solvay stood on the porch with Valencia Wilder. Beside them was a small, dark and elderly woman with a knot of black hair and a placid face.

Solvay said: "Ben-Tim brought Doña Gertrude up with a Mexican crew, some years ago. Her husband was in the crew but he died."

"I know," said Coleman and turned to her, speaking in Spanish. "Don Ben-Tim asked me to say that he is an old man and will never see you again, Doña Gertrude, but that he remembers you."

The woman's eyes grew liquid and light. "Did he say how he remembered me, Señor?"

"With affection."

The Señora sighed. Memories stirred her and she shrugged her shoulders and recaptured her placid expression. "I am old, too, I should like to see Don Ben-Tim again so that we might laugh together before we die. He was a laughing man." She showed a spark of old coquetry, as though she wished Coleman to understand the liveliness of her younger years. "He was gallant, that Ben-Tim. You are here now in this house?"

"I am in this house now," answered Coleman and told her his name.

"You will have the bedroom on the right," said Doña Gertrude. She cast a glance at Valencia Wilder. "She will be in that room, too?"

"Señorita Wilder is a guest."

"Ah," said Doña Gertrude, "then the room across the hall." She divided a quick glance between man and woman and a smile lay behind the glance and she seemed pleased as she said in English, "Señorita, I will show you the room." Valencia Wilder followed her into the house.

"It will just be for a short while," said Ben Solvay. "And thanks."

"What's your name?" asked Coleman. Solvay told him and offered his hand. Coleman shook it, giving Solvay a thorough looking-over. This man was pretty much as he appeared on the surface, square and not easily stampeded. He had a grip to his jaw and practical blue eyes. "Ben," said Coleman, "you heard the talk in the hotel. That makes this ranch a pretty poor risk for a woman."

Solvay had already thought of that possibility. "They'll think it over for a week before they move. It'll take that long for those fellows to agree. Not that you won't have trouble, later. You will."

Coleman said: "They were in two groups, one on each side of the room. What ran between those two groups, Ben?"

"The river," answered Solvay. "Stuart and Bill Yell and Tabor and Gunderson, and some others, all graze the other side of the river. The rest live on this side. Frank DeLeon's north of you and Clyde Medary north of you. Back of you, south, is Hoby Spade. The river does it."

"Where's Trumbo?"

Solvay studied his answer before giving it. "Just across the ford and to the south. A small outfit." Then he added in a reserved voice: "You see things quick."

"Who's that other girl, Ben?"

"Ann Stuart," said Ben Solvay and looked at the doorway through which Valencia Wilder had gone. He had a desire to see her and suddenly he reached down and lifted her trunk and went into the house. Coleman heard the two talking and in a moment Doña Gertrude came out and stood silently at the doorway. The long, black-haired kid loafed in the sunshine near the bunkhouse, his insolence traveling the entire length of the yard.

Ben Solvay returned, showing some confusion, as though he had permitted himself unsure emotions. He jammed on his hat, said "See you later," and rode immediately away. Doña Gertrude, Coleman noticed, looked upon the departing Solvay with disfavor; she was a woman of the old school, loyal to her ranch and everything upon it. So

now she murmured: "Your woman, Don Tracy, or his?"
"His," said Coleman.
The woman's eyes looked upon Coleman with wisdom. "What a fool he is then to leave here here."
"She is safe on this place."
She gave Coleman a placid smile and a lift of her brows. "Safe is a dull word to a woman and not a word used by Texans."
Out on the flat, meanwhile, had been the palpitation of a horse's running. Looking about he saw a rider coming in, gaunt and long-legged on the saddle. "That man you must watch," said Doña Gertrude, and walked into the house.
Fifty feet from the porch, George Pairvent pulled his horse to a stop and stood stiff on the stirrups, both hands flattened to the horn, watching Coleman with his never-trusting eyes.
"Get down for a talk," said Coleman. He observed the quick way Pairvent left the saddle and kept himself in position to meet trouble. The foreman advanced to a porch post and laid the point of a shoulder against it. He was, even in that relaxed attitude, ready to jump. Coleman sat down in one of the rocking chairs. He tipped himself idly back and forth. "Little late getting here, George."
"Had things to clean up in War Bonnet."
"Have a good talk with Trumbo?"
Pairvent's eyes widened somewhat. He didn't answer.
"George," said Coleman, "it is time to be honest. What kind of an outfit you been running here? I heard something said this morning about this being an outlaw bunch."
"Man can always hear talk."
"How much beef we got?"
"Don't know. Two thousand, maybe."
"Where's the rest gone?"
Pairvent delayed his answer a long while, finally saying: "Ask the fellow that called us an outlaw outfit. Everybody wants Horsehead. It has got no friends. You listening to people who're not friends?"
"Trumbo," said Coleman, "seems your friend."

Pairvent again hesitated, meanwhile searching Coleman's expression. "Maybe I have made my arrangements with him from time to time," he admitted. "I have had to tie up where I could. Horsehead has got to do the best it can. But we're talkin' too much. Say what's on your mind."

"You have been boss and foreman here. I'm the owner now. You stay on as foreman."

Pairvent now relaxed sufficiently to make himself a cigarette. A gray shine of satisfaction showed on the slate surface of his eyes. "I see you been doin' some thinkin'. You know this crew walks out on my say-so. You know you can't get another crew."

"So," said Coleman, "you stay on as foreman."

Pairvent drew in a deep breath of smoke, expelled it. "All right," he said and left the porch, leading his horse back toward the bunkhouse. He had won a point and his attitude reflected it.

Turning into the house, Coleman came to a living room and a small desk. There was a pencil-drawn map tacked to the wall and, standing before it, Coleman saw the lines of Horsehead Range as Ben-Tim Howlett had sketched it years before, the areas of the other outfits also indicated. Coleman took time to memorize those boundaries.

At sundown the easy wind came with a high mountain chill strange to his Texas blood; and from the porch of the house he watched the colors of the land run and change along horizon and high peak and timber-blackened draw. The supper bell rang once, its round-shaped echo striking out and on through the land's great stillness. He went back through the house to the dining room. The crew had already gathered and Doña Gertrude sat at the foot of the table, dark and still—and waiting; and this same sense of waiting was with the crew. Looking about him, he knew at once what they waited for. The seat of authority on any ranch was at the head of the table. George Pairvent sat there, usurping a place he no longer rated.

Valencia Wilder came in. Coleman drew back a chair for

her, but as she came to it he touched her and stopped her, and then he looked at the crew and at Pairvent. "Stand up," he said.

Pairvent stopped his coffee cup halfway to his mouth. He braced himself for trouble; he had planned for it and now waited for it. Yet he had not planned for it to come this way and as he looked at Valencia Wilder the surly, eager light in his eyes lessened and he put down his cup and silently rose. Taking cue from him, the rest of the crew likewise rose. Valencia Wilder took her place beside Coleman. The Mexican woman watched Coleman from the end of the table, her eyes dye-black, every partisan instinct in her outraged at the insult of Pairvent's sitting where he had no right to be.

Coleman ate, saying nothing; and the meal was a hurried, silent chore soon done. Pairvent, feeling himself victor in being kept on as foreman, now rode his victory hard. When he rose the rest of the crew got up, half showing their thin amusement at Coleman's challenged authority. The feeling of their triumph remained behind them after they had gone.

Doña Gertrude sighed an exasperated breath; she had not touched her food at all. Valencia Wilder looked at Coleman. "You didn't need to do that for me. I want to cause you no trouble. Why are you smiling?"

He had risen and was smiling. He made up a cigarette and lighted it and his lips stretched against the white heaviness of his teeth; and his eyelids came near together and wind swept steadily in and out of him, drawing deeper from his chest. "The air in here," he said, "reminds me of the South. Always sticky before a storm."

"You're angry," she said. "You're angry clear through."

She walked to the porch with him. Twilight had gone and gray darkness lay over the land and the sharper wind bore down from the surrounding slopes. Far out on the flats a single rider moved in small, scudding echoes. She watched him face the open country, the glow of the cigarette laying its dark-yellow light along his cheeks. By this faint reflection his face made a heavy show, the bones of his cheeks flat and ridged beneath the covering skin. He turned to watch the bunkhouse. Over there was the sound of men idly talking, of one man laughing. Doña Gertrude was a smoldering presence somewhere on the porch.

He turned into the house and reappeared with his belt and gun; he smoked the last of his cigarette, and threw it into the dust of the yard. He went down the steps and ground the cigarette beneath his heel.

"Do you have to do it?" she asked.

"Yes."

"There's five of them," she murmured.

"We'll see," he said.

"It is Pairvent," she said, her voice tight and quick. "He is your enemy, he thinks you're afraid. Whip him. Break him. Make him humble."

He came up the steps, stopping directly before her. He looked down at her face. "You want to see a man hurt?"

"Hurt—or be hurt. You're alone. So have I been. The world is not kind. It will shrivel all the sweetness in you, it will starve you, it will destroy you. If it can. You're alone, against a pack of dogs. If you beat them they'll cringe. If you don't they'll tear you apart. I have been through it all. I have learned that if you do not fight you'll lose."

"Why," he said gently for so big a man, "you've been through hell," and then he put his hands on her arms and drew her forward and kissed her. He stepped quickly back and left the porch. She stood motionless, hearing his boots scuff around the house. From the deeper shadows of the house she heard Doña Gertrude's soft voice:—

"Was it a good kiss?"

"It was pity, Señora," murmured Valencia.

"So, he has a heart. The other kind of a kiss will come."

"What kind, Señora?"

"A foolish question. You know the kind of kisses men give. As for this other man—this Solvay. He is not your man, or he would not have left you here."

"I came for shelter."

"Ah," said the older woman, "what is shelter? I never asked for shelter. I asked for a man. So do you. That is why you came."

"Should I go, Señora?"

"That," said Doña Gertrude practically, "will answer itself in time."

Coleman crossed the yard with the light of the bunkhouse before him. One man stood against the bunkhouse wall, a thin shadow against other shadows; the rest had gone inside. He heard the murmuring of their voices until he reached the bunkhouse doorway. When he stepped through the doorway, talk ceased and he faced the eyes of these men—the arrested, expectant attention in those eyes.

Three of them sat at the room's small table—Pairvent, the brown-skinned man and the green-eyed rider with the half beard. A deck of cards lay on the table and a rack of poker chips, but they were not playing. They sat by, waiting for him. Ray, the chunky hand with the straight blunt face, lay on a bunk, half-turned so that he also could watch. Therefore the man out in the shadows would be the tricky kid. Coleman thought of the kid momentarily and then forgot him.

The two hands at the table had meanwhile made up their minds at the same moment, both now rising and stepping away. Pairvent remained, both his hands lying flat on the table; but he betrayed himself even as he thus seemed idle, for Coleman noticed the back of those hands show pressure. The foreman, so closely watching Coleman, presently seemed to see a new thing for suddenly his feet shifted slowly beneath the chair. Coleman said: "George, I didn't make myself plain to you," and flung over the table with his arm.

Pairvent rose and kicked the chair away at a single motion; and his hand fell upon his gun and lifted it. Coleman came at him, half-turning as he jumped. He caught Pairvent's arm with both his hands. He twisted Pairvent's arm as he turned and he struck Pairvent's chest with his indriving shoulder and flung Pairvent back against a bunk frame. He buckled Pairvent's arm downward and inward until the foreman gave a high yell and dropped the gun. Coleman knocked it aside with his foot; he stepped back and hit Pairvent on the side of the jaw with his fist and moved away. "George," he said, "this time I'll make myself plain."

Pairvent cast a wild, searching glance toward the corner of the room where the gun lay. This was his unguarded moment. Coleman came in and struck him on the side of the head, half-spinning Pairvent; he caught the foreman at the waist and whirled him across the small room and slammed him against the bunkhouse wall. Pairvent's breath gushed out and he lowered his head and drove it hard against Coleman's face. Coleman took that shock on his lips, he felt the skin of his lips crush in; it staggered and stopped him and Pairvent's fists beat him on neck and chest and belly.

Coleman ducked aside. He drew back, watching Pairvent follow; and he ducked again and came in, catching the foreman once more around the waist. Pairvent's knees smashed into his crotch and he heard Pairvent's teeth snap, close by his right ear. The foreman was a barroom fighter and now jabbed his thumb straight at Coleman's eyes, and missed and whirled and jumped and brought the sharp weight of his boot heel down on Coleman's instep. Coleman hung on, braced his feet, and turned Pairvent around with a full pivot and let him go like a rock out of a slingshot, throwing the foreman backward into two punchers standing on the edge of this fight. They caught Pairvent and kept him from falling and Pairvent, dizzied by his turning, threshed around and hit the bearded puncher full on the face before he realized it. The puncher cursed at him and backed away. Pairvent, turned mad, suddenly seized a steel stove poker hanging to a bunk end and whipped it full length at Coleman.

Coleman took it on a shoulder. He reached forward and down and seized one of Pairvent's long legs and dumped the man. Pairvent, flat on the floor, rolled and suddenly shot a boot heel straight up at Coleman's face. That heel tore along Coleman's cheek. He seized the foot and he bent it and turned it and heard Pairvent's shouted agony; he dragged the man out of the narrow space between the bunks and he reached down and sledged him twice on the temples with his fists; and stepped back. Pairvent groaned and lay on his side, made dumb by the beating.

The kid stood in the doorway, his big, sullen eyes filled with desire. Coleman whirled on him so quickly that the kid jumped back, fear cracking the sullenness. Coleman said: "Never stand behind me."

"Where the hell's behind you when you're turnin' like a top?" muttered the kid.

"You takin' part in this fight?"

"No," said the kid. "No."

Coleman ran the back of a hand across his cheek and brought it away red. Pairvent's boot heel had scraped him like a razor and Pairvent's head had crushed his lips so that he tasted blood. Wind came heavily out of him and ran full in, lifting and dropping his chest. The brown-faced puncher and the rider with the half beard stood by the wall, saying nothing: Ray lay on his bunk, watching with a gray pleasure.

Pairvent rolled and sat up on the floor, pale and momentarily sickened. "You've raised hell," he said.

"Some doubt in your mind about me," Coleman said. "I wanted to put that straight." He looked at the man on the bunk. "Ray what?"

"Miller," said the chunky one. "What good does that do you?"

Pairvent pushed himself erect and tried weight on the twisted leg. He sat down on his bunk. "You've laid me up."

"You can sit and rest," said Coleman. "But not at the head of the table."

"To hell with the place," said Pairvent.

"If you're runnin' away from a fight, go ahead and run."

"Who said anything about running?" asked Ray Miller in an easy, round-toned voice.

Coleman looked at the other two. "What names you men use?"

"Ed Drum," said the whiskered one. "And it's my real name, damn you."

The fellow with the stained brown face only grumbled: "Baldy."

Pairvent stared at the other men, at Ray Miller. "What the hell do you like about stayin'?" Ray Miller smiled, saying nothing. Coleman turned from the bunkhouse and walked back to the porch. Valencia stood waiting there; Doña Gertrude was a shadow behind her.

"Day's work is done," said Coleman, and laughed quietly. He heard Doña Gertrude give out a long sigh. Valencia touched his arm and held it. "Can you trust them?"

"No," he said. "Not at all."

"Trust nobody."

He looked at the round, pale darkness of her face, he heard the deep-seated bitterness in her voice. "Somebody's left his hoof marks all over you. Listen—you can't live without trustin' somebody."

"You will be hurt if you try it."

"Everybody gets hurt. But you can't hide in a black cave and live small."

She said: "You know why I can't believe in people. You knew it when you offered me your cigarette."

"I knew," he said. "I know something else, too. There's more to you than that."

The pressure of her fingers grew quite strong on his arm. Her voice changed and filled with disturbed feeling. "There is," she whispered. "There's so much more. But what good is that now?"

"You came up here to start over, didn't you?"

"I did, but it won't work. He saw what I was. It is no use."

"Solvay," said Coleman, "is a fool."

4

ANN STUART

Shortly after the fight in Horsehead's bunkhouse, the kid with the stringy black hair saddled his horse. Ray Miller was at the moment in the shadows and hailed him. "Where you spookin' now, Alvy?"

Alvy's voice was sullen. "Air's too close around here."

Miller said: "Alvy, damn a man that plays all corners of the board."

"What's that?" asked the kid, swinging in the saddle. But Ray was too tough a man either to fight or to bluff; the hard steadiness of his return glance made the kid drop his eyes. It was always like this with the kid. At twenty he wanted to be a man like Ray, deadly and caring for nothing; but he had no wisdom and none of those gutty qualities which made a man very good or very bad. He was a mass of emotion and self-drama, unstable as river sand, treacherous and thoughtless; he was forever carrying a quarrel to men better than he and always therefore being cuffed around. All this festered in him and made him worse.

Ray Miller dryly drawled: "Better watch out, kid."

Alvy rode away. He saw nobody on the porch of the main house and he thought to himself: "I wish he'd show up there. I'd let go at him." Then he discovered Coleman's shape in the deep shadows; and thin fear washed through him and he put the horse to a gallop and ran full tilt into the night.

After he forded the river he swung to the south, crossed the open plain and entered a low pine ridge. The trail carried him over a shallow summit, directly into Drew Trumbo's yard. There wouldn't be anybody else about, Alvy knew, for Trumbo had only a small range and did his own work except in busy season. Alvy circled the house and found Trumbo on the porch. Trumbo's ears had picked up his approach. There wasn't any light on the place; therefore the kid said, "It's me – Alvy."

"What goes on?" asked Trumbo.

"This Coleman came on the place. Had a talk with Pairvent and made a dicker for Pairvent to stay as foreman. George figured Coleman maybe wasn't very sure of things. So George ran his string out a little and took head place at the supper table. After supper Coleman came to the bunkhouse and beat hell out of George."

"Pairvent going to leave?"

"I guess not. There's a woman on the place, too. That girl who's Ben Solvay's girl, I guess. Solvay brought her."

Trumbo said: "That's good going, Alvy. Be sure to keep me posted."

Alvy said: "What's it look like to you now?"

Trumbo only added: "Keep me posted, Alvy. I'll remember you."

It was always like this for Alvy. He did his part, hoping for better. But he was always crowded out. He never made a fit with men like Ray, or Trumbo. He sat awhile in the saddle, sullen and self-pitying. "All right," he said at last, and rode back into the ridge, never knowing that he passed within ten feet of Tap, Dan Stuart's foreman.

Tap came out of his covert as soon as the sound of Alvy's travel died in the pines. He traced Alvy at a distance and watched Alvy's shape grow into a black point on the grassland. Thereafter Tap turned north and in an hour reached home. Stuart sat on the porch with his daughter Ann, and so Tap simply paused his horse and made up a cigarette and moved on. He put away his horse and stood against the corral, waiting. Having dropped his signal he knew the old man would come up. It was a half hour before Stuart arrived. Tap said: –

"That kid – Alvy – carried news of some kind from aHorsehead to Trumbo."

"He's done it before," said Stuart. "He's a go-between for Horsehead to Trumbo."

"Or spyin' on Pairvent for Trumbo," said Tap. "The kid's no good. He'd do anything. But now here's a new thing. You think maybe Coleman's usin' him to send word to Trumbo?"

"They don't know each other yet. Anyhow, Trumbo wouldn't work with Horsehead. He's out to get Horsehead and make a big fellow out of himself. Little fellow into a big fellow." Then he fell into a long silence, reviewing possibilities.

Tap said: "Wouldn't take anything for granted, Mr. Stuart. This Coleman's not foolish." He always put a handle on Stuart's name. It was the way Dan Stuart wanted it to be and Tap, who knew his boss inside out, took care never to offend the man's tremendous sense of dignity. Stuart wanted to be king and Tap, therefore, wanted him to be king.

"Coleman's out of luck," said Stuart. "He's got no crew to fight with. Those fellows will do what Pairvent wants done. Pairvent will buck Coleman at every turn, wantin' things for himself. So they'll get into a fight and Pairvent will beat Coleman to the draw. I see that coming."

Tap said: "Before he left War Bonnet, Pairvent had a talk with Trumbo. Then he went back to Horsehead. I been watching the ford all day. He's still on Horsehead. Maybe Coleman made a deal with him. Maybe there's a deal between the three, Pairvent and Trumbo and Coleman."

Stuart drew a long sigh of increased anger. "God's bells. There stands Drew Trumbo with his pint and a half of grass, trying to beat me to Horsehead. A kid, a latecomer, a schoolboy with a slingshot against a man with a cannon. If he thinks he sees a way of schemin' me out of Horsehead – "

Tap made up a cigarette and let Dan Stuart's temper boil. He lighted the cigarette, he held the match in his hand, narrowly squinting at its dying flame. He said: "You been trying to do this the roundabout way. You been trying to get all the neighbors together on it. All you got out of that was a split Basin. Trumbo's got a couple men, maybe three, on his side. He's made some sort of a deal with Hoby Spade and Frank DeLeon and Hack Dobbin. The rest of the crowd may be stickin' with you, but the price of that is a slice of Horsehead to each of 'em when you take it. What's that leave you? The more you slice it up the less it is worth the fight. All or nothing. If I were you I'd step in and take it while everybody else is waitin' around. Take it and keep it all."

"That," said Dan Stuart, "is my intention."

"Then move in now."

"Wait till Pairvent and Coleman quarrel. That will just leave Pairvent for me to run off."

"Wait that long and Trumbo may be before you."

Stuart grew irritated at Tap's insistence. "Sometimes it is best to let the other man reach first. I think I'll let Coleman reach first."

Tap had offered his advice up to this point. Now that Stuart had made a decision, Tap remained still. Stuart was the law and as far as Tap was concerned that law was sufficient. Star Cross was his life entirely; for it he lived and to it he gave his complete loyalty, knowing no other allegiance. All he said was, "Let it be so then," and turned to the bunkhouse to sleep the five short hours he permitted himself.

Dan Stuart returned to the porch and found his daughter still there. He said impatiently, "Thought you'd gone to bed."

"What's Tap so mysterious about?"

"Nothing."

"Don't let him talk you into anything."

The suggestion that he could be influenced by another person affronted him greatly; for he was a man who loved power for its own sake and the fat streak of aggressiveness in him would not let him bear the thought of interference. "By God," he said, "nobody talks me into anything. I have my own mind, Ann."

"Then don't talk yourself into anything."

"I will do as I please," he said. "Why don't you go to bed?"

He faced her as a stranger and talked with a stranger's cold irritation. He had no softness in him; and she knew he resented sharing his affairs with her. He had never forgiven her for not being a boy and her earlier memories were cruel memories of having been raised, motherless, at his rough hands as a boy would have been raised. Somewhere along the years he had seen the uselessness of that and instead of accepting the fact gracefully, he had turned from her. She was a woman to run the house, nothing more.

"Dad," she said, "someday, when you're older, you'll look back and you'll wonder where the nice memories are. You're destroying them and there won't be any. You drive people away. You have driven me away little by little. Do you want me to leave Star Cross?"

"Leave?" he echoed. "Where in hell would you go? This is your home, isn't it?"

"Is it?"

He stared at her, comprehending nothing. "Women are fools for thinkin' things that make no sense." He grew impatient. "Why can't you take things as they come instead of mooning up funny things that are nothing at all? I'll be damned if I like the way you tear around the country on your horse. I never know where you are. If you were a boy I'd take the steam out of you by workin' you sixteen hours a day."

"If I were a boy," she said, "I would have left you long ago."

He said: "What were you doin' down at Gateway the other night?"

"Riding," she said. "Just riding anywhere, away from Star Cross."

"Was Trumbo down there?"

"You let me into none of your affairs. I'll let you into none of mine."

His fiery temper flew up. "Keep away from Drew Trumbo! I want nothing to do with him and I'll refuse to have him as a son-in-law." He looked at her and hurled his half-suspecting question at her. "You're a good girl, ain't you?"

"Yes," she said.

He stood silent and then one of the things she had previously said came back and struck below his thick hide. "Why would you leave me if you were a boy? If you were a boy you'd be in line for this place. You will, anyhow, as a girl."

"What memories could I have of Star Cross?" she asked. "You grasp and you shout and you curse. You give nothing good to me or to any living thing. Someday you will see that."

"When you were nine years old," he said, "I had to lick you. Then I tried to show you I wasn't really put out, so I kissed you and you hit me in the face. I never forgot it. I never will. Anything that lifts a hand against me is nothin' I want around. If you'd been a boy I would have broken your bones for that."

She turned away from his ungovernable temper. She stepped into her own room and lighted a lamp and stood in the room's center, a tall girl with yellow-gold hair and a face now softened and sad. On the dresser before her was a framed daguerreotype of her mother, a woman she had never known. Now and then, when particularly alone, she tried to reach back into her very earliest childhood memories to evoke some image of her mother, some tone, some fragrance, some soft touch; and always failed. Even so, the picture of her mother was the closest companion she had in a solitary life. Out on the porch her father steadily tramped his restless path on the boards, heavy and dominant – a great egotist of a man, a caged bear with a passion for victory and a temper which knew no bounds when crossed. She did not hate him and she did not fear him; in her was enough of his own gift to turn her face somewhat stern as she thought of him.

She was on the porch at ten the next morning when a rider dropped from the western ridge and came on at a canter and at a walk. She watched his arrow-straight course for a full twenty minutes and recognized him as Tracy Coleman when he came into the yard. Her father meanwhile appeared with Tap and Coley Blaine. These three men stood together as Coleman came up.

He turned the horse, glanced at the men and then looked at Ann and removed his hat. He held his hat in his right hand, his arm full length. It was a gesture which disarmed him before the men and Ann, knowing her father and the jealous instincts of Star Cross, was troubled by it. Coleman gave her the same kind of easy and appreciative smile she had noticed before at Gateway; and the smile removed the short-cut angles around his mouth. He was slimmer in the saddle than on the ground, but even in the saddle he had muscular bulk.

Her father called immediately out: "You're on wrong ground, Coleman."

"Payin' a call," said Coleman.

"Pay no more. I will not ask you to light."

Coleman said: "I have been lookin' over Horsehead grass this morning. You've got your beef eating all over it. Naturally beef strays around. But roundup time is when outfits drive their cattle back to their own range. Roundup's just over and nothing's been driven off Horsehead."

"Let it stay," said Stuart with a cold, deep antagonism.

"I have been looking at that beef," said Coleman, "and I see some Horsehead brands with a vent on 'em, and your brand below. In the books of Horsehead there's no item of sale to you of any Horsehead beef."

"It's on my books," said Dan Stuart.

"Let me see those books, the date and amount of sale and the money paid to Horsehead."

"Ride out," said Dan Stuart. He held his temper longer than was natural to him, Ann thought; and this was somewhat of a concession to Coleman. Her father was studying the man with his hostile eyes, weighing him and making up his mind.

Coleman said: "I am going to cut through that beef and take every cow with a vent mark back across the river. I recognize no sales."

Dan Stuart let his temper go. "You're telling me Star Cross rustled your stock!"

"Let me see your books and the signed sales slip of the Horsehead agent."

"Ride out!" cried Dan Stuart. "Don't let me catch you within a mile of a cow bearin' my mark! I told you yesterday there ain't any more Horsehead. All beef which was Horsehead is maverick stuff in the Basin, open to any man's iron!"

"You're lookin' for a private war?" asked Coleman.

"If you wasn't in my yard," cried Stuart, "I'd shoot you down."

"You are going to have a private war," said Coleman.

"Who's fightin' with you?" demanded Stuart. "You come up here, tryin' to hold something which went back to public property three-four years ago. You try to run an outfit which has been stealin' from other Basin men. All that vented Horsehead stuff you see with my brand on is beef that once belonged to me, was rustled from me, which I have retaken. You're tellin' me you're going to rustle it back. Ride right straight down to Gateway and out of the country or you'll never see another month alive."

"I was in a neighborhood war once," said Coleman, casually. "It was bad. I gather from your talk that you are after me. That makes it plain both ways. When I see you, or any man of yours, comin' at me, I will consider it to mean trouble and I will draw without talk. I also propose to collect Horsehead beef wherever it is and I will follow its tracks if it takes me into your kitchen. Since you propose to drive me out of the country I will let nothing stand in my way to drive you out."

"With what help?" said Stuart, holding the same gritty, insolent contempt in his tone.

"As to that," said Coleman and bent a little in the saddle as he spoke, "just how many friends do you think you have?" He looked again at the girl and bowed his head to her, saying in a much gentler voice, "I regret to speak like this before you." He put on his hat and turned squarely against the Star Cross men and rode away. That was a moment when Ann Stuart felt fear and looked sharply at her father who stood with his cheeks red as brick dust in the sunlight. She was not sure to what lengths he would really go, and as she watched him she noticed that Tap and Coley Blaine were also watching him, ready for his nod. Stuart drew a great breath. He slid a close look at his daughter, shook his head and wheeled around the house. She knew then he had been very near the impulse to shoot Coleman out of the saddle. Far out on the yellow land, beyond gunshot, Coleman put his horse to a canter. Ann watched him until a ridge took him from sight. Afterwards the thought of him remained and her interest grew.

5

HORSEHEAD'S CREW

After his interview with Stuart, Coleman passed over Star Cross grass to the low pine hills in the west, followed the road through the warm, timbered shadows and came out to a point from which he viewed Horsehead Range as it rolled on to the river, crossed over and continued to the mountains lying westward. Along the distance he saw scattered cattle grazing. Earlier during the morning he had scouted that beef. Some of it was Horsehead, some Star Cross, and some was Horsehead with a vent brand on it, which indicated a sale, and Star Cross below the vent—indicating that Stuart had purchased it.

It was only a way of giving legal cover to a steal. There were no records on Horsehead of such a transaction; and if Pairvent actually had sold the beef to Stuart, the money had not been accounted for. In any event it was no transaction he proposed to recognize.

Now instead of crossing the open grass to Cloud River, he took a forest trail south and arrived at a right-angle ridge, and turned west. During the afternoon he saw Drew Trumbo's ranch quarters below him in another small valley—identifying this from Ben-Tim's map. Trumbo was a man he wanted to meet, but on some other basis than an outright call; and so he moved on and in late afternoon suddenly found himself sharp against the rim of the river's canyon, about five miles below Horsehead Crossing.

At the ford the stream had been smooth and fast and shallow. Here it was well embarked upon its wild-running drop to Gateway, crowded into narrower violence by the three-hundred-foot canyon, rushing over immense-rocks, slamming in white, wicked massiveness from wall to wall. Below this point, around a long-turning bend, arose the sound of still more furious collision and explosion. The power of the river was a steady beat coming up through rock and soil to where he stood. He felt it in his legs. Far down at the lower bend he noticed a narrow gravel bar on which a man squatted and seemed to rock a gold pan.

He left the saddle and sat with his back to a tree. Luke Wall had said that the river was death and Ben Solvay had later mentioned that the river was everything. Now that he had seen Stuart he partially understood what those two had in mind. The river was a kind of drumbeat which got into a man's system; the Basin was a shut-in world which made a man different after he stayed long enough.

Thinking back on the scene, he was troubled by his own reaction. This Stuart was a grizzly who proposed that nothing should stand in his way and he had laid down the law clearly enough. That in itself was nothing new; what surprised him was the way his own temper had jumped out from beneath his control. He had been ready to fight without taking much of a look at his chances. Maybe it was the country already working on him.

He heard a horse in the timber before he saw it, making dampered echoes on the soft soil, and he sat facing the pines and presently observed Ann Stuart ride out of the trees. She said, "Whoa-up," and sat still, slanting a small smile at him; the last sunlight burned against her hair and brightened the most expressive eyes he had ever seen.

"Good tracker," he said.

"In these hills," she said, "I could find you on the darkest night of the year." His compliment had clearly pleased her. She got down and stood before him, but it was not apparently to her liking so to command a man, for she dropped to the ground. She had clean-running physical lines and her face was a mirror which changed as her feelings changed. She took up the powdered forest soil and let it slide through her fingers and even in that small act she was graceful. He saw laughter below her eyes and he saw pride; yet something smothered these things, like a cloud.

He removed his hat before her. She watched this casual gallantry with a sober interest and her lips made a small change at the corners and became soft with the caught interest of a woman. "I should tell you something," she said. "You will find Horsehead beef all over these hills, vented and rebranded with other brands. It is not my father alone who has that kind of beef. Horsehead was closed out as a ranch some time ago by the other owners. They now regard every Horsehead cow to be a maverick in the Basin."

"A man's brand is a sign of property. It doesn't change unless the man changes it. Nobody can vote him out."

"This is the Basin," she said and explained it all by that phrase.

He said: "At Gateway you laughed like a woman who had no troubles at all. Now you're sad."

She gave him a surprised glance. "My friend," she murmured, "you have sharp eyes. They should be seeing other things than the things that come and go across a woman's face."

He sat idle, soaking up the final sunlight, watching her and not answering. She made a little gesture with her shoulders and her lips stirred with a pleasant expression. "In the Basin the expected thing usually happens, and the worst thing. I like the unexpected thing for a change. It was like that in Gateway. My father does not like Drew Trumbo. I do." Then she grew increasingly serious. "You should not have come into the Basin. The ranch is lost because Ben-Tim let it go too long. Other men want it. The fight for power is everything here. But that is not all. Pairvent is a rustler and so are the men with him. That has gone against Horsehead. You can't stay."

"I'll stay."

"I suppose you'll try," she murmured. "But you'll be alone and you'll lose."

"Not alone."

"You're keeping that crew? I'm sorry for you."

He bent forward, his solid face lightening. A woman could draw his interest at once, and perhaps many had. She thought of that with some doubt and gave him a considerable inspection. A man like this could be gallant to women because he held them cheaply, or because he had some deep feeling about one particular woman. He had strong, straight eyes which revealed warmth as his humor changed. "What's to be sad for?" he asked.

"Have you been much alone?"

"Usually."

"Then you should know."

"I guess I do. I have looked at a lot of stars, wonderin', and I have ridden in and out of a lot of towns, just lookin'. Hate to think of all the miles I have covered with nobody along. A man does a lot of thinkin'. Nothing usually comes of it."

She got up and she turned from him. There had been something in his voice that hurt her and made her sad because it reminded her so much of herself. "What are you looking for?"

He didn't answer. She caught the hanging reins and stepped to the saddle. She looked down at him again and noticed that he was near to smiling. He seemed on the point of answering her question but in the end he shook his head. "Maybe I don't know."

The feeling she had at the moment astonished her. "Yes you do," she answered. "But it isn't here for you. Ride on out of the country. Is it so hard to give up? Is it so necessary to fight?"

"Not for the fightin'."

"Then why?"

"A man comin' out of nothing toward something can't turn and go back through nothing. I know what's behind me.

That country is all empty. I do not know what is ahead. Maybe something I'm after."

"If you stay and if you win there'll be no kindness left in you." She spoke with quicker feeling. "Do you want to be like these men in the Basin? If they pull you into their troubles they'll make you that kind of a man. You were sitting here when I came, thinking of other and nicer things. If you stay you'll not think of those things again."

"Cleanness and dirt are always together," he said. "We go through both, every day."

She moved away and swung about. "Don't hate the Stuarts more than you can help," she said, made a casual gesture of farewell and galloped through the timber.

He rose and turned to the horse. In the saddle he paused a moment to watch the solitary man crouched far below on the gravel bar. "That man's free," he thought. But this was only a half judgment. For if the man were free it could only be because he wanted nothing; and if a man wanted nothing he was old, all the fire was out of him. As long as the fires burned and strange pictures were before him and hunger was awake, no man could be free.

He passed through the trees, traveling downgrade to the north. When he crossed the ford he felt again the pull of the tricky waters and he pushed the horse ashore and looked back at the river with his eyes half-closed. The river was alive; he had felt it reach for him. That was what Luke Wall had meant. He arrived at the ranch in the late blue twilight and washed and went into the dining room for supper. Valencia Wilder came in and sat with him, watching him with her chin rested in her hand; her silence was like a feeling in the room. She wore a gray dress which had a thin thread of scarlet in it and her shoulders were small and square within the dress and her breasts were round-pressed plaques against it. An opal ring burned out its color on her right small finger. Her hands were brown the skin of her face faintly stained by the sun.

"News?" she asked.

"I saw Stuart."

"One of your enemies," she said.
"Full of war and breathin' fire."
"You're alone," she said. That was all she said until he lifted his eyes to her. She continued to watch him and he saw once more the way she opened her glance to him, letting him in. Then she added: "Except for me."
"Solvay guessed you'd have a safe week here. You may not."
"A week?"
"He thought it would take a week for you to make up your mind about him, didn't he?"
"He doesn't want me."
"How do you figure that?"
"Would you have waited a week?"
He got up from the table and circled it. He stood behind her, looking down on the top of her black hair. She sat still, her arms on the table; she didn't turn or lift her eyes. He put his hands behind him, solidly holding them together. She hated the world for what it had done to her. She had no faith, no trust. But her desires were live-burning in her and her stillness was the stillness of a bomb ready to explode. Nothing had touched her spirit. It was strong and ready to venture, even after all her hard experiences; and he guessed that regardless of her hurts and her hate, she still wanted something to believe and to love. She couldn't stop her spirit, she couldn't kill the flame. "No," he said.
"He doesn't want me at all," she said.
"What the hell does he want?"
"A plain woman," she said and then rose and turned. Her eyes were black and bright and he thought it wouldn't take much for her to cry. "You know what he means by plain? He means good."
"Only a fool thinks he knows the difference between good and bad."
She touched his chest with her hand and looked long and closely at him; and suddenly dropped her hand. Her voice was small. "What do you think about me?"
"I won't think about you as long as you're Solvay's girl. But

if I were Solvay I'd ask no questions and I would have married you yesterday."

"I wonder," she murmured, her voice long and interested and speculative, "what kind of a woman's in your heart."

"None."

"So you think," she murmured and changed the talk. "That thin boy, Alvy, is a traitor. I can see it in his eyes." She took his arm, small beside him, and walked with him to the porch. He made up his cigarette and smoked it silently through and ground it beneath his heel; and then he slipped into the other half of his character. He thought of her and his face held its light and its desire, but now the old roughness returned and he was no longer thinking of her as he left the porch and crossed to the bunkhouse.

Pairvent and Ray Miller were stretched out on their bunks, Ed Drum and Baldy sat at the table playing cribbage. All these men ignored him; they felt his presence and resented it and grew inwardly angry—and that feeling reached him. He nodded his head at Baldy. "Baldy, but not bald. How did that come?"

"Black bear tore out the rear end of my pants once. I been Baldy ever since."

Coleman stepped into the room and spoke over his shoulder. "Alvy, come out of the yard."

The kid was a long time coming; and entered at last nursing his sullen air. He stood in the doorway and pretended not to be interested. Coleman took an empty chair and tipped it against the wall and sat in it. Pairvent watched him. Ray Miller, the coolest of the lot, slowly turned on his stomach and hooked his head over the bunk frame so that he might look on.

"George," said Coleman, "you been selling Horsehead beef to Stuart?"

He heard Ed Drum move his hands across the table. He heard the silence grow thin, he felt its thinness. Pairvent stared at him. The foreman's eyelids sprang open and closed down. "No," he said. "Never did."

"He's got our stuff vented, his own mark underneath."

"You'll find that all over the Basin," said Pairvent. "You heard the rule, didn't you? Horsehead ain't an outfit now and its beef is maverick. That's what I been up against. You can listen to me on that, or you can listen to somebody else. But if you listen to anybody else you're listenin' to a man who is not Horsehead's friend. We're alone."

"Mighty big smoke for a little fire," commented Coleman. "I haven't heard it all. But I can guess some more. You been foolin' with somebody else's beef?"

Pairvent let out a long-held wrath. "I been makin' my own way on this place—any way I can! You try to do any better! A man that lives under the gun is entitled to some profit!"

"Then that's why we're closed out."

"Listen," said Pairvent and swung himself to a sitting position on the edge of the bunk. "They'd use any excuse, or they'd go ahead without one. You can take Horsehead, but you're going to be a damned dead man if you try to hold it."

"We'll hold it," said Coleman.

"I'll make no fight for it. I'm through fightin'."

"George," said Coleman, "I heard you were tough. You don't sound that way."

Pairvent groaned and looked at his revolver hanging beside the bed. He stared at Coleman. "You'll swallow that someday."

"In the mornin' I'm going over to the edge of Star Cross and I'm bringin' back every vented animal I see."

"You can try," said Pairvent. "Maybe you'd be fool enough to try."

"You boys have been backin' up without a fight. The Basin has got your number. Maybe you're no better at fightin' than they figure. You've eaten well around here. You're a fat bunch and you're sour. I don't think you can stand a fight. I'm leavin' early in the mornin'. If anybody feels stout enough to go along, that'll be fine."

He had felt the never-relaxed attention of Ray Miller's eyes—and that was a man he felt had something in him. He didn't look at Miller. He kept his eyes on Pairvent who sat still and nursed his festering rage. Then he added: "But if you've sold that beef to Stuart you wouldn't be in such a good position to go out there and help get it back, would you?"

Pairvent gave a long sigh. "I will go and I will watch you get knocked out. I'm a fool, because I'll get knocked out too. I wish to God I'd never seen you."

Ray Miller said: "Always wonder about a man that talks large. I'll just go along and see. Lot of wind in Texas. Maybe some if it got up here."

The two men at the table said nothing. Ray Miller spoke for them, and Miller grinned as he spoke. "We'll all go."

"No," said Coleman, "the kid won't go." He turned his attention to Alvy. He said: "And if you leave the yard tonight I'll tie you up and drown you in the water trough." He looked back to Miller. "You like to fight, Ray?"

"Friend," said Miller, cool and grinning. "I'll fight anything, anywhere. The bigger the jag, the better I like it. If you're promisin' me some fun, that's fine. If you don't deliver the fun, I'll take it out of you."

Coleman came from the house after breakfast and saddled his horse; and found the crew, including Alvy, waiting by.

"Alvy," he said, "I don't want you along. Stay back and don't leave the place."

The kid had some strange pride in him. He stood by his horse and showed Coleman a humiliated, resentful face. "I can handle my end," he said.

"The question is," said Coleman, "which end are you on?"

"I'm workin' for Horsehead, ain't I?"

"I don't know."

The kid drew a deep breath. "If I stay behind everybody in the Basin will say I didn't have the nerve to ride with the outfit. I got to ride with the outfit."

The rest were mounted and ready to go. Alvy stood by his horse, holding his eyes on Coleman and waiting for an answer. Coleman said, "Go get a rifle, Ed," and pulled at his morning cigarette. The inside of the kid was like quicksand all churned up; he wanted to be a man but he was still a boy.

There were all sorts of youngsters like this, full of ambition and wanting to be great men like other great men. Somewhere along the line the wrong kind of men crossed their trails and set the example after which they patterned themselves. Maybe, if a good man had come along first, Alvy's way of looking at the world would have been different.

Maybe. Could a kid with bad streaks in him be made good, or could a kid who had the right things in him be made bad? He had a responsibility to the kid and it was hard to know what to do. Ed Drum came back with a rifle over his saddle.

"I got to keep with my outfit," said Alvy.

Alvy had a streak of loyalty in him; and loyalty covered a lot of sins. Coleman jerked his thumb upward, and Alvy straddled his horse at once. He pulled his hat down over his eyes and his long lips came together and formed a tight fish-mouthed crease. The other men had said nothing at all; they had simply sat by. They knew Alvy better than he did but they offered him no information.

"Alvy," he said, "we're going out for some Horsehead property. But that is all, unless Star Cross meets us and gets nervous. I don't want to see you draw a gun unless I draw mine. If you start shootin', I'll shoot you. That clear?"

"All right," said Alvy.

"All right," said Coleman and let his horse go. Outside the grove of the trees he looked back to see Valencia Wilder on the porch. She raised her hand at him and he lifted his own hand and steadied himself on the leather.

The sun was round in the east, directly above the hills, and the air was crisp and clean at this hour, and the great mountains in the west stood very near. He pointed at the ford, Pairvent and Ray Miller riding abreast him, Baldy and Ed Drum and the kid directly behind. This was his crew, these were the men with whom he went into action, and of whom he knew nothing except that they had played a crooked game. It was possible that Pairvent would sell him out sometime during the morning, for Pairvent was a schemer. Still, it was a gamble he had to make; for only by a show of force could he expect to hold Horsehead. If he sat tight he lost the ranch by the gradual encroachment of the ranchers surrounding him.

They came to the river, its surface all asparkle in the fresh sun; and the smell of the river lay in the shallow canyon and the sound of the river was a steady growl below them. He led over and noted how carefully these men took the ford; none of them were easy about it. When he climbed from the shallow canyon, Coleman turned toward the low hills in the south. Half over the open land, Pairvent broke the silence. "You're goin' the wrong direction," he said and pointed to the ridge in the east. "Star Cross is beyond that."

"We'll circle," said Coleman. "Never pays to walk headfirst into a battle."

They went up a grade and passed into the pines, whereupon Coleman turned east with the spine of the ridge, followed it three or four miles and then swung north, thus going along the line of hills separating Star Cross Range from Horsehead. Now and then, through breaks of the timber, he saw cattle grazing below him on the Star Cross side.

"You're sayin'," Pairvent at last spoke up, "that you expect to be met."

"I told Stuart yesterday I'd be coming," said Coleman, and looked upon Pairvent long enough to see the lengthening and the tightening of the foreman's face. Ray Miler was to his other side; turning to him, Coleman noticed that Ray Miller's thick chops were fixed in a grinning cast.

Within another mile Coleman struck an east-and-west-running road. He turned and followed it downgrade toward Star Cross and halted when he had reached the edge of the timber. Half a mile beyond him, on the plain, lay a scatter of beef; five miles beyond that stood the shape of the Star Cross quarters. Coleman pulled into timber beside the road and halted. Ray Miller gave him a glance and a grin at this maneuver. Pairvent pointed to the road's dust. "Been somebody along here this mornin'."

"Likely," said Coleman. Somewhere in the timber's warm and resinous silence a woodpecker launched its quick attack on a tree, that sound shuttering on and on through the ridge. Far over on the northern edge of Star Cross grass he made out a cloud of rising dust. Miller laid his eyes thoughtfully on that while Pairvent suspiciously scanned the surrounding trees.

"We go out there," said Coleman, "and round up the vented stuff we find in that nearest bunch. We drive it back this road, straight to the ford. One of you stays here at the edge of timber to cover us. If Star Cross comes along we'll do a little talkin', no doubt. If you hear it turn from talk to something else, use the rifle." He looked at Pairvent. "Who stays here, George?"

"Baldy's the best rifle shot."

"You stay, Baldy," said Coleman and nodded at Drum. "Give Baldy the rifle. Let's get on with this."

He led the others out of the trees, down the last slope of the hill; he pointed to the beef grazing directly ahead. "Scatter and weed it out," he said. Pairvent struck off to the left at once and Ed Drum and the kid went rushing by him. Ray Miller stayed beside him, the grin never leaving his big mouth; there was excitement in the man and excitement pleased him. They circled the beef and dust began to lift out of the grass, making a signal that would be seen from Star Cross quarters, or from the ridge if Star Cross men were hiding there. Coleman heard Ed Drum yip at the beef; he turned in and out, spotting the vented cattle, and his horse cut them and moved them out. It was a short job. In twenty minutes they had their cut moving back toward the ridge. "Twenty-three," said Miller and brushed the sweat from his heavy cheeks. His glance kept running out to the north toward the growing ball of dust. He pointed at it. "Comin' up."

They had the beef at a trot as they reached the ridge's incline. Ed Drum's yipping got sharper and more frequent. The man, thought Coleman, was growing nervous under pressure. He went forward, reading the vent brands on the beef, and he found one that had a straight Star Cross mark. He cut that cow out and let it drift. Pairvent rode beside him, saying: "You're particular."

"I don't want a rustlin' charge against us."

"Driving this vented stuff home is rustlin' in the Basin's judgment."

"Illegally vented," answered Coleman. "Stuart's been rustlin' from us."

"Maybe," said Pairvent, "you ought to hang Stuart for bein' the rustler." His temper was short and his nerves wound up.

"That time may come," said Coleman. "Somebody's going to hang or die."

Pairvent grumbled and fell to the rear of the column. They were within the timber, moving along the red dust of the road. Baldy came out of the trees to join them but Coleman called to him. "Keep behind us some distance." He joined Pairvent and Miller at the rear while the kid and Ed Drum rode swing, holding the cattle in the road. Ahead of them the road started downgrade into the grass again, into Horsehead grass. The river ford was five miles due west and the sun crawled toward the top of the sky. Ray Miller steadily sweated and his eyes were small black lines beneath his closed lids and his cheeks were red. Pairvent's survey swept the country ceaselessly and when they had gone a mile onward he pointed a hand to the north. "There's your fun."

The dust ball which had been visible on the Star Cross side of the ridge now was here on the Horsehead side. He saw the thin black point of the group coming on and once he saw a flash of light against some piece of metal. All the Horsehead crowd had seen it. Baldy galloped forward from his rearguard position and Alvy looked around at Coleman and showed a drawn expression. The kid was suddenly afraid, all his thoughts of bigness gone. Coleman called at him: "There's the timber, Alvy. You can run for it."

Alvy turned his head away suddenly. Ed Drum ceased his shrill yipping and now rode with his glance riveted to the west where lay the ford. Pairvent began to swear in a quiet, bitter way. "God damn you, Coleman, this was a fool thing to do. I should have known better. We played right into their hands."

Coleman said: "How many do you see in that bunch, Ray?"

The oncoming group was about two miles away, the men now fanning out. "Six there," said Miller.

Pairvent's glance covered the whole distance around him. The ridge was two miles behind them and to the south of them; the river and the safety of the river's width was three miles ahead. They were in the open, no shelter at either hand; and Pairvent's narrow face expressed all this, showing a kind of disgust at the tactical error made. "Better get this clear between us now," he said. "What do you propose to do? Run or stand? Wait and argue, or start shootin' when they get in range?"

"Wait until they get here. We'll meet whatever bet they make."

"Well," said Miller in a practical voice, "they're just about here."

The oncoming riders closed the distance, spreading as they ran. He heard the steady scud of the horses and he saw Stuart's big body and he got the outflung echo of Stuart's voice, the words not clear. Coleman made a short signal with his hand and rode outward from the beef; the rest of Horsehead came up and sat beside him. Alvy crowded his horse beside Pairvent. Ed Drum pushed in toward Alvy. Coleman said: "Spread out—spread out. No firing unless they fire first. Alvy, remember that." He said no more to them. Star Cross rushed in and stopped thirty feet away and the dust of their running came on over them and moved cloudy across the gap and its gray silky substance touched Coleman's face and became a taste in his mouth.

6

THE SHADOW OF A HANGING

There were six of them, as Ray Miller had said. Coleman had seen three of them before, Stuart and Tap and one other man—these same three standing together in the Star Cross yard the previous morning; he had noticed the creep of desire in their eyes then, and he noticed it now. It was clearer now, and Stuart's vein-netted face was gray with strain, with pleasure.

"You," he said. "Stand fast. You—kid there—hold your hand away from your gun. Turn around, all of you. Start ridin' for timber."

Tap dryly spoke. "Better unbuckle 'em first."

Stuart said: "Put up your hands. Ride toward me. You first, Coleman." Then he let his satisfaction have its brutal play. "One hour from now you're six thieves swingin' on the rope, the buzzards pokin' at your eyes."

Coleman sat still, hands folded on the saddle horn. His legs were straight down in the stirrups and his shoulders were rounded and somewhat bent. He looked from beneath the brim of his hat at Stuart, so that his face was shadowed and flat. He held Stuart's eyes as he would have gripped the man's shoulders with his hands; he neither moved nor spoke.

Stuart let out a passionate yell. "Move up!"

"Old man," said Coleman, "this beef was never sold to you

and it never belonged to you. I'm takin' it back. Then I'm goin' to comb your range until I get every cow that's mine."

"Move up!" repeated Stuart in his high, half-strangled voice.

"We're not movin'. We're goin' over the river with this beef. It is up to you to start the fight. Think carefully before you do. You're old and you're fat – and how long has it been since you tried to beat a man to the draw? You can't do it. When you draw, old man, you're dead. But try it if you've got to."

"Shoot him down," said Tap's voice, as though from a great distance. "Shoot him down."

"Ray," said Coleman, "Tap's your meat if he moves."

He had never ceased to watch Dan Stuart, whose eyes were crowded with the greatness of his desire to destroy. The man, Coleman guessed, had never been seriously crossed, his temper had fed on easy victories and on a power that had not been challenged. This is what he had guessed the day before in the Star Cross yard, this was what he had sensed. The stand he made now was based on that guess, and so he held his motionless attitude and he continued to meet that violent stare. Stuart, having spoken and having been refused, now remained silent – and his silence seemed to be odd to his crew, for Tap said again: "What will it be, Mr. Stuart?"

"Your boss," said Coleman, "is tryin' to figure whether this is a good day to die."

He slid it gently at Stuart and he saw the big man's face lose its harsh lines of triumph. He saw doubt creep into lip corner and he recognized an expression of remote breakage, of deep inward shame and loss of certainty. Before him, as these tight hot moments went on, a man changed and in changing he destroyed much of himself. It was Stuart who in the end took his eyes from Coleman and dropped them. He put his hands on the saddle horn and he stared at his hands, and the corners of his shoulders lost their squareness; and then his own riders caught the sense of what had happened and certainty went out of all of them and Tap cast a bitter glance upon Coleman for the destruction accomplished and seemed to grit his teeth together. Abruptly Stuart turned his horse and rode away. He had left no command behind him; therefore Tap murmured, "Let's go," and led the crew on Stuart's heels. Coleman waited until Star Cross was well beyond gunshot.

"Now," he said, "we'll move on."

They pulled the strayed beef together and moved it westward, Alvy and Ed Drum riding swing. Baldy once more dropped back with his rifle. Pairvent and Miller were at the rear of the stock with Coleman; and nobody said anything. They wasted half an hour at the ford getting the cattle across. Once west of the river Coleman said, "Let them drift," and set off for the ranch with the outfit, arriving there in the middle of the afternoon.

The kid, he saw, had a swagger to him as he moved away. The kid was making himself big again, and riding for another fall. He stored the thought in his mind, meanwhile observing Pairvent. The foreman had brooded over the clash with Star Cross all the way home. "I do not understand," said Pairvent. "I never saw Stuart back up before a man before."

"Who," inquired Coleman, "has stood up to him recently?"

Pairvent pulled his eyelids together as he thought. "Can't rightly remember."

"He was runnin' on a reputation."

"How'd you know that?" asked Pairvent.

"I made a guess."

"Damned long chance to take on a guess."

Coleman made up a smoke, his back propped to the corral post. Ray Miller was near by, listening to the talk, a set grin on his rough face. Coleman got the cigarette lighted. "Not so long a chance, George. A man can be the world's best fighter and still be stopped without a shot. There are few men in this world who will stand in front of another man, twenty feet away, and risk a pull unless they're dead sure they've got better than an even chance. Stuart wasn't sure."

"I will tell you something," said Pairvent. "You sent him down in the eyes of the Basin. You made a monkey out of him. He will think about that until it turns him crazy. Then he'll go at you in ways that ain't white. There's a streak in Dan

Stuart like the bloody streak in an Indian. He won't rest now until he's got you fryin' over a fire."

"I observed that," said Coleman.

Pairvent growled, "You observe a hell of a lot." Then he remembered his own position and the thought turned him sour again. "Since you're so good with your eyes—what you think I'll be doin'?"

"You'll play this hand through with me until you figure a chance to get me in a corner," said Coleman. "I have got to watch out for you, George. You want Horsehead."

Anger danced hot and dangerous in Pairvent's secretive eyes; he turned on his heel and walked away. Miller's grin increased. He was laughing without a sound and after that he did a curious thing—he struck the top corral bar with his fist so hard that the bar sent out a hollow echo as it vibrated and he gave Coleman the benefit of his sly amusement and strolled toward the bunkhouse. That brute power had come out of him like a gust in an otherwise windless day, unexpected and unexplained. Going on to the main house, to Valencia waiting on the porch for him, Coleman tried to fathom the man.

Ann Stuart watched her father leave Star Cross early in the morning with the crew; from the house porch she followed the dust of their traveling as they scouted in and out of the low hills. She knew the reason for it and she therefore understood the meaning of the second cloud of dust straight to the west around ten o'clock. The cloud later vanished and the dust of her father's party faded out into the timber farther north. Thereafter she could only wait, and the waiting was hard. Near noon she saw a party come out from the hill road, straight west again, moving slowly—and at last identified her father at the head of the Star Cross men. All six were along, which caused her a great deal of relief, but the slowness of her father's traveling puzzled her and when he came into the yard the grayness of his skin and the droop of his shoulders also puzzled her. There was nothing to be read on the face of Tap, or on the faces of the others. They pulled away at once and went to the deeper part of the yard. Her father stepped from his horse, came to the porch and sat down.

She said: "What happened?"

He shook his head, no more communicative now than at any other time. Still, there was a difference in him. He looked old and he looked tired. The heavy thrust of intolerant energy was gone. His face was sallow to her and bitterness made its claw scratches at his mouth corners. He sat motionless in the chair with his hands lying palms up on his lap, and looked out upon the land as a man might do whose active days were over.

She tried once again. "Did you have trouble?"

"Don't talk," he said.

She went back through the house and out into the rear yard. Tap sat in the shade of the pumphouse, nursing a cigarette, brooding over some injury. "Tap," she said, "what went wrong?"

She hated the man, as he well knew, and therefore he was always civil and evasive with her. Yet on this occasion he spoke readily, as though he had to talk. "We came cross that fellow Coleman with his crew, runnin' our beef back to his side. We stopped him. This Coleman—" and here Tap stopped and appeared to review the incredible thing in his mind—"sat tight and faced your dad down. That was all. We came home like cur dogs. Coleman took the beef."

"That vented beef?"

"Beef which was on our grass," he said. "Vented or not."

"But he claimed it to be Horsehead's?"

"That," said Tap, "is not the point. The point is he faced us down and we gave out. That is the point."

Tap was suffering as her father suffered. It tore at his loyalty to the ranch, it poisoned his faith in himself, and presently he said in a dead tone: "It happened. I do not know why. I think I will have to kill that fellow myself. There'll be no rest for me or for your father until it is done. By God, I will do it, too!"

She went back to the house and stood in the living room, watching her father through the open doorway. He sat like an invalid whose strength came to him drop by drop; and she knew then, from Tap's explanation, how great were the gaps torn in his spirit and how increasingly his wounds would pain him. He was a man who had never been crossed and he had built a legend around himself and lived by that legend. Now it was partly destroyed and the shock had stilled him.

She could not feel sympathy or sorrow for him. Those were emotions he had driven from her heart; but she did feel pity, and she went out and put a hand to his shoulder. "Goes bad sometimes," she said.

He had no grace to receive pity. It stung his vanity and he moved his shoulder until her hand fell away; he gave her a familiar glance of dislike. He got up from the chair and went to his horse and he stood by it, thinking. Presently he said: "Next time you see Drew Trumbo, ask him to come see me."

"You hate him. Why should you want to see him?"

"That's not important right now. Go see him and tell him."

He reached the saddle after a slow pull and rode north. It was then one o'clock or after; at three he reached War Bonnet, took a pair of drinks at the saloon and went on to the Alma. He sat there, alone again, and again thinking of his injuries. By and by he got some paper from the clerk and returned to his chair and found a pencil and slowly wrote a notice on two pieces. Having done it he left the Alma, crossed to the general store to buy a box of tacks, and returned to the hotel. He tacked one of the notices to the hotel wall and left town, riding toward Gunderson's ranch. A few miles out of town he put up the second notice on the side of an abandoned log hut.

Coming out of the hills, Ben Solvay saw and read the notice. He tore it from the wall and started for Horsehead, thirty miles away.

It had been one of late summer's hot days and now at twilight, Coleman sitting on the porch steps, heat came up from the earth to render out the keen blends of the earth. The moon rolled along the edge of the mountains, reddened by summer's dust. Valencia came quietly from the house and stood near him; and at last, with a quick motion, sat beside him. There was, away over to the north, the small run of a traveler; that and a coyote's cry. Valencia said: "He's against the world, too. He has no friends."

He turned and he saw the small smile she had. He felt the turbulence of her spirit around him as a man might feel strange currents cut across the wind's major run. She was a white core of light in darkness, a personality of fragrance and will, a stubborn spirit set against the world. She had wanted many things and had been betrayed by her wants; yet she still had them. She was still proud.

"Tracy," she said, "they will never drive you away." The fighting streak in her made her voice lift. "Never let them! Tooth for tooth and claw for claw."

"Kind of a sad world that way," he reflected.

"You're strange. Everything's been hard for you, and you are hard. But not hard in the way I know men can be."

"Known men like that?"

"Most of them have been like that." All the heat and resistance of her experiences seemed to rise from her. "My trouble was in asking for too much. It was never money or clothes, even though those things seemed wonderful to the daughter of a poor woman. It was more than that—to be alive and to be important. Not to be beaten, not to grow fat and afraid, not to be just a piece of dust lost in the road. A man would call it adventure. But men do not like a woman to hunt adventure. It makes the woman cheap to them. That has made me bitter. I have had to fight and hold my own part. I could never be very soft. Men watch for softness in a woman and then betray the woman. My own ambition has betrayed me. I have believed too much. I have hoped for too much."

"I see softness in you."

"I have let you see it," she said, and turned to him. "I wanted you to see what I really am. Goodness can't die out just because of a mistake. A shadow can be perfect, but we weren't made to be shadows. I have been lonely. I have never found what I wanted."

"Why," he said, "neither have I."

"I know," she murmured. "It is in your eyes. What is the woman like—the woman you want?"

He sat still and made no immediate answer; wherefore she knew the question reached into his deepest places. The picture of that woman was in him, colored and rounded and given life by all the dreaming a man spends upon his private images; she knew men well enough to understand that. Yet there were no words which would completely describe what he felt, and even if he found the words which came closest to his desire he would be reluctant to express them. She sat near him, wanting him in a way she had wanted no man; and wanting to be seen by him not as the world judged her but as she knew herself still to be, a woman of depth and goodness, with loyalty crying in her to be claimed, with a faith that once fixed would be as rock all her life. And then she asked herself a forlorn question. "What have I really lost that a man needs?"

He hadn't answered and she knew he would not answer; and so she understood that his feeling in the matter was very strong, as she had suspected. She watched his face—the sometimes homely and sometimes recklessly expressive face of a man who lived his life in action. He felt her glance and turned to her and he smiled and then he was a man of charm, a man aware of her closeness, a man straining on the leash of his reserve. She sat still, waiting for that reserve to break; wishing for it and making herself desirable to him by her smile. His thoughts came hard upon her, so near she saw the change in his eyes, and she thought: "Perhaps now."

Out on the flat grassland a rider moved rapidly, inbound. Coleman rose and stepped in the yard, waiting; the horseman came in, wheeled to a stand and announced himself. "Coleman? This is Frank DeLeon."

"Light," said Coleman.

The houselight touched him as he dismounted and walked forward—a tall man made thin by long years; he had white mustaches and a face seamed by weather and natural wisdom. The wisdom had given him kindness and kindness was printed on his face.

"I have heard news of you," he said. "You went over to Star Cross and took Stuart's beef?"

"Horsehead beef with a sale vent on it – and his brand below. There have been no sales from Horsehead. That beef belonged to us."

"So," said Frank DeLeon. He considered Coleman over an adequate silence, an old man who had seen many a year run by, witnessed many a sad thing, and had seen some happiness. "I have heard of this venting business," he said at last. "None of it on my place. I liked old Ben-Tim. He was my friend."

"That is what he told me."

"He would be the man to remember," said DeLeon. "A high wind goin' down the road – that was Ben-Tim. I do not doubt the beef was illegally vented and I do not deny it belongs to you, wherever you may find it now." He paused to consider what was best to say, and how far he might go in speaking. "But you will have difficulty in claiming it. The Basin never likes to see grass goin' to waste and after Ben-Tim left this place to foremen it went sour. The Basin declared it a maverick outfit. Just threw it back to open land, free for the fellow that claimed it."

"Who claims it?"

"Ah," said Frank DeLeon, "the boys never got around to agreein' on that. They been jealous of each other."

"I have seen a lot of country," said Coleman, "but I have never before seen a vent brand used to cover a steal, except by rustlers."

"This is the Basin," said Frank DeLeon, "and the Basin is different. Matter of fact it is a clever idea. They will claim they bought it. When you come to take it back, with that vent mark showing a sale, you will be the rustler, son. Not them. They will have public reason to hang you higher than a kite."

"Let them prove they bought it."

"Can you prove it wasn't sold to them?" pointed out Frank

DeLeon. "You can't. You're new here. They know that. As I said, it is a clever idea."

"Cleverness has an answer. I will make it."

"That," said Frank DeLeon, "is what I have wondered." Once again he put the search of his old, blue eyes on Colemen. "I believe you will. You have backed Stuart down, which is a mighty queer thing. But he will come again. Therefore you had better know the politics of this country. Stuart does what he wishes pretty much. He drags some of the rest of the boys along simply by the power of his heavy hand. Gunderson and Bill Yell and Mitch Lovelace and Hack Dobbin are under his thumb. If he raises a posse after you he will draw on that crowd. Then there's Hoby Spade and Clyde Medary and me. I will not be against you. Spade and Medary may be against you, but they will not fight for Stuart. They do not like him. More likely you'll find Spade and Medary doing whatever Drew Trumbo does. There's your man. Find out what he's going to do."

"What's he want?"

"He wants Horsehead."

The flat sounding board of the prairie lifted the echoes of another traveler. "Coming fast," said DeLeon. "In this country trouble always travels fast." He returned to his horse and stepped up and he sat in the saddle, considering the yard; and then for the first time noticed the girl who had been so quietly placed in the shadows. Automatically he lifted his hat to her, his gesture an old-fashioned full sweep of his arm. Coleman said: "My guest, Valencia Wilder."

DeLeon bowed deep in the saddle. "Solvay's lady? My congratulations to him." The rider on the flat grass came in at a long-reaching gallop. Frank DeLeon said: "Good luck," and faded into the pines. Hardly had he done so when the new rider whirled before the porch and brought up. "Coleman," he said, "you have started your fun." His horse carried him into the beam of house light and he stepped quickly down. It was Solvay, his square cheeks a little more wooden than usual. He saw Valencia and said, "Good evenin'," and searched himself and brought forth the paper he had pulled from the cabin on the road to Gunderson's. "That's for you to read," he said and handed it to Coleman.

There were other ears in the yard. Pairvent moved forward from the darkness, and Ray Miller came along. Pairvent said: "What's up?"

Coleman first read the note to himself and then aloud: –

NOTICE TO THE BASIN

Today at eleven o'clock, on the flats of Star Cross just east of Monument Ridge, I came upon the outlaw members of the Horsehead crew, led by one Coleman, in the act of running some twenty head of Star Cross beef west to the river. Summoned to stand and deliver said cattle, Coleman refused and drove the stock away. Witnesses in this act of open rustling were five members of my crew. The following men are the rustlers: – Coleman, George Pairvent, Ray Miller, the kid Alvy, Baldy Bickle, old Ed Drum.

For each of these men I offer the reward of five hundred dollars, to be paid by me on evidence of their capture, or on evidence of their being killed resisting capture. The same sum for each. At the same time I give notice of the intention of Coleman to continue rustling, as stated to me, and I hereby call on volunteers to surround Horsehead quarters and take the said Coleman and his men into custody. Failing this aid at the hands of the other respectable men of the Basin, I propose to move against Horsehead myself and hang the crew.

DAN STUART

Ben Solvay said: "There's your fun, Coleman."

Pairvent murmured: "I told you he'd put the rope over us all. We played into his hands, like he wanted."

"Our beef," said Coleman.

"By God," flashed out Pairvent, "what difference does that make? The man's got us."

"We'll be here when he comes," said Coleman.

"Talk for yourself," said Pairvent.

"Sure," said Coleman. "You can run away from the charge of bein' a rustler. Which makes you one, all the way down the trail." He turned and he gave Pairvent a square, head-on glance. "I can't stand a man around me without guts!"

Pairvent brought a hand straight down before him, striking air; he wheeled about and groaned and walked into the black. Ray Miller, on the edge of the shadows, looked at Coleman with a rough grin and retreated.

Solvay stood in his tracks, listening. He watched Pairvent and Miller go and he followed Coleman with his glance as Coleman moved to the porch. Then Solvay saw the girl and noticed how closely she kept her eyes on Coleman. It hauled him up from his other thoughts.

"Ben," said Coleman, "do you know of a better place to put Valencia?"

Valencia swung her glance swiftly to Coleman, astonished. She murmured, "I'm not afraid."

"No," Coleman said, "you wouldn't be afraid."

Ben Solvay was angry at himself. He thought: "You damned fool, what did you leave her here for?" Then he said aloud: "No use of her movin'. But I'll stay. It might be somethin' new."

He still watched Valencia and he wished he knew, as she turned her eyes to him, what lay behind the brief and curious glance she gave him. It didn't last long; she put her attention back to Coleman. Ben wheeled and grabbed the reins of his horse and led it to the rear yard's corral. He took off the riding gear and he moved over to a stack of hay and threw several armloads into the corral. He took up his gear and strolled to the bunkhouse.

The Horsehead crew had gathered there and they gave him a cold shoulder. He stared back at each man and he said in his dry, common voice: "You can quit cheerin' anytime."

"You're a damned long way from home," said Baldy, giving forth no welcome.

"And in damned poor company," promptly replied Ben Solvay. "You got any notion to crowd me?"

"What's the hell's your hurry?" growled Baldy.

"If I'm hurryin'," said Ben, "it ain't backward." He paused and awaited the fruit of this remark. Baldy shrugged his shoulders and concluded to push no farther; whereupon Ben Solvay picked himself an empty bunk and climbed into it. He hung up gun and belt on the bunk's edge, he removed his hat and shoes; having undressed, he rolled the saddle blanket around him and lay back to stare at the bunkhouse ceiling.

He was in a frame of mind both injured and self-condemning. He had given over the girl to Coleman and the blame was his. Yet had he not said he would be back to claim her within the week? To himself he honestly admitted he had never intended coming back – but it was a blow to return and to find her looking not at him but at Coleman. He had felt poorly at himself for proposing to welsh on his bargain; what stung him was that Valencia had changed her mind ahead of him.

He lay wholly still and had it out with himself. This was not the woman, plain and straight, he had in his mind at all; she was something else and he did not want her. Still, she had stayed with him every moment since he had left her, a picture that would not leave his head, and she had drawn him here and she had raked up in him painful and unreasonable feelings he had not previously known.

He rolled a cigarette and smoked it through. The rest of the crew had turned in and one of the men had already begun to snore. Pairvent blew out the light. Long sleepless in the dark, Ben Solvay saw no answer. He did not want her, yet he had not the power of breaking her picture in his mind.

Coleman was still smoking on the porch when Valencia rose. She said, "Good night," and paused long enough to see his face turn in the shadows to her. He answered her and the sound of his voice played through her like warmth as she went to her room. She made herself ready for bed and she turned the light low on the stand and thought of him because she could think of nothing else. He knew what she was and still when he looked at her it was with good eyes, a decent man looking at a decent woman. He saw something in her other men had not taken time to see; he made her sure of herself again, after long unsureness.

She thought: "If he should want me in any way at all, I'd open the door. Perhaps he knows that too. But I wish it were possible for him to want me the nice and right way. Is that too much to hope? If he did I'd scrub these floors and be happy."

She heard Coleman's heavy steps go along the hall and turn in to the opposite room. She thought he walked slowly and that made her heart beat faster; she listened to his boots fall to the floor and she heard his weight sink into the bed. Quietness came to the house and nothing stirred on the ranch. She remained long wide-awake, acutely aware of the big man across the hall, half-fearing and half-hoping to hear him rise and cross to her door. Even as she had seen the good things in his eyes, she had seen also the man-hunger there. He was of that mixture.

In his room, Coleman did the small, methodical things he had always done. He wound his watch and laid it on the stand. He hung up gun and belt over the bed's post and laid his boots together directly at the bed's side so that he could swing immediately into them. He draped his pants over a chair and made up three cigarettes; one he lighted and two he placed on the chair within hand reach – one for the middle of the night if he awoke and one as soon as he rose for breakfast.

As he smoked he sat on the edge of the bed, feeling the nearness of Valencia. She was a powerful enough influence to be felt in the whole house and the image of her troubled him. He thought of her with a heavy, insistent appetite. He pulled his mind away from her by force, but his mind went back. He brought his jaws together, scowling and dissatisfied with himself, and he passed a hand over his face and got up in his bare feet and prowled the room. He came to his door and stopped and his swift desire to open the door jarred him. He had his hand on the knob. Heat came into his face, sticking his skin like needles. He moved away from the door and made a complete circle of the room and sat down on the bed again. He bent over, bringing his hands together. He thought: "She deserves better than that. Man's full of evil.

What have I got to hope for, thinkin' like this?"

He turned out the light and rolled into bed. It had been a long day and he was weary; the last ten minutes had raked him hard. He was ashamed of himself.

7

GAME OF FREEZE-OUT

When Dan Stuart returned from War Bonnet he found his daughter had not left Star Cross that day. "You didn't go see Trumbo?" he asked.

"No. You've got a scheme up your sleeve."

"If I'd told you to stay away from the man," he observed savagely, "you would have gone to him at once."

She met his iron-surly eyes; she shook her head. "I never dreamed you'd be willing to turn me over to a man you hated for the sake of getting what you wanted out of him."

He flung his fist unexpectedly at her. Just before he struck her he opened his hand so that the flat of it caught her on the shoulder and threw her against the house wall. He stood before her, heavy of breath, unashamed and brutally aroused. "If you were a boy I would have smashed in your face!"

"You have hurt me much worse in other ways," she said to him.

"You're like your mother—your head is full of empty fool things!"

"She must have been so sad, so lonely."

"Why?" cried out Dan Stuart. "I gave her a home and I fed her and she hated me for it, like you."

"She had to endure living with you," said Ann. She had never before permitted herself to say so harsh a thing; and the effect of it in him was immediate. He gave her a glance of uncontrolled hatred. "Your mother," he said, "set herself against me, like you're doing. She would never see things my way."

"You wanted somebody you could whip and bully and you wanted her to crawl back and lick your hand in gratitude."

"You know nothing of it!"

"I did not know her. I know you."

He was always a dangerous man when stung. She felt herself to be in danger now, and she faced him with her cool calm manner and knew he hated this above all. He could not endure resistance. He drew a great breath. "We have got to have a talk when I get this other business settled. If you are not with me, then you are against me—and if you are against me you cannot stay under this roof."

He stamped heavily across the yard and found Tap. "Ride over to Trumbo's and tell him I want to see him."

Tap was a loyal man but the suggestion that Star Cross should traffic with one of its enemies offended him. "He's not good for us," he complained.

"Go do it," said Stuart.

Tap went off, saying no more. The idea rankled him all across the desert and into the timber. This was a sin against Star Cross and a flaw in Dan Stuart. If a man was your enemy he could not overnight be your friend. You stuck to what was; you didn't change. This is what he thought as he came carefully down upon Trumbo's yard and hailed Trumbo from the house. Remaining in the shadows, Tap said: "Mr. Stuart says he'd like to talk to you," and rode away.

Trumbo listened as Tap's horse ran upgrade into the timber. A small wind came from the south, softly washing through the treetops. Trumbo built a cigarette and reached for a match, but before he lighted it he looked carefully at the dark yard and then turned to the wall and cupped the match so that it would not betray him. He played the message around his mind, seeking the meaning of it. Stuart despised him. Stuart, never a fool, had smelled ambition in him and Stuart could not stand ambition in other men. There was but one throne and one king to sit on it; all others aspiring to power were dangerous.

Something lay behind the message and he did not propose to move into a trap. Stuart, maybe, would be wanting a solid Basin front to move against Coleman. Trumbo, who was no sentimentalist, had an amused afterthought: "Just to make the steal look a little better." Still, it was hard to believe that so tough a fellow as Stuart would be asking for help—and therefore lay himself open to payment for that help—against Horsehead. How could Coleman fight back, with a crew that was no good at all? "More to it than I see now," he thought. With that in mind he saddled his horse and headed for town.

He reached War Bonnet near midnight and stopped at the saloon for a drink; and there he heard the story of the day. Coleman had backed Stuart down, Stuart had posted his notice; the long expected close-out of Horsehead was finally coming. Trumbo got all this from the saloon keeper, Snass Moran, during the course of a drink. He went on to the Alma and took a room and sat on the edge of the bed, thinking it over. Presently, he grinned to himself and went to bed.

With breakfast under his belt next morning, he struck out for Horsehead, arriving there by eight o'clock and catching Coleman in the yard. The crew was back by the bunkhouse, horses saddled and ready to travel. Pairvent was moving forward but as soon as he saw Trumbo he halted, stared a moment and wheeled away, to vanish behind the house. Coleman said: "Mornin', Trumbo. Light."

Trumbo got down. He was as large a man as Coleman, with a breadth to his shoulders and a naturally ruddy face in which sat a pair of bold blue eyes, a hawk-shaped nose and a firm, laughing mouth. He had complete confidence in himself and he displayed a worldliness that said plain as words: "All men have a price."

He didn't offer his hand when he came up. "Came for a visit," he drawled and noticed Valencia come to the porch. He lifted his hat at once and smiled. The smile was slightly off, somewhat knowing, and Coleman felt a slow ruffle of temper go through him. Coleman said: "Had breakfast?"

"At War Bonnet. I hear you played hell yesterday."

"Any vented stock over your way?" asked Coleman bluntly.

He never would have asked so pointed a question elsewhere. The Basin manners had gotten at him. Trumbo grinned but the grin was guarded. "A sudden way of putting it."

"I'll be collectin' from now on," said Coleman.

"Let's wait until you get my way before we discuss it," said Trumbo. All this while, Coleman understood, the man was figuring him. "I wanted to talk business with you."

Valencia's steps went over the porch, retreating, and for a moment Trumbo's glance followed her and the sight of her made a feeling on his face. He brought his eyes back quickly, as though he had permitted himself an unguarded moment.

"Talk it," said Coleman.

"There was a notice posted—"

"I saw it," said Coleman.

"He would have been after your hide sooner or later. You've just rushed matters."

"I'll be here when he comes."

"You backed him down, true. But he'll have help when he comes again."

"You'll be with him?" asked Coleman.

"Maybe," said Trumbo. "Maybe not. He's sent his bid to me, which is a strange enough thing, considering how he hates me."

"Why should he hate you?"

"I want Horsehead, same as he does," said Trumbo. "You see? If he wants me enough to forget a grudge it means he's comin' after you full tilt. But he knows I won't work with him unless there's something in it for me."

"What's he offerin'?"

"I don't know," said Trumbo and gave Coleman a full stare. "What are you offering?"

"What do you want?"

"All of Horsehead east of the river," said Trumbo. "It will make me a nice range—and it will leave you plenty."

"No," said Coleman.

"Man," said Trumbo, pointedly patient, "you need some help—and where do you think you'll get it? You've got no aces up your sleeve." Trumbo watched him a long while. "No," he decided, "you've got none."

"Sooner or later," said Coleman, "I'll be over your way, lookin' for beef."

Trumbo's smile grew keen. "You'll be gone from here before that happens. Listen to me. I am in this Basin for all its worth. I play my own hand strictly. If Stuart's got a good proposition I'll take it and I'll be back here with him. Don't make any mistakes about me. You caught Stuart off balance. I am never off guard."

"Glad to know it," said Coleman. "You want to try it now?"

Trumbo ceased to smile and he ceased to be casual. He became cold and careful and his temper came up within him, but not a temper that made him rash. "I never do anything just for fun. I play for chips."

"Whatever Stuart offers you," suggested Coleman, "he'll later take away. Play with him and you're a sucker."

Trumbo's edged humor returned. "If he makes a deal with me, he's the sucker. He doesn't know me and neither do you."

"So long," said Coleman.

Trumbo returned to his horses, mounted and wheeled away. He went twenty feet and returned to Coleman. He was dissatisfied with the scene and he wanted it right. "I talked to you straight, figuring you to be a fellow that didn't fool around with a lot of soft ideas. You're here for what you can get. If I didn't think that I would not have wasted my time coming. I like to get straight to the point. Life's too short to take the roundaboutway. I figure you a tough customer, but you have made the mistake of playing me down in your mind. When I come back you'll find me right in front of you and you'll find me right on your trail."

"So long," repeated Coleman.

Trumbo looked closely at Coleman and he shook his head. "With my help you could keep half of Horsehead. Otherwise you will lose it all. That is too bad." He turned again and this time moved straight out upon the flat grass at a swinging canter. As soon as he left the trees Coleman lifted his voice.

"George," he called, and waited for Pairvent to come forward. "George, has he got some of our beef?"

"I'd guess so," said Pairvent in a guarded voice.

"We'll go after it."

Pairvent shook his head. "I won't ride on his range."

"That's what I wanted to know. You sold him the beef and put the money in your pants."

"God damn your eyes!" growled Pairvent. "You got to see everything?"

Coleman smiled a little. "Not holdin' it against you. I can handle Trumbo without you. Meanwhile, you'll stay. We can use each other up till the showdown."

Pairvent murmured: "What showdown?"

"When you think the time's ripe to turn against me."

"Coleman," sighed Pairvent, "I wish I knew you."

When Drew Trumbo reached Cloud River he came upon a rowboat slipping downstream stern foremost, close-hugging the edge of the bank. Old Tam Malarkey sat in it, checking the boat's speed with his oars. Old Tam was in his fifties, a gaunt man burned to leather by the sun and showing a pair of rawhide wrists below a frayed shirt. An extra set of oarlocks had been fitted to the boat and second set of oars lay unshipped across the seats; and a woolly dog with one calico-colored eye sat on a pile of groceries near the stern and showed a pink tongue as it panted. Old Tam had rowed upriver through the easy water, moored his craft and had gone shank's mare into War Bonnet for a month's supplies, carrying a hundred pounds on his shoulders back to the boat. Now he would slip carefully down the river to the brink of Number Seven Rapids, tie his boat and carry his supplies into the depths of the canyon by devices and footholds which only he seemed to know. Tam had been in the canyon twenty years, panning gold lodged in the gravel.

Trumbo hailed him and Tam pulled in to the shore with his old man's slow and sure pace, wasting no strength. Tam put a foot over against the gravel, holding the boat still; he pulled out a pipe with an enormous bowl and filled it and lighted it up, and laid a wary glance along the glass-bright surface of the river, a veteran fighter sizing up a long-known and respected opponent. Presently he turned to Trumbo.

"On the wrong side of the river, ain't you, Drew?"

"Payin' a visit."

Old Tam sucked at the pipe until smoke made a stench around him. "I never thought I'd see this change."

"Everything is just as it has been. You're a smart old fellow, Tam, but that river's going to take you downhill someday and you'll be the new man in Luke Wall's graveyard. Why don't you get out of it?"

"I like a simple life," said Tam, "and I got it that way. Me and the river. Nothing more. I know where I stand and I know where the river stands. Maybe you can say the same thing, but I doubt it."

"Findin' much gold?"

"A little," admitted Tam. He pulled his foot aboard and let the boat drift, his oars poised. He watched the river with shaggy-browned eyes; and then he looked back. "Good thing there's just a little. If there was very much I'd have to watch out for you fellows who want things big and easy. What I got ain't enough to be worth your time. But if it was, you'd be after it." He had ignored the river for twenty seconds and that was long enough; he straightened his boat with his oars and coasted down the slick and bright water, alert and careful.

Trumbo swung east from the ford, considering the strangeness of Tam who wanted so little. The point of living was to leave a great scratch upon the world for everybody to see; to fight for power and to use whatever set of rules would bring power. In that respect he had always figured that Stuart had lived a good life, a life true to the things which drove him. Only in one respect did Stuart show weakness: he had a mind that never changed. Knowing error, he would continue with the error, and someday would be destroyed. Trumbo had analyzed the man many times, he had used Stuart as a text and a lesson, and he knew he was sharper and more flexible than Stuart. Therefore he would survive.

Arriving before the Star Cross house late in the morning, he first saw Ann. She was on a horse, moving out from the yard, and came immediately to him. He lifted his hat at her and he smiled, but he knew at once she wasn't pleased.

"Your father," he explained, "wanted to see me."

"I'm sorry you came."

He spoke out his surprise. "It would be a nice thing to be welcome here, wouldn't it? It would mean a lot to you and to me."

"Do you know why he wants to see you?"

"I can guess," he said. "He wants help."

"Would you make a deal with him?"

She was a fair, tall girl whose presence, whose smile and voice never failed to stir him. She liked him and he thought they were near something better than that. At Gateway one night he had taken her into his arms and he had looked down at her. She had not protested; she had lifted her eyes and she had watched him in her thoughtful way. He had tried to kiss her and immediately she had slipped out of his arms and after that her voice had gone cool, as though he had pressed too far too fast. She was not a girl to be at once known; she had strong feelings and fixed standards and now he searched himself carefully for an answer which would not bring to those eyes the shadows of judgment of which he was really afraid.

"Wouldn't you want me to be on your father's side?"

"Not if it is the wrong side, Drew."

She had never told him of her personal affairs; she was very quiet about her own life. Therefore her point of view puzzled him. "Star Cross is your side, Ann."

"Not if Star Cross is wrong," she insisted.

Stuart came up to the corrals and stopped near the porch. He said: "Trumbo, I'd like to see you." He tried to make it civil and agreeable, but even then it fell short. He was doing something now against his will, under the greater pressure of his needs. Ann rode from the yard, bound toward the northern hills at a reaching canter.

Trumbo advanced to the porch and got down, Stuart's eyes following him with their loaded harshness. Stuart growled: "Take a chair."

Trumbo walked to the chair. He stood near it and then he turned and caught a quick glimpse of Stuart's face again—its deep-lined, domineering strength, its blind self-faith. This man had in him greater capacities for straight brutality than he had so far shown the Basin. Trumbo said "I'll stand."

"Stand then," snapped Stuart.

Trumbo smiled his short, pressed smile. "What can I do for you?"

"You remind me of myself when I was a younger man," said Stuart. "You can grin well enough and you can sing and drink with the boys. But you're cold as a fish. I spotted that a long time ago."

"Sure you did," said Trumbo. "You've been layin' for me a long time, too."

"I never let a man get as big as I am," said Stuart. "You've got the idea of tryin' to be. You got a piece of land too close to me. I knew what you were up to—building your stock by slippin' a calf at a time away from Star Cross. The oldest trick in the world."

"It wasn't necessary," said Trumbo, still smiling. "Taking Horsehead beef was easier. I can put a vent brand on their beef as well as you can."

"Except," said Stuart, "that you had Pairvent bring it to you. You paid him to rustle his own outfit."

"Easier that way," agreed Trumbo. "You're sore because you didn't think of it first."

"Then," added Stuart, "not bein' sure of Pairvent, you paid Alvy to spy on his own outfit for you."

Trumbo's eyes widened. "Know that, too?" he breathed.

Stuart's temper pressed at his self-control. "You have tried to pull some of the ranchers away from me. I have heard how you proposed to split Horsehead between yourself and Spade and Medary, leavin' me out of it."

"Not hard," said Trumbo. "I can get along with those men. You always use a club over them. I offered those boys a piece of Horsehead for their trouble. What have you offered? You want them to help you take Horsehead but you don't want to give them any of it. If you're going to use a man for a sucker, Stuart, you've got to give him something."

"What do you want?" Stuart said, throwing the thing at him bluntly.

"Give me the Horsehead ranch quarters and the range west of the river – and the stock on it. That leaves you the country east of the river. The river's a proper boundary."

"Why don't you ask for it all?" said Stuart, using a heavy sarcasm.

"Because," Trumbo coolly answered, "I'm not big enough to take it all."

"Or any of it," retorted Stuart.

"What did you call me here for then?" demanded Trumbo.

"To give you a chance for a little gravy," said Stuart. "Not for the whole meal."

"You've tried to get the other outfits to help you clean out Horsehead," guessed Trumbo. "But they held back. So you sent for me. You wouldn't play pool with a man you hated unless there was no other way out of it. I'm here but you don't like me any better than you did – and you never will. Point is, you need me."

"All you've got is one set of arms," said Stuart. "No crew."

"I'll tell you why you called me in. You're too old to lay a gun on Coleman and come out first best. You can't figure any of your crew doin' it either. It is a tough outfit you're proposin' to fight. But you know I can meet him and you know I can pull faster."

"How would I know that?" said Stuart.

Trumbo gave Stuart a long, straight-pushing glance. "You went to a lot of trouble, some time ago, to look up my record before I came to the Basin. I heard about it from some of my friends down the trail. You found out didn't you?"

"I found out. You were too fast with your gun too many times."

"That's why you want me, said Trumbo. He was smiling, now knowing he had his man. Stuart stood glum and bitter on the porch, hating every bit of this scene. But he had a greater hatred, rising from the humiliation Coleman had put upon him. So he said in a heavy voice: "It is a deal. I will see Hoby Spade. I want him along. I'll be by for you when the right day comes."

Trumbo went to his horse and climbed to the saddle. He looked back at Stuart and he thought he saw a changed expression on the man's face, a half-hidden satisfaction. Stuart was thinking that he had done this piece of work well; that when Coleman was out of the way, it would be no great thing to put Trumbo also out of the way. It was on the end of Trumbo's tongue to say this much, but he held his peace and rode on. He had his own schemes.

He rode over the yellow grass to the Star Cross hills and turned to keep within the timber as he traveled home. Now and then he saw the Horsehead plain below him through the pines, all yellow with summer; and presently he noticed a flare of dust far out near the river. He kept his eye on it as he rode, now losing it as the trees thickened, now seeing it again. It was, he thought, a string of cattle moving toward water; but in another ten minutes he stopped and looked more closely. Cattle, by their own impulse, never trudged along that steadily or that fast. Therefore they were being driven. Suddenly, struck by forewarning, he left the ridge on the run and pointed west.

It took him an hour to reach the driven stock. Long before he got there he knew what had happened. He counted five men with the beef and he counted the beef itself as it strung along. There were seventy or eighty head moving steadily away from his range. He began to curse aloud long before any of the Horsehead crew could hear him; he cursed the ranch and he cursed every man on it and when he came to Pairvent he cried out: "I will kill him, by God I will, for playing me both ways!" He looked for Pairvent and then saw that the foreman was not with the crew. Three hundred yards away he pinned his glance to Tracy Coleman and he drove at Coleman straight on; and only the deep calculating cold streak which was in him saved him from drawing as he came. He stopped, watching Coleman quietly turn his horse half-around. Coleman's face was bone-hard and his eyes were wide-open, wicked and quiet.

"Damn your soul!" cried Trumbo.

Coleman laid a flat order on Trumbo. "Keep your hands on that saddle unless you mean to fight."

"I met worse men than you and lived to see them buried!" snarled Trumbo.

"Watch your hands," repeated Coleman. "I will not tell you again."

"Why didn't you rustle my range when I was around!" yelled Trumbo.

"I told you I'd be over. Now I'll tell you something else. You've got a lot of fat stuff grazin' your grass, mostly borrowed from Horsehead. I'll come again."

"No," said Trumbo, "you'll never come again."

"Say your piece," said Coleman, "and do what you plan to do. We're wastin' time."

Trumbo sized up the crew, holding himself on even balance. Alvy the kid was at the head of the column, walking as the beef walked, but looking back over his shoulder. Ed Drum and Baldy moved on. Coleman stood fast and behind him was Ray Miller, showing a squinted smile. Trumbo gritted his teeth together. "You're waitin' for me to be a fool." He gripped the pommel with both hands and he squeezed his strength into them and sighed. His coolness returned. Raising his reins, he said: "I will see you in good enough time," and trotted away.

Miller looked after Trumbo, until the latter was far beyond range. He said to Coleman: "Now there's a boy which has smelled powder somewhere. Didn't realize that till just now."

"It is written all over him. Time to push on."

Ray Miler's weather-tight grin remained. He said: "Now you're a great hand to figure—and you been figurin' the boys on Horsehead pretty close. How you got me figured?"

Coleman looked at him. "Rather have you on my side than against me, Ray."

"I like most any kind of a fight," said Ray. "Always been that way with me."

"One's coming."

"Then," said Ray, "I'm with you. I like the way you work."

8

A SMALL DREAM DIES

Ann Stuart rode over Star Cross grass to the near-by southern ridge; and when she reached the trees she looked back to discover that Trumbo had finished his interview and was riding west. Therefore she followed the ridge, paralleling Trumbo's course, and at last reached a junction trail and waited. At the end of a half hour he had not appeared and so she continued until she was on the main road directly behind his house. It was then near noon. Drew came along not long after. She noticed at once that he had been through some considerable scene and had been left the worse for it. He neither lifted his hat nor smiled.

"Did you quarrel with my father?"

"No," he said. "We got along all right."

"You're in a bad frame of mind."

"I just met Coleman and his crew driving my beef back over the river."

"Was it that vented beef?" When he nodded, she said: "I'm sorry you took it. Never mind what rules the Basin laid down—it wasn't right."

"I'll have it back," he said.

"You're like my father. You give nothing up and you don't change easily."

He sat still, not trying to follow her thoughts as he usually did. The niceness and the consideration were gone and the irony which leavened his spirit was missing. She had never been too certain of his character but she had liked him well enough to be interested in his future. What she now saw was a gambler's calculating ambition, and this hurt her. "What did my father want?"

"Help."

"He wants to destroy Coleman and he wants Horsehead. He has always wanted it. What did he offer you?"

"Your father never gives anything if he can help it. I had to make the offer—all of Horsehead west of the river for me. All of it east of the river for him. He accepted."

"Coleman won't run."

"It will be a fight," he said, "if he can make his crew fight."

"You have agreed," she said, "to help kill him. That is the bargain."

He had grown irritated at the way her talk pushed him unfavorably back. "Take another look at it," he said. "If Coleman hadn't come here that ranch would have been split up in another three months without a fight. But Coleman comes. Look at him carefully a minute. What is he? Another man fighting to get a piece of land—just like I am. Is he any better than I am?"

Her logical mind supplied an immediate answer. "Horsehead still has an owner. You are not the owner."

"The Basin says different."

She shook her head. "I have watched all of the Basin ranchmen when they spoke of opening up Horsehead. In the eyes of every one of them, Drew, was a look that wasn't quite square. They know they're not on sound ground."

"Square or not," he said, "somebody in the Basin will take over Horsehead. I want my part of it."

"Horsehead," she repeated, "is an owned ranch."

He shrugged his shoulders, he grew frank. "I am the smallest owner in the Basin. A man like me, with nothing to show for his years, gets sour. I have got to cut my notch. These big owners came here when everything was open and they took what they wanted—men no better than I am. Your father did it. So will I."

"Don't grow big on other men's bones. Go where the range is still open."

"The world is gettin' small. The free grass is just about gone. I am a little too late to be one of the pirates lookin' out on a million acres of range. But I was born to be one of those fellows and I'll be one. Horsehead is my last chance."

"Drew," she said, "I have been waiting to see one man strong enough not to be changed by the Basin. I had thought you were that man."

"Why," he said, "nothing changes me. Whatever you see about Drew Trumbo is something Drew Trumbo always had in him."

She was grave and thoughtful; she shook her head. "I am disappointed."

He went toward her and put his hands on her shoulders. She didn't move but as he watched her, closely and with anxiousness, he saw little doors close against him which once had been half-opened. He tightened his fingers on her shoulders. "Don't turn against me!"

She looked down from him. "It is more than disappointment," she murmured, and when she looked up there were tears in her eyes. He brought her against him and he tried to kiss her. She pushed against him and stepped aside.

"Ann," he said, "you want me to be a little fellow carryin' a hoe?"

"You will be what you are," she said. "A man may try to change and a woman may think she has changed him, but it is only an outward thing. He remains the same."

He shook his head. "What do you want in a man?"

She closed it out with a gesture, and changed the subject. "When will you be doing this?"

She was sorry she had asked the question. His eyes became different and his character was another character, all in the space of a moment. This man, she well knew, had loved her and still loved her; in every meeting it was a feeling that came from him to touch her. Yet this suddenly had he the power to pull away and close her out and look upon her as an enemy to his plans. She stepped back to her horse and mounted. "So long, Drew."

"I'll see you again," he said. He came up to her and for a little while he recaptured his smiling manner. But it was too late then. She had never really given him her heart; in all their moments of closeness she had held herself away from that final step. It wasn't only that she was not quite certain of him; she was also unsure of herself, sometimes wondering if the lonely search of some personal answer for herself might not lead her to a false decision. But he had always known – for she had let him see it – that he was closer to her and more desirable to her than any other man. The rest might have followed. Instead, he had chosen to put another desire before her. "I'll see you again," he repeated. "I'll come to you someday, a man with something to offer."

"An offer of land and cattle?" she said. "Drew, you're blind. Good-by."

She rode through the trees, checking the horse to a walk, meanwhile thinking of Drew Trumbo from her first meeting with him onward to the last one. She recalled his words and the tone of his voice and the unsaid things in his voice and the times he had pleasantly lifted her spirit out of its loneliness and as she thought of all this she took Drew Trumbo from her heart little by little until at last there was only an empty spot where he had been.

She rode the hardest mile of her life; and halted and sat still, knowing there was no living person who now had a claim on her, and no living person on whom she might have a claim. She was as thoroughly alone in the world as if there were no other thing alive on the planet. All her search for color and warmth, for the comfort of some man's closeness, had ended with this great solitariness. She had left only her convictions of right and wrong – and so turned downslope toward the river's ford.

She came to the Horsehead yard in midafternoon, finding Valencia Wilder on the porch. She had heard of the girl's being there, and the reason for it. Such news traveled with something near the speed of light in the Basin; and it had aroused Ann

Stuart's natural curiosity. She wondered about Coleman. Even though this girl was engaged to be married to Ben Solvay, what would her closeness to Coleman do to him? For her first meeting with Coleman had told her at once he was a robust man, something in his voice and on his face betraying the quick currents which ran within him. It would be natural for him to seek the beauty and the comfort of a woman.

Valencia Wilder said: "Will you get down?"

Dismounting, Ann came to the porch. Valencia was a smaller girl than she, very dark and with a spirit glowing like hot coals in her. Her smile was a small lightness around her mouth and her eyes were sharp and alert for trouble; she was far prettier, Ann thought, than the grapevine rumor had indicated. She wasn't hard – Ann looked at once for that – but she had a self-sufficiency, and she was on guard.

"I'd like to speak to Tracy Coleman if he's around," said Ann.

"He's back of the house," Valencia said. She stood a moment, openly interested. "You're Ann Stuart. You know my name, I imagine, and my reason for being here."

"We've got a good system of gossip in the Basin," said Ann.

"Unkind, I suppose," said Valencia, her expression slightly hardening.

"If there was unkindness," said Ann, "men would keep that to themselves."

"But not women."

"I seldom see other women. This is mostly a man's country."

"Yes," said Valencia, "they make the rules."

"You don't have to follow them."

"I don't," said Valencia.

Doña Gertrude came quickly through the doorway, untying an apron. She said: "Welcome to our house," and her smooth old face lighted. "It is long since you have been here before. Things go well?"

"Things go well, Doña Gertrude. You have not visited us."

Doña Gertrude's face turned regretful. "The men of this ranch and the men of your ranch –" she said, and conveyed the rest of it with a shrug.

"Miss Stuart wants to see Mr. Coleman," said Valencia Wilder. She looked at Ann and she permitted Ann to see one small, possessive streak. "I will go tell him."

But Doña Gertrude said: "You would not wish to leave your guest alone. I will do your errand for you." She moved placidly back through the house.

"Something out of the old, old past," murmured Ann. "And very nice."

A rebel note came to Valencia's voice. "To Ben-Tim, I gather, she was a chattel to remain with his property when he left."

"Perhaps," said Ann, "they thought it better to be apart. They were both growing old and maybe they wanted to have their memories to live on."

Valencia said: "You make people better than they are."

"Badness and goodness are close together. It is better to think of the goodness."

"I would worship the memory of no man," said Valencia. "If he didn't care enough to hold me forever I'd hate him."

Ann gave Valencia a close inspection and shook her head. "You are deceiving yourself."

Coleman came up from the rear of the house and turned to the porch. He had been trying out a tough horse and his face was red from the pounding and when he removed his hat sweat rolled down from his forehead. He grinned and reached for his tobacco and divided a look between the women. "You've met?"

"Yes," said Valencia.

He had his eyes then on his hands, rolling the cigarette. The tone of her voice lifted his glance and he watched her a considerable moment, and it was that long look which Ann wondered about. He was a man with sharp eyes. What did he see in this dark strange-willed girl and what were his thoughts of her? She already knew what Valencia Wilder's thoughts were of Coleman; as soon as he stepped to the porch Valencia's face showed change.

"I wanted to talk a minute with you," she said to Coleman.

Valencia Wilder moved back into the house, not speaking yet leaving something of her disturbing self behind.

"I'm surprised," said Coleman. "Your father and I are not friends." He paused and soberly added: "Nor is Trumbo my friend."

"I know. That's why I'm here."

"Thanks," he said. "But you must not get into my troubles."

"You got into mine, at Gateway. I'm paying back." She saw Pairvent standing down the yard near the bunkhouse, tall and rigid and motionless on the ground, his glance pinned to her. She said: "Ride out from here a short way," and went to her horse. She waited while he walked to the rear of the house and rode back. They moved together out upon the plain. "How far can you trust your crew?"

"Far as I can keep my eyes on them. Except for two men. Solvay and Miller will do."

"Miller's tough. He killed one of Gunderson's crew last winter in the hills."

"He'll stick. He sees a good fight comin'."

"What a terrible judgment of a man." Then she thought of something else and was slightly surprised. "Ben Solvay's good. How did it happen he came here?"

"Came to warn me last night, about your father's notice. Then he saw his girl again." He rode the better part of a hundred yards before adding, "I think he regrets his decision to leave her here, and now stays to be near her."

"Probably he feels she needs more protection."

"Probably," he said.

She looked at him quickly; he had an odd expression on his face and in a moment, because of the increasing smile in her eyes, he turned red. Suddenly she put both hands down to the saddle horn and laughed in uncontrolled amusement. The wry, embarrassed expression grew on him and he smiled a little and that made her laugh again until she had to hunt up her handkerchief and dry her eyes. "Oh, Tracy," she said, "the expression on your face was so funny. Have I hurt your feelings?"

"No," he said.

"I wouldn't want to do that. You're a very honest man. She's quite pretty, too."

"I suppose," he admitted cautiously, "she might be considered so."

She tried to suppress her laughter but could not. "I suppose," she jeered, "you've had no time to notice it. Ah, but you are transparent. And that is of course why Ben Solvay decided to stay and defend his interests. Ben is not a fool."

"I wouldn't have left her to another man's care," he admitted.

"Was it," she inquired with a very gentle malice, "entirely Ben's idea."

He showed embarrassment again. "Why would she think of it? She came here to marry him."

"She saw you at Gateway, didn't she?" said Ann, in the same idly provoking tone.

"What of that?" He eyed her with doubt. She had her glance thrown forward into the lengthening yellow rays of sunlight; she was serene, and humor disturbed the corners of her mouth. "Well," he admitted, "if she were my girl I'd not be tradin' her around."

"If she were," said Ann, still looking ahead, no longer amused. He rode on with her, content to wait out what she had to tell him; and so they came a good deal later to the ford. She looked back across the plain and showed surprise. "I didn't realize I had carried you this far from home."

"The ride," he said, "was pleasant to me."

She gave him a pleased glance. "You have a nice way of putting things." Then she remembered the reason for her visit. "I do not agree with my father or Drew Trumbo or the Basin. I think Horsehead is an owned ranch and I think that vented-stock idea is just as crooked as open rustling. I have to tell you this, otherwise you might think it unnatural for me to say the rest of it. My father and Trumbo intend to raid you. Soon I think."

He sat still on the saddle, looking out upon the river. His nerves were well-covered, not easily touched by little disturbances or rumors. She got the renewed impression, as she watched him, of a man wholly confident of his chores in the surface world but greatly troubled by other and deeper things.

At times he could be quite homely. He was now as he turned to those fighting impulses which seemed his natural life; his face showed its stout bones and his lips lay in close rolls and everything in him—his fancies and his lightness and his easy moods—were put aside.

"I wish," he said, "you had not come to me with this."

"You are under no obligation to the Stuart family."

"Maybe not. This fight will unroll, regardless of you or me. Still, you came." He looked at her with a straight suddenness. "I will think of that when I do something which hurts you."

"My father?"

"I see no way of duckin' it." He gave her another direct glance. "I do not quite understand how it is between you and your father."

"It would be too long a story to tell."

"And I do not quite understand how it is with you and Trumbo."

"That," she said slowly, "is a story which is ended. My father made a deal with him. He accepted it—and so he will be against you."

He listened to her and she felt he took in her words and understood them and that his mind went on and grasped the things she had not said. Gradually the plain homeliness went from his face. "There's right and wrong—and many things half-right and half-wrong," he observed. "I have quit judgin' people. We are all in the same wagon, passin' through the same scenery, bound for the same place. But every man has a different set of eyes, and there's the beginnin' of right and wrong. That is why I'm here with you, and why your father will move at me. It does no good to talk about it. But I hate to think of hurtin' you."

She sat up in the saddle, startled at the change in him and what the change did to her. He was more than he had been the moment before; and he had become more to her simply by speaking from deeper places. He was saying things that might have come straight from her own private thoughts—said with a faintly saddened note, an unsure note.

She said: "I had no intention of riding you so far. But you

let me laugh and I needed to laugh. It's been a long day."

He looked at her with the same directness. His thoughts were so fully on her that they made a feeling in her, warm and embracing. "Long day. I noticed that in your eyes. Nothin' comes the way you think it should be and the world is blind and dumb to what you see. Finally you figure it is something that doesn't exist—that you're just makin' pictures on water."

"Yes," she said.

"I wish to God I would not be soon hurtin' you."

She turned the horse into the water and crossed it; she didn't look back, even though she knew he was still watching her. She climbed the low bluff and as he struck out at a long run over the flatlands she was openly crying for the first time since childhood. Then the tears quit and she kept her mind on him all the way home; and suddenly she no longer felt like laughing at the thought of Valencia Wilder in his house. The tolerance left her and dislike of the other girl came.

Coleman returned to Horsehead through the long last sunlight, hearing the gong-strike of the dinner bell; and he sat at the head of the table, not speaking at all while he struggled with his close thoughts. Stuart had six men and Trumbo made seven. There might be another outfit throwing in with Stuart. Against that he had these six men at the table. Which of them would fight, which of them could he trust? He thought to himself, "I had better send Alvy on his way before he gets another chance to betray me." Solvay would have to pull out with the girl. That left four.

The crew ate and departed and Doña Gertrude silently vanished. Valencia remained, watching him. He heard Ben Solvay impatiently tramping back and forward on the porch. He looked at Valencia. "He wants you."

She said: "He didn't want me four days ago."

"Changed his mind. You can see it on him."

"Maybe I have changed mine," said Valencia. "Can you see that on me?"

He said: "You've got to pull out tomorrow. We're going to be paid a visit."

"They would never touch me."

"If some fool starts shootin' there's no way of pushin' a bullet aside." He got up in the twilight of the room; and she rose and moved at him. She stood in front of him, looking up, her eyes turned to the color of slate, and wide-sprung. There was a heavy expression on her mouth. "What did the girl want of you?"

"She wanted nothing."

"Everybody wants something."

"Yes," he said, "everybody does. But few of us get what we want."

"Nothing can stand against that stubborn mind of yours, once you decide upon a thing. You can have whatever you want." She held herself before him and she held her arms stiff at her sides, waiting. She watched the effect of her nearness go through him and she knew she had unsteadied him, she knew she had broken his will for that moment.

"Tracy," she said, "after all I have been through, I'm still good. The best of me has never been given away. I feel it, all of it, right inside where it has always been. If there had ever been a man big enough to see it there, it would have gone to him. There never was such a man. Do you believe that?"

"I've seen it," he said. "It's there." He held his talk, searching himself for the right word. "When you're not thinkin' of the world you hate so much, it is like the light in a young girl's eyes, clear as crystal."

"Tracy," she said, her voice crowded and trembling, "can a man see that—and forget the rest? Can he ever?"

"There are men who would," he said.

But, listening with her whole private world waiting on him, she did not quite hear the one thing she wanted to hear, and at that point she gave up the good standard she had set for herself. If she could not have him one way she would try the other. She murmured: "You kissed me the other night," and she put her arms to his shoulders, lightly resting them there; and reached up and kissed him. The reserve in her vanished before the heat of her wish and she held him with all the strength she had.

He touched her gently, hearing Ben Solvay's boots stamp back through the house. Valencia stepped away, sighing. Solvay was at the dining room's doorway. He said in a short, cranky voice: "Ten minutes is long enough for anybody to eat supper, isn't it?"

"Ben," said Coleman, "this ranch is to be raided. Take Valencia out of here tomorrow."

In the gathering darkness of the room he witnessed the relief come to Ben's round cheeks. "Tonight," Solvay said. "Right away. I'll find an extra saddle. Never mind the trunk. I can come back for it."

He took Valencia by the arm, going through the house. Coleman followed to the porch and found the crew collected under the trees. Pairvent said: "What's on your mind? What'd the girl tell you?"

"Stuart's comin', with Trumbo. Don't know what other outfits."

"Tonight?" asked Pairvent in a knife-keen tone.

"Soon. Maybe tonight, maybe not."

Ben Solvay left the porch and cut around to the rear yard. Pairvent passed a hand across his wedge-shaped face. "I know Stuart. He never lets a thing wait. God damn you, Coleman, you have whipsawed us into it. Alvy, get your horse and ride to the ford. Watch-see if anybody crosses. Don't dream, boy!"

"No," said Coleman. "Get your horse and keep goin', Alvy. I don't want you around at all."

"Listen," said Pairvent, "if I'm foreman, don't go over my head. I'm not goin' to throw a man away. If he tricks us I'll kill him, but we got to use him."

Alvy murmured: "This is my outfit."

Coleman said: "All right—all right." Alvy ran back into the yard, making a scarecrow shape through the shadows. Coleman called after him. "Get a horse for Doña Gertrude. She'll ride away with Ben and Miss Wilder."

Pairvent said: "What'll it be, Coleman? We can stand off our own size but we can't buck too much weight."

"You're stayin', George?"

Pairvent spoke from his long-held-anger, from his grinding resentment. "I'm stayin'. I nursed this place along three years. I would have pulled it through. I had my deals made and they were good enough to keep the Basin from movin' in. You have played hell—and it is your chestnuts I have got to help pull out of the fire. I'll do it. Then we'll see whose ranch this is, yours or mine."

Ben Solvay returned with three led horses. "Time to go," he said. Alvy came by at a headlong run, rushing for the open land. "Time to go," said Ben Solvay again.

Coleman murmured: "Nothing's happened yet. Slow down."

Doña Gertrude moved slowly forward. "What is this foolishness, Don Tracy? What is this talk of going?"

"There is a reason for you to leave here," said Coleman. "It will not be for long."

"I will stay," said Doña Gertrude, firm and calm. "This is my home. Do not command me to do a thing which I cannot obey."

Pairvent said: "What'll it be, Coleman? Make your plan while you got time to make it."

"Never plan too far, George. A man can't scheme against ghosts."

Ben said: "Valencia, you'll have to try ridin' side saddle on a straight horn. Come on——"

She had not stirred from the porch; and did not now. The night wind rose and ran through the trees with its blends of dust and grass and pine. The heat of the day slowly moved against Coleman, the night silence had its edge of suspense. He had not felt it before, and now stood quite still, wondering whence it came. The crew was around him, waiting—and maybe they made the tension which lay upon him as a growing weight. Ben started to speak again but Coleman said: "Shut up." He took one step toward the back yard, and stopped; and he knew the night was turning wrong while he delayed. He made a circle on his heels. He stared through the increased blackness of the trees. Out on the plain he saw nothing in the shadows, and heard only the drum of Alvy's horse; presently, as he listened, he heard that come to an abrupt halt. Pairvent also heard it. He said: "Something's up."

"Wait," said Coleman. The weight pushed against him more and more and had no direction to it. He murmured: "Valencia – Doña Gertrude, get on your horses."

"Tracy," murmured the girl, "I don't want to go!"

"Now!" he said. It grew worse and worse; he took one false step to the porch, halted, and swung toward the back yard. Suddenly he broke into a run toward the corral rack. "Come on – come on. Ben, get those women out of here." He reached the corral with the crew tumbling behind him. Pairvent grumbled, "What's up – where's – "

Coleman was in the saddle when the first racket came; and the source of it told him how it was. Riders came down the hill behind the house at full tilt, crying; they had circled the grass plain during daylight to these hills, they had crept down – and they were here. He was out in the yard, the other Horsehead men swinging around him. Pairvent cursed violently and Ray Miller was laughing out his dead-toned pleasure. Coleman shouted at the porch: "Get out of here with your women, Ben!"

Stuart's voice overrode all other voices pouring off the hill. "Left side of the house! Left side of the house!"

Ray Miller answered for Horsehead; his eager answer jumped back at Stuart. "You go to hell!" It was Ray Miller also who opened the firing. Coleman said: "Drop back to the trees in the front yard." He ran his horse over there, troubled about the women. They were in the saddle and Solvay had only then started off. "Move out!" Coleman yelled. "Move out fast!" His crew had come up. Stuart's men boiled into the back yard and the steady, hard-round claps of gunfire broke into the trees and ran out upon the flats and echoed on and on through the hillside. He knew then Stuart had found other help, for suddenly the pressure of Stuart's outfit got greater in the front yard. The Horsehead men were steady around him, shifting through the trees as he shifted, answering Stuart's fire. "Lay it on," he called. Bullets clipped the trees near at hand; he heard them sing and shatter. "Cover the yard," he said. "They've got no shelter." He saw the black weave of shapes in the yard. He heard one man's cry; and that cry took the drive out of Stuart's riders. The blackness of their shapes grew vaguer as they turned behind the house to try an approach from the other side.

Ben Solvay shouted, near at hand. "Come back here, Doña Gertrude!"

Doña Gertrude rode past on her horse. Coleman reached at her and missed her. She stopped the horse at the porch and slid down. She said in a breathless voice, "This is my home," and in another moment Stuart's men swept around the far side, firing in sudden rushes. Doña Gertrude's voice lifted, high and crying: "Ah, ah, *Dios!*"

She had fallen. Over there Stuart's voice turned crazy. "You've hit a woman! Now—now—at those trees!"

Coleman heard Valencia Wilder's voice directly behind him. "I won't leave!" And it was that one thing which took the fight from him. "Pairvent," he said. "Pairvent!"

"Here."

"Make a run for the hills."

Ray Miller heard that. "What the hell—we're all right!"

"Do as I say," ordered Coleman. He wheeled at Valencia. He said, "Go in front of me," and he ran through the pines with Horsehead moving beside him. He saw Pairvent swing into the trail and he heard Stuart's greater yell behind: "Come on—they're runnin'!" Pairvent had vanished up a trail. Coleman called to Valencia, "Follow Pairvent—go on, go on!" His horse dropped to a walk on the grade, but he dug in his spurs and forced it to a labored run. He heard Stuart once more, now from a greater distance; and he heard Horsehead's men come behind him. He called forward to Pairvent: "Keep going until you get to a good hide-out." Doña Gertrude, he realized, was dead at the doorway of the house, and Stuart had won his first move.

9

DEAD WOMAN'S HAND

The smell of powder smoke clung to the yard long after the firing had ceased and long after Horsehead vanished up the trail. Tap ranged around the front yard and through the front trees. He circled the house and came again to the group standing near the porch. He said: "Mr. Stuart, you're doin' wrong, standin' here. We should be after him."

He could not understand the silence and the weariness which had come over this group. There were ten of them, Stuart and the Star Cross men, and Trumbo, and Hoby Spade with two of his hands. After the last firing they had all stopped in their tracks. Tap had gone onto the porch, bent over Doña Gertrude and come back to report her death. "Bullet in the chest." The group around him had changed at that moment—the wind punched out of their bellies. Now he again said: "We should be after the man."

Spade murmured: "We go rammin' through that timber and we'll run into a beautiful trap. He's probably layin' for us up there." Hoby Spade's voice gave him away; he was sickened of the business.

Stuart said: "He won't be comin' back." Tap listened to Stuart, hearing nothing familiar. The Star Cross owner's sureness was gone.

"Why won't he?" asked Trumbo.

"Nothin' to come back with. That crooked crew will keep right on travelin'. They see the writin' in the sky. He's alone with his woman. Tomorrow this time they'll be over the range."

Tap thought to himself: "That is strange." For Stuart was talking cautious.

Spade said: "I'll pull out. Nothing to stay for now. Good luck, Drew."

Trumbo had lighted a cigarette. He reached up and pulled it quickly from his mouth. "Hold on."

"For what?" asked Spade.

Trumbo pointed at the porch. "Doña Gertrude."

The chill, uneasy silence came again. Stuart said at last: "Take the boys, Tap. Hunt up some shovels. Dig a grave somewhere." He made a step toward the porch and wheeled back. "It could have been a bullet from the Horsehead outfit just as well as one of ours. It may have been."

"I hope so," Spade murmured. "It is a pretty grisly thing to remember. I don't like it."

"Well," said Stuart, "it is done. Can't make a cake without breakin' eggs."

"Can't put the wrong eggs back together again either."

"You don't need to keep talkin' about it," said Stuart. He raised his voice. "Get about it, Tap. Get about it!"

Trumbo said "The Basin won't like it. We're in a bad light."

"Why did she have to run straight into us?" grumbled Spade.

"Might have been Horsehead's fire," repeated Stuart.

Spade suddenly thought of a possibility. "Any chance of keeping this quiet?"

"You think anybody's goin' to mention it?" asked Trumbo.

"No," said Spade. "But she'll be missed sooner or later."

"Let Coleman answer for that," said Trumbo.

"Somebody in his outfit will talk," Spade said.

Stuart broke in. "Who'll believe those fellows?" Then he added in a different tone: "There's that woman."

Tap called from the trees. "Solvay, too."

A strange sound came out of Stuart, half a groan and half a sigh. Trumbo dragged in the smoke of his cigarette and threw it to the ground; and he stood with his head lowered. They remained like this, all of them hard-caught by the situation they were in. Tap called, long afterward: –

"This is deep enough. Get Doña Gertrude."

"Go get her, Tap," said Stuart.

Tap, who had never disobeyed Stuart before, didn't move from the shadows of the pines and he didn't answer. Stuart jerked his head upward and said with a return of his old arbitrariness: "You hear?"

"Mr. Stuart," said Tap, "I will not touch her."

Trumbo suddenly swung toward the porch. Doña Gertrude had reached the house's front door and had fallen there, her small body blocking it. Lamplight came out of the doorway and touched her. She lay as a little heap of black clothes, her two hands drawn up toward her shoulders. Trumbo stepped over her into the house and went on to a bedroom, finding a blanket. He came back and spread the blanket on the porch. Nobody else had come forward. He lifted Doña Gertrude onto the blanket and rolled it about her and he carried her out to the trees. He stepped into the grave and laid Doña Gertrude on the bottom and got out. The crew began to shovel in the dirt; at the sound Trumbo whirled on his heels and went back to the group. The sound followed him and suddenly he removed his hat.

"It is a bad break for us," he said.

It didn't need to be said; they knew it. They were thinking about it and they were trying to slide away from it. He saw it on Hoby Spade's face; he saw it on Stuart whose eyes, even in the shadows, showed their hard, sly gleaming. Both of these men would try, in some way or another, to put the affair on him. Spade said: "Time to get out of here," and walked away. Trumbo turned and followed him; when they were alone, beyond hearing distance of the others, Trumbo caught Spade's arm and whirled him around. He put his face close to Spade's. "You're not backing out on us. You've got what you wanted. You made your deal with Stuart. You're stickin' to it."

Spade said: "This thing will stink up the whole Basin. No use, Drew. Mistake's been made. I'm through with it now."

"How do you propose to get rid of what's already done?"

"It's done. But I won't make it worse by takin' Stuart's pay for it."

"You'll do what you set out to do," said Trumbo. He put his strength into the grip on Spade's arm. He saw Spade's expression tighten and he knew he had put fear into the man. "You were in this when it looked easy. You'll stay in it when it is gettin' hard. If I call for help from you, I want it. If I don't get it I'll come after you!"

Spade pulled his arm free and moved away. In a moment he raced from the yard with his two punchers. The man had less bottom than Trumbo had thought; and his very weakness might betray them all. He moved back to Stuart. "Spade," he said, "is trying to slide out."

Stuart said nothing. Tap came up and all the Star Cross men stood by. Trumbo rolled a cigarette and lighted it. He held the match suddenly close to Stuart's face and watched the man. The light went out. Stuart said: "Well, time to go."

Trumbo said: "You think it is finished?"

"We drove him off," said Stuart. "It's done."

"You're wrong—and you'll see why in a few hours. It will just ride back home with you."

Stuart walked away. Trumbo stood still, watching the Star Cross men fade to their horses and swing back; they returned through the yard on the run and in a little while vanished. For a moment the murmur of their traveling remained in the air and then that died and the silence began to flow around Trumbo, thick and disturbing. He had not finished his smoke but he dropped it and walked to the house. He moved to the lighted lamp in the living room and turned it down. He put his hands in his pockets and went from room to room. Fire burned in the kitchen stove and the coffee pot was still warm. He lifted the pot and drank from it; and stood still, listening for outer sounds. He left the house by the back door and put his shoulders against the house wall, facing the slope of the hills.

Spade was full of fear and Stuart would be steadily scheming to put the burden of this affair on him, on Trumbo. Stuart, he knew, had never intended going through with his bargain, and did not intend to go through with it now. The killing of Doña Gertrude had set him back; but it would be only an added prompting to work the deal around to his own advantage if he could.

There was no sound at all on the place; silence pulsed around him like the pulse of his own heart. He stood still, straining with attention. His muscles were tight and his jaws bitten together. He slid along the wall and returned to the front yard. He took his horse into the front pines and he squatted down there; and he saw something now that he hadn't seen before. He was alone on this place with Coleman moving somewhere free through the hills. He was trapped on Horsehead, as Coleman had been a little while before. Coleman had traded positions with him – and now Coleman had the advantage of surprise and attack.

Stuart had probably thought that same thing, and had been quick to pull out from the ranch and leave him alone. Trumbo struck his fist into the soft soil. He rose, walking through the trees. Doña Gertrude's grave was a dark patch on the ground before him; he swerved aside and turned about, at that moment realizing another thing. If he remained on the ranch he would be admitting that Doña Gertrude's grave was of his making; if he stayed to claim ownership of Horsehead he also stayed to claim the grave. Maybe Stuart had thought of that too.

He went to his horse. One pure stream of cold feeling shot through him when he came to think of how close he had come to permitting Stuart to outmaneuver him. He smiled bitterly into the night. "The man who is saddled with Doña Gertrude's death is dead in this Basin. He figures to have the Basin find me here."

He rode out upon the flat, headed for the river ford. They had driven Coleman from the place; but Coleman had not lost. Coleman was alive. Until he was dead neither Stuart nor he would be free men!

As soon as Stuart crossed the ford he halted to face his crew. "The whole thing dies right here. Let no man carry it farther."

Tap answered with a trace of resentment. "Unnecessary to mention it, Mr. Stuart."

"Never does harm to speak plainly."

"We'll not be speakin', but you got a lot of other tongues to consider."

"Trumbo," said Stuart, "will say nothing. Nor will Spade. The information, if it comes, will come from Horsehead—and there's no man on that outfit with a name for honesty."

"Except Ben Solvay," said Tap. "Then, there's the woman."

Stuart sat silent, considering those two; and presently he spoke in the way of a man who traces his thoughts aloud, very quietly and with no stress. "The woman does not count. As for Solvay—he will have to be killed. He's the only man who would be believed by the Basin."

"That's tough," said Niles Peck. "Ben's not a bad hand."

"If he speaks," said Stuart, "he speaks against us. I have got a job for you, Niles. Break off for town. Just drift into the saloon and say you were crossin' Horsehead Range tonight and heard some shootin' over that way."

"Which there was," commented Niles Peck. "What else do I say?"

"Nothing. But somebody will ride that way in the morning, out of curiosity."

"Whut'll they find?" asked Niles.

"Trumbo," said Stuart. "Trumbo and a grave."

The crew pondered this a moment. Then Tap said:

"That's all right. That will put the load on Trumbo. Go ahead, Niles. Get a drink or two under your belt before you talk."

"Won't be hard," said Niles Peck and sloped away into the night. Stuart took his outfit on, Tap riding abreast him. Starlight showed thin and bright against night's moonless black;

and in the wind was the first thin bitter-sweet odor of fall. Ahead of them the low hills lay in round shapelessness and beyond that stood the great ragged bulk of the main mountains. Tap fell into a spell of coughing, the dust and the weed pollen touching off an asthma which had cursed him all his days; and the sound of his lungs was like the pumping of an old dry-leather bellows. He calmed himself, and said: "I wondered why you took to Trumbo so sudden. It did not seem natural. I see now." Then he later added in a puzzled way: "But how'd you know there'd be the curse of a thing like Doña Gertrude to put on the man?"

Stuart made no answer.

Niles Peck made it to town in an hour. There was half a crowd in the saloon, the busy time of roundup now over and men drifting in to soak up the dryness of summer's abstinence. Gunderson sat at a poker table with Frank DeLeon and Bill Yell, the three of them buried deep in a game that would not end for a week. They would play until they were hungry, and eat; and play again until they were half-asleep and then would sleep and play again. Doc Fallon stood by, idly watching; the out-driver of the Gateway stage came in for a drink and a try at the lunch counter.

Niles Peck wigwagged for a drink, took it straight and poured a second; he worried the second drink around the bar with the point of his finger. Buck Gadsby, the saloon's nightman, had a moment to gossip and stood by. He said: "Where's the rest of your bunch?"

"Driving some stuff down from the high country," said Niles Peck.

"You bein' the gentleman of leisure?"

"No, I just came off the west side. Was up at that old Cliff cabin." Niles Peck swallowed his second drink, closed both eyes briefly the better to withstand the wallop, and laid down payment therefor. "I wouldn't mind knowin' what the hell the shootin' was about."

"Where?" said Gadsby on the alert.

"At Horsehead, sounded like. I heard it away out on the flat. One long bust, like three-four guns, maybe. I kept going some faster." He turned from the saloon, got on his horse and rode from town. He thought: "I did it smooth. Lyin' might come easy to me. Hell of a ride for two drinks, though." A mile onward he had a disgusted second thought: "Why didn't I buy a pint to drink on the way? Better all drunk than just comfortable."

Gadsby washed the used glass, put the bottle behind the bar and dropped the two-bit piece into the till. He made a swipe at the small wet ring on the counter with his towel and came about the bar. He leaned over the cattle owner's table, speaking gently to Yell and Gunderson and DeLeon. "Niles Peck just said he was ridin' on the flat near Horsehead quarters hour and a half ago and heard a jag of shootin'."

He went back to the bar and resumed his chores. The three cattlemen kept on with their play. Doc Fallon had heard the barkeep's talk, thought about it and stepped to the bar.

"Did Niles say he was riding with anybody?" he asked Gadsby.

"Said he was alone."

Fallon turned and made an idle circle of the room, looking on at other poker tables, saying a word now and then to one man or another; and moved back to the cattlemen's table. He bent over. "That is a very funny thing. Niles said he was riding across Horsehead alone. Now I will say something. I stood on the bluff of the river, near the ford, about that time and I watched a bunch come over from the west side. I didn't call out or come up, since it was a night ride and none of my business." He looked at the three. "I think I know what outfit it was. If I am right, Niles was not riding alone." Having said it, he left the saloon.

Frank DeLeon said: "We'll break up this game a little before daylight. I want to go over there."

"Go with you," said Gunderson. Yell nodded.

On that night there was one other person traveling the prairie at the time Dan Stuart brought his crew over the ford. Ann, riding under the blackly cushioned stars, had followed the net of trails which wound in and through the low hills separating Star Cross from Horsehead. A lonely girl, with a lonely girl's vivid imagination, she had coursed this whole country since childhood, so that she knew every night shadow and night sound. Brought blind-folded to any piece of the Basin, she would have been able to orient herself within ten minutes by some familiar shape or scar of the land.

This night she rode to consider her last remaining duty to her father and had her painful tragic moments when she realized there could be no compromise between her father and Coleman. Her father's nature would never change. His need of power drove him and would always drive him. The clash would come and nothing could save it except Coleman's withdrawal, but as she remembered the bits of character Coleman had unconsciously revealed to her, she doubted if he would give ground. One lone silver thread of loyalty still held her to her father, after all his brutalities; yet he was wrong—and that conflict was a storm inside her.

She circled out of the hills near Trumbo's range and followed the river northward. Half a mile from the ford she saw a group suddenly come into view against the bluff; having crossed over from the west side. The group paused a moment, apparently to talk, and later a man split away while the rest moved straight east. That would be her father and the crew returning from the trip on which they had so abruptly started a little before sundown that day.

She rode diagonally across the flat, and tarried a little in the Star Cross hills, and arrived home a half hour after them. Her father was on the porch with his cigar.

Usually he had a surly question for her. Usually he said: "Where the hell have you been spookin' this time of night?" Now he only sat still, a taciturn, granite-willed man, wrapped in his own affairs. She stood near him, gradually becoming aware that something out of the way had happened; after so many years with him, she knew the quality of his temper by little signs on him. But he had nothing to offer her and she turned to her room. She lay long awake, feeling fear, and as it ran through her, she thought of Coleman and she visualized him and then she knew the reason for her fear.

At sunup she watched her father stroll around the yard, obviously restless, obviously troubled; around eleven he climbed to his saddle and headed for town, the sun slanting around his stout, truculent figure. Tap sat in the yard, working over a broken bridle. She walked out to him.

"What's up, Tap? What went on last night?"

"I would not know."

"Say it the way you mean it, Tap."

"Then," he said, shortly polite, "the truth is I would say nothing."

He went on with his work. This little man was a deadly bomb of blind zeal for Star Cross; her father had but to light the fuse and Tap would throw himself unhesitatingly into the destruction of whatever her father wished. In a way Tap was terrifyingly simple; in a way terribly malign. She idled through the yard, watching the other men of the crew, noting that none of them were anxious to meet her—that they moved off before she came close to them. Returning to the porch, she waited for her father, but as noon grew nearer she continued to think of Coleman; and at last she saddled her horse and started over the flat. For a short distance she thought of going to Trumbo. Within a half mile she gave over that idea, realizing she would meet only the same evasive silence. If there were news it would be in War Bonnet; so she turned townward.

Dan Stuart reached War Bonnet near noon and put up in front of the Alma Hotel. He walked back to the saloon, knowing it was likely some of the owners would be there—and as soon as he stepped into the saloon he saw Frank DeLeon at the bar drinking an odd mixture of beer and bitters which he had invented many years before to doctor a fancied stomach trouble. He joined DeLeon, and his pride unbent to permit him to speak first to a man, a thing he seldom did. He said, "Mornin', Frank," and waggled a finger for his bottle of

Scotch.

DeLeon soberly added bitters to his beer, murmuring, "I notice I use more bitters and less beer. Man's taste changes as he gets older. For that matter, a man changes otherwise, too." He finished his drink and turned to meet Dan Stuart's glance with a chilled expression, and left the saloon.

Stuart remained quite still. He was not entirely sure DeLeon had meant to cut him, for the man sometimes had long spells of reserve; yet the glance had been straight and seemingly deliberate. He stood with his head dropped, the debating continuing in his mind. He weighed DeLeon's manner until he grew confused and suddenly hit the bar with his closed fist and walked out. He went on to the Alma Hotel and crossed the lobby to the dining room. Three men were there—a rider from Medary's outfit, a tobacco drummer, and Fay Taggart who ran the livery.

He sat down, ridden by a growing obsession. Nobody had spoken of Drew Trumbo being on Horsehead; and he knew the Basin well enough to guess that somebody had already gone out to investigate Horsehead on Niles Peck's rumor. He ordered his dinner and when it came he ate in a heavy, disinterested way—an autocratic man who never offered friendliness or interest to anyone. He had no way of speaking casually to people, thereby discovering what he most wanted to know. So he sat glum and formidable in the warm dining room. He heard riders trot up the street and later he made out the voices of Gunderson and Bill Yell as they came into the dining room. He didn't look up. These were men he had neighbored with for many years and if nothing had changed during the last few hours they would simply turn at his table and sit down, out of habit.

When they got abreast his table he saw them from the corner of his eye and knew they were not going to stop. He looked up at them and he caught Gunderson's glance. He said, "Mornin', Sam. Mornin', Bill."

Yell nodded. Gunderson broke his stride and paused momentarily. He seemed about to say something—and never said it. Nodding, he went on with Yell to a farther table. The waitress laid a pie before Stuart; he cut out a piece and ferried it to his plate. He ate it and laid half a dollar on the table and left his seat at once. In the lobby he checked himself to light a cigar. The ends of his fingers shook and he thought somebody watched him from a back corner, but he didn't turn to see. As he walked to the street he knew something had gone wrong.

His daughter had arrived and was at the moment entering the house of Mary van Hogh, the little seamstress. He watched people move idly along the walks, and his curiosity burned harder and harder. He looked at each person he saw with the sharpest possible glance, trying to read them but reading nothing. He noticed Jack O'Boyle step up out of his saddle shop and for an instant he had a quick hope. He had always been friendly with O'Boyle and the Irishman liked him. He would go across the street and pass the time of the day with the man, but O'Boyle gave him a look and moved at once into the livery stable.

His dull suspicion could no longer be held back. Trumbo had outguessed him and had escaped the trap on Horsehead; somehow it had become known that Star Cross had raided Horsehead—and that Doña Gertrude was dead. He stood alone in town and he felt the eyes of the town upon him. He thought: "It is in my mind, nowhere else," and moved toward his horse. Oldness came upon him and his first lift did not take him into the saddle; and then his brutal anger flared up and he took a huge swing, landed on the leather and started from town.

His daughter came from the seamstress's shop and called to him. He went on, giving her no attention, but she followed and caught up with him. He looked at her and discovered the same weight in her eyes he had seen elsewhere this morning and all his repressed anger and fear rose up and punished her. "You're big enough to ride home alone! Get the hell away from me!"

She rode a full three hundred yards before answering him; and at that point pulled her horse half-around. "That's what I am about to do," she said. "Stop a moment."

He reined in, growling: "Don't need to make a ceremony of ridin' away."

"I'm never riding back to Star Cross. There is only one thing on it I want. Mother's picture. I wish you'd leave it at Mary van Hogh's someday."

He said: "I put up with the fool dreams of your mother a long time. I don't want to see them in you. Let me alone."

"Better listen. I'm saying good-by to you."

He looked at her with his redly formidable eyes. The desire to strike her was on his face; his temper had punished him all morning and now he was dangerous, cruelty making its wild thresh through him. He looked around him quickly, at the open prairie, at the town four hundred yards behind them. He looked back at her. "Leave and be damned! What man you going to? Tell me his name and I'll kill him for what he's probably done. Is it Trumbo?" He fired this at her quickly, indecently; and then his mind swung back and he added in a changed voice: "Why?"

"You know, don't you?"

"I know nothing."

"You raided Horsehead last night—and Doña Gertrude's dead. Where's Coleman?"

He said with a sly swiftness: "Who told you all that?"

"Almost anybody in town could tell you."

He turned his eyes from her, staring into the western sunlight. She saw the age on him, the breakage beginning to show on his red face; she saw the cruel, small down-slanting lines at the corners of his mouth. She searched him for some soft quality, for some kind memory to carry away, and failed. Still looking away from her, he said: "If you leave me now you'll be lending truth to a lie."

"Is it a lie?"

He said with his old impatience: "I never explain anything to anybody!"

"Someday you'll want one thing I have tried to give you. When you want it you'll want it worse than water or food or all the land you ever dreamed of. It will be the last thing you'll ever want—and you'll call for it, just as you call your dogs to you. But it won't come."

"What would I be wanting from you?" he challenged her.

"My love," she said. "But it won't come. You did a good job of killing it."

"I told you once," he said, "that anything that lifts a hand against me is something I never want around. You leave now and you never come back."

"That's the way it will be. And I will be against you."

"Against me?" he cried out. "By God—" He would have hit her then if she had been within reach of his big arm. He brought his horse nearer and she saw temper slash through him and turn him crazy. "I'll watch you and I'll watch the man you go to—and I swear I'll kill the man!"

She had never lifted her voice out of its repressed calm. "Can't you let me think of you in any nice way at all? Do you have to send me away with so much hate and venom?" She wheeled her horse, walking it back toward town. He watched her go, a long fierce flare in his eyes, the old and massive intolerance dominating him. When she had traveled a hundred feet he called out, "Wait up," and rode to her. "I'd never ask you to come back in a thousand years. I beg nothing of any human being—never did, never will. The door's open until midnight, on Star Cross. After that it won't ever be open to you."

"You can close it and lock it now."

"I never knew the queer things that went through a woman," he said, half to himself. "All right. I'll send you a hundred dollars. Don't want Dan Stuart's daughter to be beggin'."

"I'm stayin' with Mary van Hogh. Send me nothing but Mother's picture."

"That," he said, with a fresh revival of temper, "I will smash into a thousand pieces tonight!" She didn't answer him but he knew he had hurt her and he was pleased for it. She started on. He watched her in his gray, incomprehending way; and then he called one more thing after her—and this rose out of a place beyond his close guard, escaping from a source of which he had no knowledge at all, and when he spoke it he knew not why he had done so.

"You're my daughter, ain't you?"

She had her face away from him and he therefore had no way of seeing the tears running down her cheeks. He watched her until she had entered War Bonnet's main street; after that he set out homeward. She was in his mind a full half the distance and his thoughts were unclear about her, turning from odd questions to destructive impulses, and back again to a baffled wonder. Long later it occurred to him to remember why she had left him. Everybody now knew that Doña Gertrude was dead. The blame was on him and would remain here. "That," he said, "will never be proved until the Horsehead outfit comes out of the hills. They'll never come out. I will have to go after that bunch."

10

IN THE HILLS

Two or three miles up the black hill trail Coleman called ahead: "Move off the trail and wait for me," and rode down-grade. There was below him the grunt and the pound of a horse coming along, and the occasional rattle of a branch. Coleman listened carefully until he was sure it was only a single rider; and lifted his gun. He stayed in the trail and he watched the black shape of horse and rider move into vague view below him.

The rider's horse felt or saw the obstruction in the trail before the rider, and dropped to an uncertain walk. The rider's voice began to swear softly. "Go on—go on." When he heard that voice Coleman lowered his gun.

"Hold up, Alvy."

Alvy's breath made a steamy in-and-out report. "Coleman?"

"What's behind you, Alvy?"

"Nothin' I know of. I heard the shootin' and I came back. I got on the edge of the trees and I heard Stuart talkin'. I figured you'd be on this trail."

He had never been sure of Alvy and was not now. "What made you think we'd come this way?"

"If you'd crossed the flats I'd heard you. This is the only

other way. Somebody in the yard was talking' about Doña Gertrude. They said she was dead."

"Stay here a minute, Alvy."

Coleman went by Alvy, dropping down-trail another hundred yards. A wind ruffled the treetops and in that wind drifted the keen smell of winter, distant yet true. There was nothing else. So far Stuart was not following. He turned and rejoined Alvy; the two moved forward at a walk. "You recognize anybody else in that bunch?" asked Coleman.

"Trumbo was there. All of Stuart's outfit, I'd guess. I heard Stuart sing out Tap's name. I heard Trumbo call to Spade."

"How much of a crew has Spade got?"

"Two-three."

There had been ten or eleven against him. Except for Valencia Wilder's presence he might have stood off the attack with his crew. The girl had made it impossible to carry on a fight. He plugged methodically up the hill until he thought he had gone a sufficient distance, and sent a careful call outward. "Pairvent."

Pairvent's "All right" came from the near-by black.

"Find a good place to hole up for the night."

The main party came into the trail and moved upward again. Coleman said, "Go ahead of me, Alvy," and took the rear position after Alvy passed. He dropped back, occasionally stopping to listen into the night, puzzled by the lack of pursuit. He had been driven off Horsehead, but until Stuart and Trumbo had destroyed him they could not say the job was completed. They were smart enough to know that. Perhaps, then, it was fear of hurting the girl which held them back. He considered this as he rode along the winding, rising trail. There was no moon and the timber around him held a kind of blackness that absorbed everything; nothing broke that blackness except overhead where the trees bordering the trail struck against the starlit sky.

Maybe fear of hurting Valencia had kept them from following; but it would not long restrain them. For they had the death of Doña Gertrude on their hands, which was a fact which would never let them alone. A lot of things would come out of her death. It would change every man who had charged across that yard; it would make a difference to each one of them. Tonight or tomorrow or next week Stuart and Trumbo would start after Horsehead again. They would have to do it to justify the killing of a woman; they would have to go through with what they had planned. If they stopped short of it Doña Gertrude's ghost would rise upon them. Their act was incompleted. They would now have to complete it if it killed them all.

An hour or so onward Pairvent's voice drifted to him: "We turn off here," and the single-file column left the road, passed between high rock shoulders and came upon some kind of a mountain meadow. Water ran quick and shallow near by; the trees seemed shorter around him and a colder wind moved up. Directly ahead seemed to be the face of a canyon. The party had stopped and Pairvent was beside him.

"This will do," Pairvent said.

Coleman stepped to the ground. "Put a guard back on the trail, George. We'll take turns at it." He unsaddled and let his horse stand. He said, "Valencia," and heard her small, tired voice answer. She was still mounted. He lifted his arms and she came heavily against him as she stepped down. Her face brushed his head and she whispered a single, soft word he didn't catch. He led her back to his blanket. "There's your bed," he told her; and returned to her horse. He got the blanket from her horse and took it to her. He crouched down near her. "I'll find a way of getting you out of this tomorrow. Ben will know how to circle back to War Bonnet."

Her fingers closed about his arm. "Doña Gertrude's dead?"

"Yes."

"I liked her. She was kind in her judgments. It would be nice to grow old with so little meanness." Her tone quickened. "You're not running from them?"

"I do not know yet."

"Don't run," she said. "You were never made to give up. Remember what I told you—you can have anything your stubborn mind wants." The pressure of her hand held on; and her voice was a quiet whisper for him. Somebody moved slowly forward and stood still. A match broke the intense black and

Coleman saw Ben Solvay's face outlined by the sudden glow. Solvay let the light burn to its last guttering bit of flame while he looked down at Valencia and at Coleman. He had a stony, unhappy expression on his face. After the light died he spoke in a gruff way: "Better get to sleep, Valencia."

Valencia drew her hand away from Coleman; he heard her faint whisper: "Stay near." He settled back, hearing the horses stir and hunt for grass.

Early morning's fog was a cold steam rolling through the canyon; and the chill wetness of it collected in Coleman's bones. He rose and put on his hat and he rolled a cigarette and had a quick smoke, noting how peacefully Valencia slept; he had heard her turning restlessly during the small hours.

Northward stood a ragged chunk of rocks, through which they had apparently come the night before. South lay the up-and-down canyon wall, something like two hundred feet high, and at its base ran a creek which at this point was a slow-moving pool. Watching it and the mists which were beginning to rise from it, he saw a trout jump. Farther on, to the east, was a widening of the canyon into a kind of meadow. The timber made a solid mass northward.

"Alvy," he said, "take the horses over to that grass."

He walked to the creek, washed and took a deep drink to fill the emptiness in him. He was hungry in the sharp and painful way of an active man who sees no hope of food; he stood in the lightening fog and felt hunger's transient irritability. Pairvent came up, the rest of the crew straggling behind. Ben Solvay remained with the girl.

Pairvent said: "You still givin' orders for Horsehead?"

Coleman watched the yonder scene between Solvay and the girl with interest. Solvay was stiff and displeased and appeared to be saying unpleasant things to her—the long-brooded things of a jealous man's mind. Coleman's eyelids drew together, temper ruffled through him. The girl appeared to be answering with softness. She smiled at Solvay, but he turned on his heel and moved toward the group. When he arrived he gave Coleman a crusty stare.

"Or," said Pairvent, "are you goin' over the hill and leave this mess the way you made it?"

"Why should I run?"

Pairvent's dry sarcasm grew more pronounced. "I'm askin' that question—not answerin' it. But you got every earmark of a man on the run. Last night we could have taken a chance of standin' those fellows off. It might have worked. Long chance, but I gathered that was the kind you liked."

"We had the girl with us."

"Damn the woman," said Pairvent. "Send her away."

"George," said Coleman, "that's enough of that."

"All right," said Pairvent, "what're you thinkin' to do? We can't stay here forever."

"Where are we now?"

"Five miles from the ranch. The big canyon of Cloud River is a couple miles east. You're two hours' ride from the summit of the range. Ten from there downgrade to Gateway."

Coleman pointed west. "What's that way?"

"No use thinkin' of it. Too rough to get through." Pairvent pointed at the canyon wall. "Just a lot of that."

"Can we cross the big canyon?"

"A trail goes down to an old mining shaft near the river. It will do you no good. No way of crossing."

"Baldy," said Coleman, "ride back through those rocks and keep an eye peeled. We'll stay here until something else seems in the cards."

Pairvent grunted, drawing Ray Miller and Ed Drum after him as he moved off. Coleman watched them huddle up near the trees and talk it over. Alvy joined them.

Solvay said: "Want me to pull out now?"

Coleman looked carefully at Ben Solvay. Something stuck in the man's craw and would not budge. He said, himself on edge: "Spit it out, Ben."

"Maybe," suggested Ben, "I shouldn't have left her on Horsehead."

"You were a fool to leave her on Horsehead," Coleman bluntly told him.

"I took you for an honest man."

Coleman gave Solvay a gray, grim smile. The crankiness of hunger clung to him and influenced the way he talked. "You gave her away when you brought her to me. You're such a damned pure character that you didn't want her. Now you've decided you do."

Solvay grew red and disturbed and angry. "Never mind me," he said. "But I expected you to leave her alone."

"What do you think I've done?"

Solvay wanted to speak out but the thing in his mind needed decent covering before he could show it, and so he searched himself for words. The conversation went on between Pairvent and the rest of the crew, over at the trees; they were in deep debate—Pairvent doing most of the talking. The girl walked idly through the rocky area; she had been watching Solvay and she had at once known, Coleman guessed, that she was being discussed. Solvay said:—

"When you and I stand together in front of her, she looks at you. Not at me. If the things I'm thinkin' are right—"

"Ben," said Coleman, "I'll draw a picture of you, and it is nothin' you should be proud of. This girl came to Gateway and you took a look at her and saw she was better than you had a right to expect. That made you suspicious. You drew four aces, so you figured the deal was crooked somewhere. You've been disbelievin' your luck ever since. You brought her to Horsehead on the high and mighty statement that she needed to be safe for a week. You didn't mean it. What you meant was that you had changed your mind about wantin' her. You went away and figured maybe you were through with her. You found you couldn't ride far enough to quit thinkin' about her. Now you're back, wanting to take up a bargain you threw over. You cashed in your chips but you're standin' at the table tryin' to run the game. What the hell are you so proud of, my friend?"

Solvay's practical face showed injury and embarrassment. He seemed to restrain himself, he seemed to make himself listen; and then he dropped his head and considered it all—and lifted his glance. "In all that you are right. I want her back."

"Better let her alone, or quit askin' yourself questions."

Coleman looked long at this steady, unimaginative man, seeing in him many fine things; but seeing in him too that puritanical strain which would hound him and hound the girl. He said as a last rough blow: "She's better than you are."

He watched Solvay tramp away; he crouched by the creek with his back to the Horsehead men. Their voices kept murmuring and Pairvent's voice occasionally got sharp. Sunlight broke into the canyon; he turned his glance to the rim and watched it a long while. Pairvent would stick until Pairvent saw a better scheme. Miller would stick because there was a fight coming. Of Ed Drum and Baldy he could form no conclusions. Alvy was a question mark. These were men he had to depend upon.

He called, "Alvy," without turning his head, and heard the lad's boots crunch along the gravel. Alvy circled and stood near the water's edge before him, tipping his callow, characterless face downward. "Alvy," said Coleman, "I want to give you a chore. This is important."

He had judged the depth of the boy's rank pride; he saw the way it swept across Alvy's face. Alvy said in a throaty tone: "I'll do it."

"Slide down the hill and get where you can watch the ranch. Watch it a long time. I want to know who's there. Middle of the morning now. Be back by the middle of the afternoon."

"I'll do it," said Alvy.

"Alvy," said Coleman, "there's only one important thing about a man. Good man or bad one. When he gives his word he'll stand on his word if it kills him." He didn't look at Alvy but he knew his talk had effect, for Alvy's voice was guttural with importance. "I'll do it," Alvy repeated and went away.

Coleman watched Alvy trot to his horse and leave the canyon; the strike of his horse's shoes came back for a little while as clean, tapping runs of sound. Coleman rose, meeting Pairvent and the rest of the crew as they came up. "Sent Alvy down to scout the place," he said.

"A pail with no bottom to fetch water with," said Pairvent. "He's been afraid all mornin'. It was a grease creepin' out on his face. He'll run."

"Maybe he'll grow up."

"He'll run—or he'll get into trouble and die. There is no sense in him."

"Grow or die," said Coleman. "It is time he did one thing or the other."

He crossed to where the girl stood with Ben Solvay. Something had passed between them. Solvay stood irresolute and troubled before her, a flush on his cheeks. The girl had not changed; this scene was within her grasp. She held it with her self-possession, she had bettered Ben and had left him helpless. She spoke to Coleman. "If Ben takes me out of here you will have one less man. You can't spare a man."

"It is not his war," said Coleman. "I want you to go. Now."

An expression of helplessness replaced her certainty. Ben, a man made wise by jealousy, saw this and abruptly turned away. Coleman called after him. "Bring up her horse."

Valencia took his arm and murmured: "Don't send me away."

"Don't want you hurt," he said. "You go down to Gateway."

"I'll never see you again." She looked away from him, seeing visions not in this meadow and not in this day. "A man failed me once. Noting else has mattered much since then, until now. Now I've failed a man. I wish it didn't hurt so much." She paused, and added: "Should I take Ben?" and searched his face line by line with her anxious eyes.

"I don't know," he said, and once more a strange irritation churned through him. "You're better than he is."

Ben moved forward with his horse and hers. Her hand held Coleman's arm and her glance went up to him and for a moment she lifted the last reserve from her eyes so that he looked into her and saw the pure-white fire burning. To his tongue came many aroused things he wanted to say, but he only murmured, "So long." Solvay gave her a hand to the saddle and got to his own horse. Coleman reached for his cigarette sack. He had it in his fingers and he held it still. They were at the bend, traveling around it. She had swung in her saddle to watch and when he lifted his arm to her she touched a hand to her lips. Coleman removed his hat until she was gone.

Pairvent was behind him. Pairvent said in a grudging way: "I liked that woman. Now you have lost another man. What you waitin' for?"

"For Stuart," said Coleman.

At noon Solvay and Valencia reached the top of the range and traveled through a pass which led downgrade to Gateway. Far south the great yellow-grass plain ran on and on; after the rough coldness of the mountains that plain was warmth to the eyes. Valencia stopped to watch it.

Solvay said: "Long ride yet. Ten miles. Better keep going. You can put up at Gateway until this is over."

"Maybe," she said, and again his jealous-born wisdom told him that she was thinking of Coleman entirely.

"Valencia," he said. "I want to keep the bargain."

"You have changed your mind again?"

"Never was changed. The week's delay was only to let you be sure."

"You're an honest man making a poor job of a lie. You have been troubled by my past. If I married you I'd have to watch that suspicion in your eyes the rest of my life."

"I've thought of that," he said. "When you came here I had figured a sort of partnership with you, leavin' out the word love. When I saw you I knew that wouldn't do. I had to have you the way a man wants a woman—all of her. That changed things. A man in love with a woman can't forget anything about her. I will admit I am jealous. I can't help it. But I want you."

"You'd never have all of me, Ben. You'd never have more than you first bargained for."

He looked at her in a way he had not permitted himself before, burning and hungry and possessive, and was ashamed to stand so naked before her. It had never been his intention to give this girl his heart, but only to take a wife out of necessity; she had changed that for him and the change was something he could not control. She grew into him, even though he resisted her, and so at last he stood before her, defeated and wanting her and hating her past.

"I could kill the man!"

"Ben," she said, "I want him but I'll never have him."

He looked down, raked and tortured, and he groaned: "Why didn't you keep that to yourself? Why did you have to make it worse?"

"I have to tell the truth." She shook her head, sadly speaking. "If I could lie I would have been much happier."

He lifted his eyes and she saw the wreckage in him. "I still want you," he said.

"Why, Ben," she murmured, "I'm sorry I've hurt you."

"Let's get on."

They rode on a considerable distance through the timber, saying nothing. She was thoughtful, frequently looking behind her, and finally said: "You can't go back to War Bonnet. The people who are after Coleman will be after you – because you helped Coleman. You'll never be able to live in the Basin until Coleman wins. Go back and help him."

"Help him?" said Ben Solvay and showed his instant dislike.

"You don't know him. If you called on him for help, even if he hated you, he'd come. He'd stay with you until the very last, and ride away and ask nothing of you. There are not so many like that."

He stopped. "Maybe I'm never going to forget about the past. Man can't guarantee what's in his head. But I guess I have got to prove I want you. I will do a thing I do not want to do. I do it only because you want me to. Go straight down this trail until you reach Gateway. Stay until I come."

She was about to add, "Tell Tracy I sent you," but she denied herself the privilege. She crowded her horse near Ben and she bent and lightly kissed him. She drew away, smiling. "So long," she said and went down the trail. When she looked back he had disappeared around a bend; and she stopped, no longer smiling. She was thinking of Coleman when she said to herself: "I wish he knew I sent Ben back. I wish he knew I had good enough in me to give up what I came here for."

11

TIME RUNS OUT

Alvy rode out of the meadow into the hill trail, passing Baldy and hearing Baldy's warning: "Keep out of sight, kid." The kid grinned. Descending toward Horsehead, he had before him a narrow dusty strip closely girt by the pines, turning one blind bend and another. He rode with the bravado of a young man who was about important business. Coleman had told him so, and the words made strong drink to his thirsty pride. He saw himself as he wanted to see himself—a man on a desperate venture, a man crafty and resourceful, a man riding so easily into great risks that other men would be saying of him: "There goes a fighter." He thought of this so vividly that it became the truth to him.

Half-down the grade he moved from the trail to timber, pausing behind trees to scan the vistas opening before him, to listen to all stray sounds, and at last caught sight of Horsehead's housetops at the foot of the hills. To this point he had been confident; here now a chill shook and grew tight and at that moment one part of Alvy stood off and viewed the other part with shame.

He rode the last few yards in greater and greater caution and reached the edge of the pines, here stopping to study the house and the yard and the surrounding area. Two horses stood still against the corral bars, hungry and waterless the last twelve hours. A band of chickens foraged the back area of the house and somebody's underwear hung on the clothesline near the bunkhouse. There was no other sign of life on the place. Alvy waited a quarter hour to be sure of this, meanwhile playing with the idea of going inside the house. It was a risky thing to do, for the crossing between the trees and the house was fifty yards wide and made a plain target of him in the event somebody was inside. Fear was a wind in his belly; it placed an oil scum on his face. He hated himself for his weakness, and the need of crossing the open strip grew greater and greater until he knew he had to do it or never face himself again.

He moved into the open. The horses in the corral swung, scenting him in the wind. They nickered at him and the sound whirled him back to the timber. He cursed himself under his breath, turned and ran up to the kitchen door. He pulled himself from the saddle. When he hit the ground his legs shook but he clamped his teeth together and walked through the open kitchen doorway.

There was a pan of bread on the table, and a cold pot of coffee on the stove. He broke off half a loaf and moved through the house, eating as he traveled. The front door was also open and from it had a view of the Horsehead grass to the north. Nothing there. His courage crept back. Returning to the kitchen he drank cold coffee, left the house and got on the horse.

He felt like a man and the old dreaming came back and he grew reckless. "Ought to scout the flats out there," he told himself and instantly regretted it. He tried to believe he hadn't said it but his conscience taunted him until he turned the horse and set out upon the grass.

Tracks led him straight to the ford, through occasional cattle grazing. The ranch and the shelter of the foothills dropped behind him and the fear stuck with him all the way to the ford. When he got there he felt better; he had pleased his conscience again, and now he said to himself, "Ought to cross and scout the country around Trumbo's."

He crossed and turned south along the riverbank, now far

out on alien soil. Distance was all around him and the river itself was a barrier he could not jump except by backtracking to the ford. He rode with his eyes steadily moving and his breath lifted and fell upon a suddenly thin air; he played his part of a big man, but the fear never left him and when he got within a mile of the timber, near Trumbo's, he put the horse into a run and kept it there until he was in the shelter of the pines.

He stopped a moment to clear the sweat from his face and to consider what he should next do. He thought of how he would say to Coleman when he returned: "I scouted the flats, crossed the ford and went as far as Trumbo's place." He would roll a cigarette while he talked, to show his easiness in the matter. The Horsehead crowd would watch him and they would think better of him than they had before. But then he seemed to hear Coleman's voice say: "What the hell did you think was smart about dragging all around the prairie, boy?"

He wanted Coleman's approval more than he wanted any other thing. He wanted the casual nod of equality from that smart, tough man who had ridden the trail and had held his own part. For, although he did not realize it, he was a hero-worshipper and his pattern now was Coleman. Then he remembered he had played the part of informer for Trumbo, and keen shame came upon him. Coleman would despise him for that. He thought: "I'll get closer to Trumbo's ranch and see if anything's doing there," and moved on southeastward through the trees. He had not ridden fifty yards when a voice—Trumbo's voice—came at him like a bullet from some part of the timber.

"Stand fast, Alvy."

The shock of it froze him in the saddle. He was so chilled and so frightened that he did not try to move his head until he heard a horse come forward from his rear. Then he turned slowly and watched Trumbo ride up. Trumbo was smiling; there seemed to be a friendliness in the man. Trumbo, the kid thought, figured that he had broken away from Horsehead to bring more news. Maybe he could get through this by lying a little. As he thought so he caught the edge of his constant dream; he was a cool fighter facing another hard man in a dangerous scene. It was a small, soon-dying vision, for the fear hung on and made him small and he wanted to run and he wished with a passionate hopelessness that he had not crossed the ford.

"Well, Alvy," said Trumbo, "what's news?"

He was smiling and he was easy but to Alvy's fear-sharpened eyes there was a difference, there was something cloudy-black in Trumbo's glance.

"Nothing," said Alvy. "I was just ridin' by."

"Pulling out, Alvy?"

"That's it," said Alvy, and adopted the excuse thankfully. "A little too tough for me. I got nothing against the Basin people."

"Where'd you leave Coleman, Alvy?"

Alvy made a half-hearted stand and gave a vague answer. "Up in the hills."

Trumbo's voice was increasingly friendly, his smile remained. "Alvy," he said, "we're old friends. You've brought information to me before. Someday I mean to do something for you. Whereabouts in the hills?"

Alvy's mind was a slow mind. He could not duck the question and he could not think fast enough to get ahead of it. "Quite a ways up."

"At summit, Alvy?"

"That's about it."

"Everybody still with Coleman?"

"The girl pulled out with Solvay."

Trumbo's smile lessened. "That leaves just four of them?" He hit Alvy with his glance. "I always know when a man's lyin'. Be careful—don't lie to me now. Just where is Coleman hidin'?"

Alvy blurted out a futile protest. "I don't like to help get a man killed."

"Who said he'd be killed," asked Trumbo. "We're just going to drive him out. Don't fool with me. Where's he hidin'?"

"Up in the Olally meadows," said Alvy. He lowered his eyes, he sank into abysmal depths. Every dream stood in ruins and his conscience was a loud voice saying: "You're just a fool kid, you're afraid, you're crooked, there is no good in you and never was." He lifted his eyes to Trumbo and dully spoke. "That's all I know."

"Good-by, Alvy," said Trumbo. "Keep right on riding."

Alvy swung by Trumbo, obsessed by the memory of Coleman's black eyes boring into him. He heard Coleman say again: "If a man give his word he keeps it if it kills him." Never otherwise would he have attempted what he did. But the things inside him were more than he could bear and Coleman's words were alive and loud in his ears; and then he had one more great surge of bravado, one more dream of producing triumph out of disaster. Prompted by it, he swung and drew his gun.

His great moment never came. Trumbo had already drawn and now held his revolver steady on him. Trumbo said, "I thought so – you're a cheap kid," and fired once. Alvy heard the sound and he felt the bullet knock him back. He slipped from the saddle and he fell through space. The strange thing was that he seemed never to strike ground; he fell on and on through this endless space, out of the land of the alive.

Trumbo rode forward and bent in the saddle, long looking down at the lank, immature face. He said aloud, "I have not done that for three years." It would have been better, he thought, if he had not killed the kid; for the act brought forward an older pattern of his life. It took him back to his wilder days when he had made something of a name of himself as a tough far south of the Basin. From that name and from that past he had deliberately fled, wise enough to know that a man with a reputation for fighting sooner or later invited his own death.

He had run away from his record; somewhere down the trail there were men who still hunted him. This was what Stuart had found out about him. This was why Stuart wanted him. He had a skill Stuart needed. Watching the dead kid, he shook his head and regretted the act. There was no reaction of pity, no particular human feeling, and by this he knew he had not destroyed his past years or the qualities which had produced them. They had slept and now were awake.

He rode to the edge of timber to scan the open range northward and he thought, "Coleman smelled it. He knew I had used a gun." Coleman was a wise man. Coleman was the same type, except for a different strain in him. Coleman could kill, but never except for a well-grounded reason.

He was also thinking in his close way of what had to be done. Stuart had tried to trap him on Horsehead and leave the death of Doña Gertrude at his door. Stuart had failed, but would try again. The death of the woman was a shadow over them all, to be removed only by removing the spectators at the scene. Trumbo never concealed harsh things from himself; so now he ticked off in his mind those men who had to die if he were to remain in the Basin: Coleman, Pairvent, Baldy, Ed Drum, Ray Miller and Ben Solvay. There was also the woman; but if she left the country he would be content. Beyond that, there remained the problem of Stuart, but that was for another day. First things first.

He turned back to his ranch and half an hour later rode into the yard and stepped down at his porch. As he did so, Dan Stuart came out of the house and faced him.

"You kept me waitin'," he said.

Trumbo, staring at his unexpected visitor, observed the confidence in Stuart and at once swung about. The Star Cross crew was at the moment coming out of the timber. He had been neatly outmaneuvered, but even then he felt himself on sound enough ground to show Stuart a sharp grin. "Still need me, Dan?"

"That's why I'm here," said Stuart. "We'll cross the river and climb the hill until we find Coleman's outfit."

Trumbo said: "What made you figure I'd stay on Horsehead last night, takin' the blame?"

Stuart gave Trumbo a surly stare. "You're old enough to defend yourself."

"You've got gall enough for an elephant."

"I want to see Horsehead hangin' in a row, kickin' as they hang."

Stuart had gone through the same thought that he had,

reaching the same answer. Doña Gertrude was a fact before them all, unavoidable and not to be ignored. For a moment Trumbo had a strange pulse of warning. Maybe Doña Gertrude, dead, was stronger than all the living and maybe her hand would point at them forever. He shook it aside. "I'll go along."

"We'll pick up Spade on the way," said Stuart.

Ann Stuart left War Bonnet by morning and reached Horsehead three hours later, immediately noting the new grave in the pines. She stopped to call out, "Hello, house," and raised no answer. Dismounting, she walked through the house, had a look at the rear yard and put her head inside the crew quarters. She noticed the two horses penned in the corral, let them out and pumped water into the near-by trough for them.

She had so long traveled around the Basin that she took no great amount of time guessing Coleman's whereabouts. They would not, running from gunfire, go out on the flat. They would have hit for the nearest possible shelter—the ravines and deep pine thickets lying back of the house. The next question was, how far would she have to go to overtake them? The answer to that depended entirely on the kind of man Coleman was; and therefore she had her answer. He could not be frightened, and he would not give up Horsehead and so he would not be far off. She paused by Doña Gertrude's grave, remembering the Spanish woman so clearly, her gentle hospitality, her old woman's sweet-sharp wisdom; and she cried a little over Doña Gertrude's grave, and turned away.

She went into the kitchen, knowing the Horsehead men would be hungry. She found a muslin flour sack, collected half a dozen cans of tomatoes, some dried apricots, a mess of onions and potatoes, and the bread on the table; out in the cooler above the well she discovered a chunk of boiling beef. Returning to the kitchen, she ground up a supply of coffee, found a coffee pot and a frying pan, and prepared to mount. She had trouble lifting the sack to the saddle and spent some time tying it to the horn.

As soon as she rode into the trail she observed the prints of many horses feet scuffled in the dark dust; these were, for a half mile, all upward-bound prints. At that point one set came downhill; somebody had started back for the ranch.

Meanwhile she got to thinking of Valencia Wilder. The girl would be with the men, since there was nothing else for her to do—and her presence would be an extra problem for Coleman. The thought troubled her; she could not keep from her mind the question of Coleman's interest in Valencia. The girl had a dark and intense pair of eyes, beautiful hair and a face that would stir any man, even so strong a man as Coleman; or particularly a man as strong as Coleman, for precisely because of the depth and the width of his nature he would have heavy appetites. He could appreciate a pretty woman; she had seen that appreciation in his eyes at Gateway and in the hills, she had seen the flare of his sudden-warmed thoughts. He was in that respect very human. Yet though it had been a deeply personal interest it had not been offensive. Even as he had struck into her with his eyes, arousing her, he had smiled away his trespass.

What would he see in Valencia—what answer would there be for him in the girl's eyes? The thought rode with her and never quite left her mind; it was a darkness and a weight. "I thought I was almost in love with one man," she told herself. "How can I believe, so soon afterwards, that I could love another?" Then an unhappy thought gripped her. Valencia was really beautiful. Perhaps she was not better than she should be and no doubt Tracy knew that. But if he liked her he would never let that stop him. He would take her as she was. Either for a little while, or else by marriage. She changed that last part. "No, not for a little while. I don't think he'd be happy with that. But against her, how plain I am."

This inward search had nothing to do with her eyes. They rummaged the trail steadily, the trees and the tracks on the ground. She caught the smell of pines, she heard all the little sounds and knew what they were. She was a fair, alert girl with expressive gray eyes, with little changes occurring around her lips, by turns grave and humorous as the spirit moved her, and she carried herself with reliance.

At the jaws of the meadow she paused, seeing the tracks turn in. She sat still in the saddle, looking about her, and at last she called toward the timber on the opposite side of the trail. "Come on out of it."

Baldy appeared, bearing his surprise. "How'd you know?"

"A good general always puts out pickets."

"Well, keep on goin' up the trail. We just got rid of one woman. Don't need another."

She smiled at Baldy. "Had anything to eat lately?"

Baldy looked glum. "No. You got somethin' to eat in that sack?" He drew a troubled breath. "For God's sake, girl. You're a Stuart. What you foolin' around Horsehead for? Here's a bunch of men all bound for a hangin' since they was eight years old. You're doin' yourself no good."

She smiled again and moved into the rock defile. "Your heart's all right, Baldy, but I can see your stomach's got the best of you."

The echo of her horse traveled ahead of her through the stony corridor. When she turned the bend into the meadow she met Pairvent head on, his gun lifted and his strange mud-black eyes sighting at her along its barrel. She noticed his startled expression; he lowered the gun and turned rapidly on his heels as though he had committed an improper act. Coleman came up from the far side of the meadow.

She watched him with a greater attention than she realized; she was anxious to see the first reaction on his face and she found her heart beating higher. He stopped at the head of her horse, sober and troubled. His glance searched her thoroughly and then he reached for his hat and she saw a trace of a smile and the change of his eyes. It brightened the whole day.

He said: "How'd you find us?"

"I told you once I could find you anywhere. These are my mountains." She untied the thongs holding the muslin sack. "Are you hungry?"

He caught the bag as it fell and opened the top, and the broadest possible smile lighted his face. "Heaven must be owned and operated by women like you. George, you're the cook."

Pairvent came back and looked into the sack; he gave Ann a grudging glance of approval and took the sack away, calling to Ray Miller. "Catch up a fire, Ray."

Coleman had not asked her to step down, and now he was serious. "You're makin' a tough situation for yourself. Your father's probably in the hills now. How did you come?"

"Up from Horsehead."

"Better go back by Gateway."

"Let me stay a little while."

A day's growth of whiskers glittered like metal filings on his face and, except when he smiled at her, the whole set of his features was harsh. Looking down upon him she noticed the width of his shoulders and the heavy roundness of his neck muscles. She put a hand to his shoulder and at that instant she saw the flash of warmth come to his eyes. He lifted his arms and as she dropped to the ground he took her whole weight for a moment. He stepped immediately back and looked away from her. She had stirred him. Knowing it, she felt an uplift of spirit. It was good to know she had the power to do that.

He said: "I sent Alvy down to have a look at the ranch. You see him?"

"No, but there was one set of tracks going downhill. They faded out about half a mile from the house."

"Probably he's playing Indian somewhere."

"Don't trust Alvy. He might betray you. I know he used to ride over to Drew's. There was some arrangement between them."

"I suspected that. There was an arrangement between Trumbo and Pairvent also."

She said: "You still put trust in Alvy after that?"

"There's some good in the kid. I am hoping he'll grow up."

"You're a kind man, Tracy, but you've not got a single rider you can depend on."

"You can dig as deep a hole with a broken shovel as with a sound one, if you've got to."

She looked into the meadow and saw only Pairvent and Ray Miller crouched over the fire. Alvy was out on scout, Baldy hidden in the trail. "Where's Ed Drum and Solvay?"

He pointed to the rim of the sheer canyon wall. "Ed's up there. I sent Ben on to Gateway with Valencia."

He mentioned the girl's name casually but his hands went to his pocket for his cigarette makings and he looked down as he built his smoke; there was some feeling in him about her, some memory. Ann said: "Why did you leave Horsehead?"

"After Doña Gertrude was killed I couldn't risk the same thing happenin' to Valencia." He lighted his smoke and looked directly at her. "I had not meant to bring Doña Gertrude's name into it."

She said: "Do you think it was my father, or one of his men?"

"There's no name on a bullet, but it was your father who started the raid." He shook his head. "I wish you were not here."

"I told you the other day how I felt about it."

He lifted his head and she saw the regret in him. "That does not change it. It is beyond your power to change. If we met and drew, you would be between us. If I shot, it would be the same to me as though I were shootin' you."

His admission hit hard; it overfilled her heart and she had to turn away from him to keep him from seeing the things that must have come to her face. "You should not say that. You are entirely free."

"You'd better go back to Star Cross," he said.

She had intended telling him of her broken relations with her father. Now she knew she could not. His sense of responsibility was strong enough that he would make her troubles his own—and he had enough of his own. She said: "Pairvent's got something cooked up. You go eat. I want to talk to you before I leave."

He turned to the fire. Ann led her horse to the creek's side for water, her glance meanwhile running the top rim of the canyon wall. It was near two o'clock and the sun was still high; but when the light struck the canyon and the timber it was partly lost. There was a blackness upon these hills that no sun touched. she thought of many things in those few minutes, of this wild heartbreaking land, of her father, of Drew Trumbo and of Valencia; and always of Coleman.

He returned from the fire, made cheerful by the meal. He stood near her, rolling a cigarette and smiling. His eyebrows were as black as his hair and as thick. He had a short white scar to the left of his chin. She lifted her hand at it. "Where'd you get that?"

"Four years ago, when I brought some cattle up the trail. We stopped for a day at Dodge City." The memory of it made him grin. "There was a saloon called the Nugget. So we all went in and maybe we were a little bit stout. Only clear thing I remember was that a girl came over the floor and started to sing a song at me. I do not recall who objected. We fought our way out of the place, down the street and all the way back to camp. It was a nice night."

"You like your pleasures strong, Tracy."

"All a man's got at the end of life is a set of memories. Things done well and things poorly done. The great sin is to end up with nothing done." He threw away his smoke and his glance seemed to pull her forward to him. "I can't live easy and small. A man is full of things meant to be used or given away, or maybe destroyed. The more he spends the more comes back. That is all he is, something to be used, to have his fingers smashed and his body bent, to fall down and get up. To hunt and find."

"To hunt for what?"

He shrugged his shoulders, he would go no farther. Then his temper changed and he lifted his eyes to the rim, turned alert. "Alvy should have been back long ago. I do not like the smell of this place."

"If he has betrayed you—"

He turned and called to Pairvent. "George, we'll get out of here." Suddenly haste was upon him; it made him seize her arm and lead her back to her horse. He gave her a hand up and turned to her own horse. He sent a call up to the cliff. "Come in, Ed!" He put his horse to a gallop and threaded the rock defile with Ann at his heels. The sound of it had brought Baldy out of the timber. Baldy said, "What's up?"

Coleman stopped. He made a motion for silence and he looked down the trail, listening, and he faced the trail's upper side and watched it a long while. He heard nothing and he saw nothing and still it was plain to the girl how some kind of clear warning disturbed him. He murmured: "They're comin' from one direction or the other. I can't tell which one."

Ann said: "Dad was in War Bonnet this noon. He couldn't have had time to circle around by Gateway. If he's near here it will be on the Horsehead side."

Coleman swung uptrail at once. Ed Drum had meanwhile turned off the rim and now advanced down the trail. The sight of the group coming along at so fast a gait set him about; and he ran before them, on through the trees and around the short bends. A mile or thereabouts onward, Coleman called a halt.

"George," he said, "pick another hide-out."

Pairvent sat still, thinking, and seemed to find no suitable point in his mind. He said: "We got to stay away from the river or they'll box us in. As for these hills, west, I never put a horse through 'em. Maybe—"

Ann crowded around Coleman and on past Ed Drum. "I know where to go."

Coleman said: "I don't want you in this, Ann."

She looked back, almost laughing at him; and turned and led the party away. Some distance from the original starting point, she left the trail and struck straight through the thickening trees, upward into half-passable land. They dropped to a walk, the horses grunting and sighing with the heavy labor of the climb. The sun still remained above the horizon and still touched the high peaks of the range; but in here twilight had already come.

Trumbo, leading Star Cross, stopped briefly at Horsehead to have a look at the yard; and noticed the two horses roaming through it. "Somebody's been back," he pointed out. He took to the hills at once, going upward by one grade and another. Two hours from Horsehead found them in the roughest possible country, with Stuart grumbling his dislike for the slowness of advance. They made a hard, slanting descent into a ravine and toiled up its far side; and at this point Trumbo signaled behind him for a quieter approach. Sliding forward, again down-grade, they came to the edge of timber and looked out upon an open flat boxed in by a high cliff on the other side—upon the Olally meadows quitted by Coleman not quite ten minutes before.

Trumbo noticed the remnants of the fire and he made a close survey of the rocks; he swore at himself and he led the party into the meadow, turning through the rock defile to the main trail. He caught the smell of dust and he drifted down-grade until he lost it and came back, pointing upward.

"Not far ahead of us."

Tap said: "Better be a little careful."

"Go on, Drew," urged Stuart. "We're wasting time. It'll be dark as the inside of a gut in another hour."

Trumbo said: "This dust smell is goin' to give them away. We're on the right track."

"Go on," said Stuart, more and more impatient. "Get it."

12

CHANGE AND LOSS

Ann halted in a small bowl-like area lying in the heart of these massive, uptilted and fast blackening mountains. Coleman, thrown off in his sense of direction, made a slow turn. He pointed a hand and said: "That's south."

"West," said Ann.

Pairvent grumbled: "You've got us lost, girl."

"I'm not lost," she said.

"You're soon pullin' out," said Pairvent. "That leaves us in a damned dark alley. If we get flushed by Star Cross we better know where we are or else we'll head straight into a blind corral. Where's the trail?"

"That way," said Ann, and pointed. "But don't try to go that way when you leave. That will bring you to the edge of the Olally cliff, which boxes you in. Don't try the west. You could never get through with your horses unless you had me along. The way out is to the south."

Pairvent grumbled some uneasy thing half under his breath. His man-feeling was offended to be thus dependent on a woman and he had no faith in any Stuart. "We'd better go on south then. Right now. One back door ain't enough. They might close it on us."

"Neither my father nor Trumbo knows the country well enough," pointed out Ann.

Baldy said: "My God I'm hungry. Why didn't you fellows think to bring some of that grub along?"

Ed Drum grumbled: "Shut up. I'm empty too."

Blackness crowded into the bowl, sky-light was vaguely above them. Horsehead's crew stood alert and glum and uncertain. Ann had moved away. Coleman heard her voice from a far spot: "Tracy," she said, and drew him on by the sound of her voice. She touched his arm and went into the farther blackness with him until the discontented talk of the crew was a murmur. She stopped and turned and he saw the pale outline of her face as it lifted. "Tracy," she said, "a man like you never runs unless he's unsure of himself. You have been in the hills all day, just waiting. It isn't like you to wait. There's something holding you back. I feel it and the crew feels it. I can tell by the way they look at you."

"You're tellin' me to move against Star Cross?"

"I'm telling you that you must either start out of the country now, or else you must fight my father. But you cannot fight him with half a heart. It will make you slow, and if you are slow you will be killed. What I fear is that I have made you undecided. I don't want you to think of me. Do what you must do, regardless of how it hurts anybody else."

"It would go hard for you to stand over your father's body and know that I killed him."

She sighed and her voice lessened. "You are less a stranger to me than my father. It would be harder for me to know that he had killed you, than to know you had killed him."

"I do not understand that."

"It is too long a story." She wanted to tell him but she would not. Her troubles were her own and she kept them to herself so strictly that not even Trumbo had known the gulf between father and daughter. With Coleman it was somewhat different. She knew now that he meant a great deal to her; she knew it because of her desire to tell him something she had never wished to tell another. But she held it back.

"Mighty odd," he said in a grave, wondering tone, "how

a man will think of things he never thought of before. When I was twenty a good fight was the best thing in life. If anybody had told me then that I would stand in the middle of a forest, eight years later, and dodge a fight, I would have knocked him over. You're right. I am not sure." He shook his head, never having been unsure before. "I did not know that all this was in my head until you mentioned it."

"Put me out of your thoughts, if that is the reason."

"Maybe the sight of you brought it on. But it goes on from you onto other things. Those things are not all clear. Your father will drop, or I will, when we meet. That makes me think of you. But then it comes to me what piece of ground is worth a killing? And what is a man for—to seize what he wants and to hold it against all men until he's worn out, or is it to be riding free, takin' what comes and lettin' other men do the same?"

She murmured: "I can't bring you the answer."

He sat down on the ground and he rolled a cigarette. She dropped beside him, her shoulder touching him. The lighted match was a great explosion in the black night, shining dark-red on his face; he looked at her and saw the glow of her eyes, the wide attention in them. The light went out.

"A man's like a shovel, which is no good standing in the shed. It has to turn soil and get scoured bright, and be filed smaller and smaller and someday break. Then it is through—but it has seen a lot of work. Well, a useless man is small. So is a man who lives only to grab and hold. This Basin has made a lot of men small."

"It changes everything. It turns and twists everyone."

"So I have seen," he said. "Except you. It has left its mark on you, but it has not changed you. You're stronger than the Basin."

The cigarette burned bright, burned dull. Farther away the Horsehead men were murmuring. A wind ran in steady sighing through the pines, cold at this elevation. Coleman bent his big hands together, pushing his steady thoughts through untraveled places. The girl said nothing but her nearness buoyed him and then she put her hand on his arm and it was like the tug of a line on a drifting ship.

"But a man can be small by runnin' free. He spends the days and comes to no halt and someday is old and has found nothing. The world is full of drifters."

"Go deeper," she said. "What do you want?"

"All I know," he said, "is it has been close by since I've been in the Basin. Don't know what it is."

Her voice came softly at him, it pressed him forward. She was the echo of his conscience speaking. "Will you stay or go? You must know that tonight."

"What would you do?"

"I'm not Tracy Coleman."

"The sound of your voice is like—" He stopped and was long still. When he resumed talking he had pulled the warmth out of it; she felt the change and wondered, and was hurt. "A man can't run from his chores. I have led these men into trouble. The rope is waitin' for them all. Maybe it was waitin' for them before I came, but I dragged them nearer to it. That is my doing."

"If you run, they will run. They will escape. They are not part of your responsibility. No, it is what you want. You alone. What do you want to do?"

"You're holdin' me to it, hard and fast."

"Because you are uncertain. You were never made to be that way."

He threw the cigarette away. He drew a long breath. "If I left this place I'd always be lookin' back over my shoulder, knowin' I missed something I do not know what. I will have to play it out here."

She rose and stood above him. "Then do it. You will face Star Cross sooner or later. Don't think of me then."

"Too late for you to ride on tonight. Camp here until mornin'. At daylight I'll be takin' the crew back to Horsehead."

She was still not certain of him. So she said: "Once I heard you say that you did what had to be done, no doubts and no regrets. Don't change from that, Tracy. It is the only way you can live."

He rose and took her arm and walked toward the shadowy group. "Back to Horsehead when daylight comes," he said.

Pairvent murmured, "Never should have left," and moved away. Ann disappeared into the outer darkness. When Coleman found her again she had taken saddle and blanket from her horse; she had rolled up in the blanket. He crouched near her: "Ann," he said, "what are you thinkin'?"

She was silent. Her hand came up and touched him and dropped. He rose and moved away.

Trumbo stopped the Star Cross column when dark came. "Dust smell's gone. They left the trail here, but they'll have to camp. Can't travel at night in that country. We'll stay here until light."

"Which way did they go?" asked Stuart.

Trumbo thought about it. "Pairvent knows the country. He wouldn't let Coleman lead them into the big canyon. South, I think. Over the summit toward Gateway. We'll head 'em off. Daylight's about four-thirty. We'll move on at four."

They stayed in the trail and unsaddled for a cold camp. Trumbo built a smoke and lighted it, a new thought occurring to him. He said: "Stuart, where's your daughter?"

"In town."

Trumbo's mind worried the facts before him terrier fashion. "None of that outfit knows much about these hills, yet they're battin' around like it was level ground. Somebody with them knows this country like a book. I keep thinkin' of your daughter."

"She's in town," growled Stuart.

Trumbo pinched out his cigarette and settled on his blanket, his suspicions growing. Ann had said she could not be neutral in the fight. She would go to Coleman if her sense of rightness was sufficiently stirred. She was like that, following her convictions into strange places. A new feeling got into Trumbo and ate at his pride like an acid and for the first time he began to think of the personal relations between Ann and Coleman; and a furious bitterness rose, so that he was no longer the cool and distantly amused schemer that he had been.

After leaving Valencia, Ben Solvay backtracked the trail for an hour, deeply pondering his reasons for so doing, and presently his thoughts got too involved for him and he dismounted and sat on a rock to work his way through the confusion. Here he was, he told himself, a man going out on an errand he had no heart in, for the sake of a woman who wanted the man she was sending him back to help; and when that became clear to him he told himself that he would not do this fool's errand.

It was but a momentary rebellion, for he knew he would do what she wished. He had not the power to put her out of his mind. It was hard to realize that he, Ben Solvay, who did his day's chores and was content with the day, could be so greatly changed and so weakened. For it was a weakness to him that he no longer abided his own convictions. In a way it was a disease which had destroyed something in him—like Tyco Rhett in town who, having had typhoid, was no longer the same.

"When a man's alone," he thought, "he's complete, he needs nothin'. But then he sees a woman and he gives something to her. He never gets it back. If he wants to be whole again he's got to go to the woman."

It went farther. As a man alone he had nobody to please but himself; he was his own guide and his own judge and his own wants were simple. He counted his own winnings and found them good. That was changed. There was no pleasure in lone thoughts and he saw that his triumphs were stale when he could not share them; and he found himself measuring things according to Valencia's eyes.

Then—and his thoughts were moving fast and irregu-larly—he had an odd idea. Coleman once had said: "You sleep well at night and do not dream." He had not understood those words. Now their meaning came to him like the sound of a gunshot through the dark. There were other things than sleeping and eating. There were strange images before a man, and strange visions and great tides on the inward sweep; there was a world below the world he saw and in that world there were powerful feelings and agonies and hungers and shames and beauties. And this world had been opened by one woman suddenly appearing before him, and the old comforts and satisfactions of his days were gone forever and he would be going through hell and heaven for the rest of his life.

He thought: "How did Coleman know all this? Is one man born different from another, or has he gone through his torment before me?"

There would be torment for him in knowing that it was Coleman she wanted. He foresaw that as an unhealing burn inside him, the pain of it lasting as long as he lasted. When he had first heard about her he had known her love had gone to another man—now dead. He had prepared himself for that. It had not seemed important then. Now that he had seen her, it was important. Then he thought: "If she loved that fellow, how could she love another one?" He had figured love was a single flame which, once destroyed, never burned again. He went deeper and deeper into strange, unknown depths, through the black tunnels of human behavior, lost and without direction; and presently the tag end of a new thought came to him: Maybe a woman's need to love a man and to be loved by him was so much of her life that it went to the grave with one man but could not be buried with him. Maybe it was like the need of air to breathe, something that could not stop. Maybe that was the secret of living, the reason for it.

And maybe there was in people a pull, like to like. She had known him first and she had made a bargain with him. Then she had seen Coleman; and he was the man—something in the sound of Coleman's voice, in his eyes, in the shape of his body, something like that crossing the air to her. He thought it until he grew confused and shook his head. He had gone through so steady a vigil with himself and had been so disrupted and torn apart and shaken by the thoughts racing through him that he felt no particular antagonism toward Coleman.

He had dismounted from the horse as one man; in the growing shadows he returned to the saddle, humbled into another man. Wisdom had come to Ben Solvay in the shape of doubt and wonder. Nothing was positive any more. From here on even the shadows in the sky and the pattern of the trees through twilight would not be quite the same; nor would he ever see these things without stretching his senses forward to reach the things singing so strangely over the earth.

It was night when he reached the summit of the divide—a swift blackness swinging cape-like around him. Not sure of his destination, he drew off the trail, unsaddled and camped. If anyone came along the trail he'd hear and follow; otherwise he would wait for day.

13

ECHO OF THE RIVER

At two o'clock Coleman relieved Ray Miller on watch. A sharp pinching cold lay throughout the hills, and the world was a dead ball rushing through dead space. He took his blanket over to Ann and laid it around her shoulders, and moved to a far corner of the bowl. Near four a first skim-milk color diluted the coffee-black shadows; and he circled the bowl, rousing the men. When he reached Ann he found she had already wakened, and now sat upright in her blankets. He crouched close, catching the half-asleep softness of her face.

"Time to go," he said.

She rose at once. She stood still, working at the pins in her hair. "Don't look too closely at me," she said.

He caught up his blanket and saddled his horse. Baldy was quietly cursing the world. "Second day and nothin' to eat. Next time you knotheads find grub, I'll do the cookin'." Ed Drum's horse pitched along the clearing and suddenly stopped dead, brought in by Ed's quick hand; this was no morning for fiddling. Ann rode beside the group. "Straight over the mountain," she said.

"Wait," said Pairvent, a surly man turned infinitely worse by wear and suspicion. "Look at what's ahead of us."

They were still short of the crest of the big hills. That somber mass lay before them and above them, disheartening to men cold and weary and cranky. "Take us too long to get over the hump. Maybe get lost as well."

"I won't get you lost," said Ann. "I can go through here with my eyes shut."

Pairvent hated the thought of being in her hands; he was set against her and would not change. "The horses ain't had grass and they'll play out by the time we get up there. If we get chased they'll have no steam left for a run. This won't do."

Ed Drum, the most quiet man in the group, now put in his blunt addition: "Time to turn around and go home."

Miller said nothing. Baldy, stabbed by hunger, made a grunting assent. The crew, Coleman thought, had reached the end of its rope. He said: "We're goin' home. But if Stuart is on our trail he will have followed our tracks as far as the turnoff. If we go back that way we'll run straight into him. I'd rather pick my own ground for fightin'. Roundabout is the best idea."

"Hell with it," said Pairvent. "We been roundabout too long."

In that out-and-out defiance Pairvent had, Coleman guessed, Drum and Baldy with him. There was always a sour point in men which, once reached, made handling of them impossible. He could do two things, either make a show of force, or let them go as they wished. At four o'clock in the morning a show of force seemed foolish. He made up his mind quickly. "You go back to the trail in any manner you please. I'm followin' Miss Stuart to the summit. I'll hit the trail there and come back. Wait for me."

Miller now spoke out. "Never wise to split."

"No," said Coleman, "it is not wise. But it is less wise for all of us to walk straight into Star Cross."

Pairvent's jealous suspicion never lessened. "You sure you're coming back when you get to the summit?"

"I'll pass over the remark for the time bein', George. When you move on, don't start the brass band."

It was now light enough to bring up the shadows of horses and men. Pairvent said, "Come on," and rode away, Drum and Baldy behind. Ray Miller sat fast, his smart mind caught by the situation. "You're right," he said to Coleman. "We should circle. But there's no handling George when he ain't had a meal. This is bad. I better go with the crew. One more gun in case we hit a snag."

"Wait off the trail for me when you get there," said Coleman. Ann had already moved ahead and was a vanishing shadow in the shouldering blackness before them. He rode after her and closed the distance. The grade began directly beyond the bowl and rose in stiffest pitches, putting the horses to great labor. Ann tacked it crisscross, making short right and left angles. They came upon thick stands of pine and worked slowly around them; they faced layers of rock and skirted these to more passable ground; they made long slants through open growth. At daylight she stopped to give the horses a badly needed breather.

The ride had reddened her cheeks and her lips formed a turned, smiling line. "I have ridden this country a hundred times. The evil in the Basin doesn't climb this far. It is too tough a ride for men to make, and nothing here is worth enough for them to steal." She looked at him, moved to seriousness. "If men could only be pleased with what they have. They don't lift their eyes, Tracy. They raise dust and the dust blinds them."

He made a wry remark. "I am thinkin' of the coffee we threw away yesterday. Half a pot of it."

Day rose in the east and somewhere out there the sun grew bright and warm; here it still remained cold. "Once I thought Drew was above the Basin. It was his ambition to be a big owner that dragged him back to its level."

"A man and his dream."

"A cheap dream," she said.

He started to speak, and afterwards lifted himself straight on the saddle. Below them, to north and south, was the break of one shot, close-followed by another, the echoes bounding on through the hills like great balls rolling on an iron floor. No other shots followed. Coleman swung his horse about and started it downhill. He checked in at once. "No," he said, "not that way."

"It came from the trail."

"Go on, Ann. Get to the top."

She rode on, forcing her horse somewhat harder. Now and then from this high elevation Coleman had an occasional vista outward, to see a piece of the trail lying gray and brown in the forest's dark green. Farther east was the hint of the big canyon's deep slash. Away in the north lay the grass plain of the Basin, slowly turning amber under sunlight—and sunlight now began to strike through the trees as they rode.

"Two shots," said Ann over her shoulder. "What does it mean?"

"Sounds like one man tried and the other man beat him to it."

"Suppose it was a signal?"

"Pairvent wouldn't give himself away with a signal. Neither would your father."

They ran on up a more gradual slope and came finally to a summit meadow lying between low peaks, rocks bare and glittering under the sun. "Straight for the trail, Ann. Damn Pairvent, I think he walked into an ambush. How far to the trail?"

"Mile."

They went across an open area at a slow gallop. Both horses were winded from the climb, Coleman's running with its head dropped and grunting at each strike of its feet. They circled the bare peak and moved into a scattered grove of stunted trees gnarled and blistered by wind. The ground pitched downward. They left the pines behind, fell into the dry, gravelly bed of a winter's stream—and arrived suddenly upon the trail.

The girl stopped. "That way," she said, pointing to the left, "is Horsehead." He had already lifted his reins and she knew he was ready to go. She gave him a short, incomplete smile. She said: "So long, Tracy. Good luck," and turned to the right, toward Gateway. She hadn't waited for him to speak; and when he did speak it was with one sharp word that brought her about: "Wait." He was looking along the trail, half-lifted in his stirrups, and as she followed his glance she saw two men gallop forward.

Those two came to a complete stop for a moment, staring forward at Coleman and at her; and then one of them raced on and the other lifted a long yell behind him and hit into the timber. The oncoming man was Tap; he reached for his gun as he rode and although it was still far beyond a decent shot he fired once—as though signaling.

"Whole outfit right off there," said Coleman. He watched Tap coolly; his eyelids came together and she saw the bones of his face make their flat pressure against his skin. Nothing hurried him while he had his quick look and came to his conclusion. "Other way," he said and turned about. "You'd better stick with me until we're out of this." Ann ran before him, south down the trail's slope, around a bend. This closed them out of Tap's sight for a moment, and Coleman immediately called at Ann, "Off the trail and double back."

She swung left, ran through timber and fell over a rough break of land; with this shelter between them and the trail she veered left again. Coleman pulled her to a walk with a gentle "Easy, Ann." They moved quietly north. To the left of them lay the trail, not more than a hundred yards distant; and now they heard the hard run of horses along it and the shout of a man's voice. Ann turned her head so that Coleman observed the collected gravity on her cheeks. "My father," she murmured.

The sound of this fast riding came to a quick halt not

far away. Stuart's voice was a clear halloo in the thin morning air. Another man raced by and stopped, and a horse's feet crushed dead-fallen limbs to the rear of them. Coleman murmured. "Steady." Riders swept back along the adjoining trail. Ann moved ahead, dipping and rising with the potty earth. The stringer of land still lay beside them but, in another ten minutes, Ann made a sharp swing downgrade and quickened the pace. She looked around, whispering: "This is dangerous. We're drifting into the canyon. I'm trying to make a circle back to the trail below them, before they push us any farther down."

"Long day, lots of time."

One more shot broke, forward and to the left. As soon as she heard it, Ann pointed directly north. The trees began to thin and sunlight streamed down. Ann bent in her saddle, staring ahead; she made a signal with her hand and stopped, permitting Coleman to draw alongside. There was a road ahead of them. "That leads from the trail to the Star mine at the bottom of the canyon. We've got to cross it. They may be watching. Shall we turn back and try the Gateway end?"

He rode to the edge of timber and looked up the road toward the trail. He saw nothing and he heard nothing. "Over we go," he said, "on the run." He waited for her to come up and put his spurs into the horse. They left the pines, struck the deep dust of the road and fled across, and at once heard a yell sail out. "Tap—downhill at 'em! Beau—Henry—down at 'em!"

Sound poured at them from their front left quarter. Star Cross came in from that direction, hitting the rough land hard. Stuart's unmistakable voice rose and quit and presently rose again, now nearer. Coleman stopped, listening to all this racket. He shook his head at Ann. "Back—and down."

"Once we drop into the canyon we can't get out."

"Down we go."

She swung with him, slanting with the hill. The road

was directly before them but she avoided it until the ground before them got too steep, then turned upon it. Coleman came abreast and halted, listening into the air. The racket was behind them and around them; and now Stuart's voice was a stronger summons somewhere on the far side of the road, to the South. South was Gateway—and Stuart blocked that direction.

"Down," said Coleman. "Take the road."

She obeyed, throwing her horse into the road and descending with it. He came behind her, his gun lifted, and he rode with his body slung around to cover the higher rear. Thus running from bend to bend, they were sheltered from whoever followed directly on the road. At the end of another quarter mile the girl stopped. They were now at the very edge of the canyon, the road becoming a ledge cut into the canyon's wall, dropping down and down to the river's whitely broken surface. "Last chance to double back, Tracy."

He shook his head. "Keep going."

They fell at once below the rim, the horses trotting stiff-legged. Dust flared behind them and behind them was a fainter calling. A hundred feet on he saw the gray top of a mine shack below and a long dump of burnt-yellow dirt stretching to the very edge of the river. The dump made a kind of breakwater, behind which the river's edge lay calm. Beyond the dump was a smooth, fast-flowing stretch and below this, at half a mile, the river exploded into rapids as it fell deeper and deeper between the canyon walls. Heat grew thick. Suddenly behind him he heard a call, and looked back to find Tap on the high break of the ledge.

Ann turned a switchback. Following her, Coleman now looked up at Tap, and at Tap's gun. The distance was close to two hundred feet and Tap's bullet ran far overhead. Ann knew nothing of it until she heard the echo of the shot above the river's growing growl; and jerked up her head in surprise. Tap, preparing for a second and more careful shot, suddenly lowered the gun as if he had not recognized her before. He stared at her, he turned around and called back of him. Another Star Cross man came down, and Drew Trumbo rode into sight at the break. Stuart followed immediately on his heels—these four forming a watching group. Suddenly Trumbo rode into the ledge, followed by the others.

Ann pointed ahead at the slack water behind the mine dump. "Tam Malarkey's boat."

The boat swung on the gravel, its oars lying inboard on the seats. Malarkey, old in the ways of the river, had descended this far, tied up, and had gone on. There was no sight of him on the open stretch above or below them. By now they had reached the narrow gravel beach. Coleman followed Ann to the back side of the mine building, got down and took a swift glance inside the building. "No good," he said. He had already made up his mind. Having been brought this far downstream, the boat was stout enough to cross him over. The river, though fast, was smooth and he had a half-mile leeway before reaching the rapids. It seemed a good bet but, good or bad, it was the only bet. He said to Ann: "You're safe with your father, aren't you?"

"Yes," she said.

"So long." He ran at the boat before she had dismounted. She turned to watch him, then understanding what was in his mind. Star Cross was half down the ledge, and a shot harked against the canyon walls and she saw the bullet lift gravel near by. Coleman reaching the boat, made a jump into it and ran out the oars. Ann said, half under her breath: "Oh, no—you're a target!" She said it and rushed from the mine house toward the water, so running as to place herself between Coleman and Star Cross coming down the slope. She heard her father yell: "Get out of the way!" She reached the water's edge, watching the boat drift on, and suddenly she waded hip deep into the river and climbed over the bow of the boat. Coleman had begun to row. He stopped rowing and looked around. "Go back," he said, and dug his oars deep into the water, heading again for the shore.

"Keep going. Keep going! I can't go back to Star Cross!"

Coleman reversed direction and sent the stern of the boat through the slack water. Directly beyond the mine dump a hard current caught the stern and swung it down. Coleman righted the boat, nose upstream, and put all his weight into the oars. He realized then the river was a power he knew nothing about, for with all his sudden and rapid laboring, the boat ran down, seeming to squat lower as the water pulled it. He turned the bow slightly, intending to make a long diagonal for the farther shore, but as soon as this broadside came against the current the bow swung and then they were racing head on at the rapids.

Above the growing roar of the rapids, he caught Dan Stuart's long, hard-flung cry: "Pull that bow around, you fool! Pull it around!" He knew then why Ann had come aboard. Neither Dan Stuart nor any Star Cross man would fire at him now.

But that made little difference. The smooth green surface water raced on, faster than he dreamed water could go, and the glass surface began to break before little ripples, and the ripples grew into washboard waves; and suddenly before him was the churned flurry of the rapids and the steady, monotonous racket of them. He was broadside and he dug deep, forward on one oar, backward on the other, and got the stern at the rapids and called behind him: "Sit low, Ann."

The current, so far straight-running, now became a trough into which they fell, and the trough narrowed toward a boulder half-awash and half-screened by white spray. He laid all his strength into the oars; he heard the edge of the rock strike the boat and he felt the lunge of the boat as it went by. Now, looking downriver, it seemed to him the water dropped at a forty-five-degree angle, from one boiling explosion to another. He braced his feet on the cleats, lifted his oars clear and watched all this rush forward, his belly made empty by the knowledge he could do nothing more.

"Ann," he said, "I'm sorry."

"Remember," she called back, "Luke Wall ran this river."

14

MEN ALWAYS DIE ALONE

It was Tap, in whose soul burned so pure and so terrible a flame of loyalty to Star Cross, who first raised his gun and fired at the boat whirling midway in the river, his desire making him forget the girl. Trumbo whirled and knocked Tap's gun down. "You damned dumb fool!" he shouted.

He received from Tap a burning, brilliant glance of hatred. Tap lifted the gun again, obsessed and made greedy by the target Coleman presented. It took Stuart's bawled-out shout to stop him. "No firin'!" Then Stuart cried full-voice to the boat. "Coleman—pull in, pull in!"

Even as he shouted, the boat was caught in the full-out grip of the river, beyond the reach of Stuart's voice and beyond the power of recall. Trumbo watched it for a full ten seconds, his glance clinging to the girl now sitting in the boat's bottom, both hands gripped on the combing; he saw Coleman poise the oars and swing and speak to Ann. Her head turned and Trumbo had a dimmed view of her face.

He wheeled his horse and ran down the shore line. He untied the lariat from its thong as he rushed ahead, and shook out its loop and began to swing it overhead. At this point the river was not wide; from midstream to shore was not much more than thirty feet, but the boat was ahead of him and the current rushed it on. He scraped his spurs full across the flanks of his horse, ramming it to a dead gallop on the difficult footing of the gravel. The horse stumbled and almost threw him. He grabbed his horn and kicked himself upright again. He made some gain on the boat and he thought that if he had a long-enough run he might get alongside it, ride a few feet into the water and let go with the rope. He had no doubt about holding the boat once he made a throw of it.

He saw he would never get a long-enough run. The boat was now nearing the top of the rapids. At that point the gravel beach narrowed to a foot-wide ledge at the base of the canyon wall; and great chunks of rock fallen from the canyon's face, studded the shallow waters near the shore. He looked at the boat on which he was slowly gaining, he looked at the ledge; hard by the face of the cliff he brought the horse to a somersault stop, dropped to the ground and ran upon the ledge.

The canyon wall bent in a slow quarter circle. Around this the thin pathway traveled for a distance of two hundred feet, at the end of which it headed into a great boulder. Beyond that point there was no footway at all. He saw this as he ran, and he kept half a glance on the boat now bouncing in the first heavy water of the rapids. A roar of wilder rapids came upon him and wetness was all around him and he breathed from the bottom of his lungs. He began swinging his loop, building it over his head as he ran; close upon the big boulder he stopped, turning his body half-around to get a sight on the boat, and made a long high-arched throw.

He knew even as he cast that it would fall short if he held on; and in one of those instant-born decisions which come of necessity, he let go the rope before it had stretched full. He had allowed for the onward run of the boat, just as he would have allowed for the onward run of a steer; the rope led the boat, so that the boat was broadside to it when the loop came down. He watched Ann make a perilous stand, reach high and seize the loop with her arm. She dropped flat in the boat, snubbing the rope with her body. Trumbo ran hip deep into the stream, made a futile grab at the rope's free end and slowly straightened. Ann shook her head and sat down in the boat.

He had a quick stab of fright at the power of the river; he dug his boot heels into the gravel's slickness and got ashore and climbed the big boulder. The boat's stern shot high into the air and its bow dipped from sight below a roller; he saw Coleman poise the oars, lower them to steady the boat, and poise them again. The current rushed at the bend of the canyon and struck it with a slashing and a spraying, and boiled about the black and battered rocks. The girl was just visible as she crouched low; he saw Coleman suddenly use the oars again in swift, short stabs. The boat slid away from the collision of water and rock, careened until its floor boards were visible to Trumbo, and vanished around another bend of the canyon into the greater roar below.

Trumbo said to himself with a dull satisfaction: "It was a good throw." Water dripped from him; water squealed in his boots. He sucked air into his lungs and found his legs trembling. A thought stabbed into him, turning and gritting through his spirit. "I wish she had thought better of me." She would be dead in another five minutes, all of her fairness and laughter gone, her hair streaming in the river, the beauty of her face rubbed and broken and destroyed by it. He stood with sickness in him; he heard Dan Stuart calling behind him but he didn't turn. Before him, moving slowly forward on the barest edge of the shore, he recognized Tam Malarkey.

Tam shouted. "How'd they get out there?"

Trumbo shook his head. Stuart yelled again. "Drew—Drew!"

Trumbo slid from the rock. Stuart was half-along the narrow pathway; he waved Stuart back and he followed the Star Cross owner to the gravel beach. The old man's face was without its ruddiness. Pale, it showed the network of broken veins, it showed its sags and lines, its oldness and its basic cruelty. "No luck," said Trumbo. He thought to himself: "Good God, Stuart's dead inside, so dead he stinks!" He himself had some of that deadness. Twenty years more and maybe he would look like Stuart. He pushed the thought aside. "No luck," he repeated.

He stepped to his horse and turned toward the mine shanty. He had lamed his horse in the reckless run through the gravel and he rode slowly, Stuart tramping abreast. The Star Cross crew stood by the mine house, watching these two come forward. Tap stared at Trumbo, bright evil clearly shining on that narrow face. The girl meant nothing to Tap; and at the thought of it Trumbo's rage swelled in him and he stared at Tap and so desired to kill the man that Tap saw it. Trumbo thought: "He knows I'll try it sooner or later. He will beat me to it unless I watch sharp."

Somebody followed them, kicking the gravel. Trumbo turned to see Tam Malarkey move forward with his old man's loose gait. Tam stopped and scanned the group. He said: "Coleman, hey?" He knew the story then, except for the girl's part. "How'd your daughter get in that boat, Stuart?"

Stuart was too far sunk into himself to hear; or too indifferent to answer. Trumbo answered for him. "She was on Coleman's side, Tam."

Malarkey carried a rifle cradled in his arms, his right hand loosely curved around the stock of the trigger guard; his eyes drilled their holes into Stuart with an insistence Stuart at last felt. He looked at Malarkey. "Old man," he said, "get out of here."

"Old?" said Tam Malarkey. "I could walk the heart right out of you in an hour. I could pin you to your back in half a minute. I could break your neck with a twist of my hands. I have seen you ride your horse like the lord of creation, but your wind is broken and your face has got death written all over it."

"Old man," cried out Stuart, "shut that loose mouth!"

Tam shook his head both in distaste and in sorrow for what he saw. "You Basin fellers are a bunch of wolves lookin' for dead carcasses to feed on. You're here now, knowin' you pushed your daughter down the river. Think you'll ever sleep again, Stuart? Think your grub will ever taste the same? I would not care to live in your sort of a hell."

Stuart made half a motion toward his gun, driven to it by the ceaseless goading of those words. Old Tam's shoulders swung gently, thereby presenting the raw round muzzle of his rifle at Stuart. There was no answer to that; the old man stood his ground, his glance rendering out a hard judgement. Stuart walked on to his horse, gesturing his crew to follow, and turned up the trail. Trumbo delayed his departure, considering Tam Malarkey and in a way envious of this bony, rugged old man who had no worries, no ambitions cankering him. "Tam," he said, "it is easy for you to judge. There is nothin' you want. How can you judge other men that want things?"

Old Tam cast a weather eye on Star Cross going up the trail, and relaxed long enough to find his pipe and light it. His hair was gray-iron, close to his skull, his skin as smooth and dark as dressed leather. His brows made a grizzled, tangled awning over his eyes, over his long arched nose. His glance finished its search of Trumbo. "I have made my errors, son. Only way a man learns. You will have to do the same. But there is no way of knowin' if you'll grow wise from your mistakes or not. Some men do not. And some men die from their follies before knowledge comes."

"Not much help, Tam," said Trumbo.

Tam's eyes mirrored scorn. "The damned world bleats for help, figurin' it is somethin' that comes natural." He waved a hand at the canyon, at the river. "You think you'll get any help from this water or these rocks? The world will beat the livin' guts out of you if it can. You have got to help yourself or else die."

Trumbo shrugged his shoulders and turned from Tam's

uncomfortable presence. His pride was ruffled at the rough talk, his temper was disturbed; yet the distantly critical eye that looked upon his life with so complete a detachment—that ironic and self-knowing bit of mind in him—accepted Tam's words as full truth, and used them as malicious weapons against himself. There was this warp and division in Drew Trumbo, this isolated knowledge of rightness lying lonely and ineffective and mocking in him while his will and his energy carried him on through baser things. He knew his baseness, he lived with it and sometimes cringed before it; but always he kept on.

He followed Star Cross up the trail, thinking steadily of Ann. The strangest images of her came to him, beautiful images of her alive and laughing, grisly images of her torn and dead. It brought him a kind of agony and a kind of emptiness. He heard the lovely tone of her voice, felt the warm touch of her hand; he remembered how her shoulders made their curve at the points, he remembered the faint freckles at the base of her nose. He went up the canyon, sickened and weary of riding, and when he came to consider what chore lay next, he ground his teeth together and could scarcely face it. Still, he knew he would do what Stuart intended should be done; he could not go back, he could not change himself, he could be no other kind of man.

So he followed Star Cross out of the canyon to the main north-and-south trail, and rode down the trail for a mile and a half, at which point Star Cross turned into the timber and stopped.

Pairvent, Ed Drum and Baldy stood here, trapped at this spot earlier in the morning as they came out of the hills; and Ray Miller, the only man alert enough to make a draw, lay dead on the ground. Those two shots, fired by Miller and Tap, were the ones heard from a distance by Coleman. Ambushed by Star Cross, the other three Horsehead men had surrendered.

Hoby Spade and his two riders had been left behind by Stuart to guard Horsehead. Spade showed a great deal of relief at the reappearance of Star Cross. He said: "You took a hell of a lot of time. Where's Coleman?"

Trumbo looked at Pairvent when he answered. "Coleman went down the river in a boat. The boat's smashed to matches by this time, and Coleman's lodged against a couple of rocks, ten feet under water."

Ed and Baldy showed the full force of the news; they looked at each other and the starch of their last hopes went out of them. It was visible to all the watching men. Pairvent, a tough and cross-grained character in his mildest moments, shrugged his shoulders. "We never should have left the ranch. That was his mistake." Then he paid his sultry respects to Stuart. "Your daughter no doubt led him into it, as she led us into this blind pocket. I wanted to keep goin' straight down the trail."

"No," said Trumbo, "she was in the same boat that went down with Coleman."

That affected Pairvent. He ran a hand across his dark jaws, drew a breath and shook his head. "Then she was square after all. She liked Coleman."

"Yes," said Trumbo, dully furious at the thought, "she did."

Pairvent knew what lay ahead of him; it was the finish of a hard game—the only possible finish. Even so, he was tough enough to make an observation which ended any remote chance of mercy. "You boys," he said, "are sure tough on women."

Trumbo took it without an answer; and was shocked at himself. Stuart, all this while acting like a drugged man, suddenly straightened and walked at Pairvent with the red haze of murder in his eyes. "George," he said, "I'd like to stick a knife through that tongue of yours. I'd like to strangle you until it hung out, and cut it off." He raised his closed fist and swept it crosswise, catching Pairvent on the side of the head. Pairvent raised his hands in defense. He swayed from the blow—and suddenly struck back, knocking Stuart to the ground. Tap's gun raised, centering on Pairvent, and he took a steady aim. He

would have fired if Stuart had not yelled at him.
"Cut it out. That's the way he wants it." He got up and looked at the trees around him. He pointed at them. "Those will be fine." He motioned his crew to be at it; he passed by Tap and murmured a word and went on. Tap turned, following him, with Trumbo watching that little byplay closely. These two were out near the trail and Stuart said some quiet thing in Tap's ear. Tap nodded, swinging back; he held his eyes steadily before him, looking straight into the trees, but by that deliberate training of his glance he gave himself away. Trumbo stirred on the saddle and pushed his hands against the horn. Star Cross had three ropes hanging down from the trees and Tap rode from rope to rope, forming the knot and the noose in each, adjusting the length of them as casually as though he were repairing a fence; the coldness in him was as deep as his bones, Trumbo thought. Stuart said: "Bring up the horses."

Tap went back for the horses and led them up. He cut an extra piece of rope, four feet long, and unbraided it and used the single strands to catch and tie the hands of the Horsehead men. Pairvent lunged away from him whereupon Stuart lifted his gun. "Be still, George."

Drum and Baldy had given up, the closeness of death laying its frost on their nerves. Trumbo, still detached and sharp-eyed, observed this and wondered if death's forerunning chill always had the power to freeze the pain of the final passage. He hoped it was so, for he was a man cursed with an imagination, and his imagination had often visualized his own end. He hoped for a dullness just before the stroke came, but he was not sure. It seemed to depend on the man. Drum and Baldy were only half-alive, while Pairvent, by contrast, stood straight and hated every soul around him with that bitterness which had been a constant thing in him. He was a man stiff on his two feet, with a pride fierce enough to hold him intact, and he began to taunt Stuart. "Don't you wish you had my guts? Watch me die—and just remember you'll never have half the nerve. Your days are about done. Somebody's going to kill you. Your luck ran out with Doña Gertrude. The Basin hates the ground you walk on. You got no friends. You sent your daughter down the river and you're standin' here now with maggots in your mind. They'll eat you through. They'll make a pain in you worse than any pain you ever thought of. I hope the man that shoots you hits you in a spot that will let you drag on for hours, suffering every second of the time."

Stuart looked back at Pairvent, his eyes reddened by their broken blood vessels, vainly searching for some way of breaking this tall Horsehead foreman, of making him bend and cry for mercy. But he could not think of any device which would pierce Pairvent's shell. Pairvent was as strong as he was. Pairvent was stronger, for his glance clashed with Stuart's and his rigid face showed a gray smile and he put his tongue between his teeth and ejected a flat, vulgar sound. "Your insides," he said, "are the insides of a cur dog."

Stuart dropped his glance. The choleric color so characteristic of the man had not appeared since the scene at the river; his complexion was a dirty-gray pallor, like the pallor of disease, constant and startling. He said in the quietest voice he had ever used: "Get it done, Tap."

Tap called the Star Cross men forward. They boosted Pairvent and Drum and Baldy to the horses. Tap mounted and rode forward with them, a black and wicked little man acting as death's chaperone and liking the job. He dropped the nooses over each man, he cinched the nooses and coolly tested the ropes. He rode back. He said, "Stand away." He was still Star Cross foreman, obedient to his owner, and waited now for Stuart's command.

Hoby Spade was sick. He wheeled his horse and trotted fifty yards into the trees, whereupon Tap looked at him with a zealot's intolerance. His glance came slowly back, touched Trumbo and paused, and Trumbo saw once more that distant and eager hatred grow bright. Stuart looked at Pairvent.

"This is the end of a crooked outfit. If you're thinkin' the Basin will condemn me for this, you're wrong. The Basin would do it sooner or later." His anger whipped him and his basic brutality fed upon this scene. "I hope," he ground out, "the rope slips. I hope you strangle a little at a time."

"You can quit talkin'," said Pairvent.

The lines of Stuart's face deepened and all the evil of his soul filled them; and he thought of one last malign thing and almost smiled as he thought of it. "Tap," he said, "George goes last. Let him see the other boys swing."

Tap moved behind Drum. He paused a moment, lifting his quirt, methodically setting himself; then he put his horse to a run, struck Drum's horse a hard blow with the quirt as he swept by. Drum's horse rushed on, dragging Drum from the saddle. His feet whipped and churned in the air and broken, sighs came out of him; his legs moved more slowly and more slowly, and ceased to move. Stuart called: "You like that, George?"

Pairvent said nothing. Tap swung behind Baldy, raised his quirt and ran forward again. Baldy let a last, violent yell out of him as he was swept from the horse and he struggled with his hands, trying to free them. His eyes grew large and his terribly congested stare hit Drew Trumbo. Trumbo clenched his teeth together, feeling Baldy's agony. Tap went behind Pairvent.

"You like that, George?" repeated Stuart.

Spade called out from the rear. "My God, Stuart, a white man's a white man! Don't drag it out!"

Tap struck Pairvent's horse. But Pairvent, until now wholly still, suddenly made a leap upward from his stirrups, kicked himself violently free and fell with a force that broke his neck at once. The rope jerked him upward and gave a dull twang and whirled him a little; but he had died without delay. Stuart stared at Pairvent's full-length figure as it slowly swung and he spoke a lifeless phrase. "He beat me out."

Tap rode slowly into the center of the clearing. He had his back to Trumbo, he was looking at Stuart. Stuart said: "That's three of them. Now we have got to find Alvy. After that I want Ben Solvay. As for that Wilder woman, I will make sure she has left the country."

"Is that all?" asked Tap, still watching Stuart.

"No," said Stuart, "not all. Go ahead, Tap."

Tap used his legs and his left arm to bring his horse about; and as he turned his right hand dropped for his gun. He came thus face to face with Trumbo and he had half drawn on Trumbo. That was as far as he moved. Trumbo, thirty feet across the small clearing, had his own revolver centered on Tap. He had known for ten minutes that this would come.

"Too late, Tap," he said.

Tap's face was alive with his desire. He held the gun half-risen, pointed at the earth; he held it still and waited and watched. Hoby Spade suddenly ran his horse forward and stopped near Trumbo. Spade was an outraged man, a common man made brave by desperation.

"You damned Paiute! Ain't nothin' enough for you?"

"Hoby," said Stuart, reclaiming his old, arrogant manner, "stay out of this or you will go the same way. I've had to drag you through this by the heels. As for Drew, I told him to look out for himself. The two of you have made your own plans. I have made mine. Stay out of this and go home. You will never get an inch of Horsehead, either of you."

Spade called to his two riders. "Come here," he said, and waited until they had joined him. Now he added, "I see how it will be. You won't feel safe until you've got us out of the road. Trumbo and me will be dodgin' through timber the rest of our days. Might be well if we finish this business right here and now."

Stuart said sharply: "Don't be a damned fool, Hoby."

"Drew," said Spade, "you take Tap. I'll handle Stuart."

"Let them start it," said Trumbo. He looked at Stuart briefly: "Start it, Dan," and he looked back at Tap.

Stuart's red color had returned. He watched Spade steadily, reading the man and guessing how close he was to a killing. He had no great opinion of Spade, but his opinion did not sufficiently strengthen him. Therefore he shrugged his shoulders, turned about and went to his horse, well knowing Spade would not fire at his back. He climbed to his horse. He said: "All right," and led the way from the grove, Star Cross following. Tap was last. Tap reluctantly holstered his gun, reluctantly gave up his desire. In a moment Star Cross vanished down the trail.

Spade ran a nervous hand over his face. "That's not the end of it."

"A thing like this never does end," said Trumbo.

"Then," said Spade, "I think we had better finish the thing. Stuart will hound us until we're dead. We had better get him first." He looked at Trumbo, hating him and despising himself. "You got me into this deal, Drew."

"For God's sake, Hoby, play your part. You wanted some of Horsehead."

"That's true," murmured Spade. "I wanted it. Then when I saw what it meant, I didn't want it. Now it is entirely too late to mend anything." He caught the fleeting end of that thought with all its implications, and burst out: "A man can't ever quit in the middle."

"I said there never was an end, didn't I?"

"We've got to go after Stuart. That's the end of it."

Trumbo shook his head. He sat on the saddle, a ruddy and handsome man darkened by his thoughts; a man condemned to know goodness and right without the strength to follow his knowledge. It was his tantalizing insight which controlled him now. "Stuart thinks he can wipe it all from his mind by destroying the men who know of it. You think you can set everything proper by destroying Stuart. None of that will help. This thing is like the seed pod of a thistle, a thousand seeds bein' scattered around. They'll root and grow everywhere—mostly in you and me and Stuart." He drew a heavy breath. "Doña Gertrude will outlive all of us."

"What?" asked Spade.

Trumbo shook his head and moved to the trail. Star Cross had gone downhill in the direction of Horsehead Range, the dust of their passage still hanging in the bright air. He could not go that way, well knowing that from now on he would be under constant observation by Stuart; they had set out upon a course of destruction and had been partly successful. Yet he knew Stuart could never feel at ease until the last outsider participating in Doña Gertrude's death had been disposed of. Stuart would track him without conscience; neither he nor Spade could expect any relief from that.

Doña Gertrude would follow Stuart still. The time would come when Stuart, obsessed by it, would look upon his own crew as accusers; he would see in the eyes of his own men the memory of the act and then he would turn crazy, and try to destroy them. "No end," Trumbo thought. "No end at all." He turned south, moving toward Gateway. As he did so he felt for the first time in his life two alien sensations: the feeling of being hunted and the feeling of being alone.

Ben Solvay, camped off the trail near the summit, had been warned by the two shots, sounding in the north and not far away; and presently, crouched in the timber, he seemed to be the center of a good deal of crisscross riding. When that died out he got to his horse and ducked forward from tree to tree and so eventually spotted a group of men standing in a glade below him. Thus he was a witness to the hanging and was helpless to prevent it. Long later, after everybody had gone, he ventured forward and cut down the Horsehead men, immediately leaving the area. Back in deep shelter he considered his own situation and found it bad. Stuart and Trumbo had wiped out most of Horsehead and no doubt would next be after Coleman. But since he, too, had thrown in with Horsehead, it looked as though he were also a fugitive. Valencia had been right; he could not go back to the Basin as long as Stuart was in it.

He pondered this over a cigarette, very calm and very thorough; and at last he said to himself: "Why, to hell with them," and rose up, mentally buckling on his armor. He would find Coleman. He would join Coleman and help out.

15

IN THE GORGE

Coleman dug hard with the oars, making deep, short chops into the water; he got the stern squared at the white tumbling river before him, and poised the oars. They swung out of the chute and scraped past a black-edge boulder and faced the wilderness of white rollers ahead. The boat dropped stern first into a short cross trough, was thrown upward and slammed down again. Long gouts of spray curved aboard and the bottom was awash, and the thin planking of the boat began to squeal with the twisting and the straining given it.

The stern whipped aside and slowly swung beam-to. Coleman dipped his oars and had them almost wrenched from his hands by the sudden seizure of the current. He tried to backwater with the right oar, but the river ran here so rapidly that he could not shove fast enough on that oar to make pressure against the river. He put all his force into the left oar, feeling it bend. Sometimes he buried it deep into a roller skimming the top edge of the boat; sometimes he caught nothing but air as the hollows came beneath him. He got the stern straight again and rested. Sweat rolled back and forth under the brim of his hat.

"Ann," he said, not daring to look around, "you're all right?"

"Still here."

They shot on, rocked and jarred. They swayed through the eddying turbulence at the lower end of the rapids and were picked up and shoved forward by a stretch of smooth, fast river. He relaxed and bowed his shoulders and wished he had time to light a smoke. His coat was soaked and water sloshed around the boat's floor boards, high as his ankles. He heard Ann bailing.

He looked at the banks and saw nothing there. To either side the canyon rims were higher, the canyon faces steeper; down from those rims, through the hundreds of thousands of years, huge boulder chunks had fallen, and these boulder chunks were great black teeth on either side of him, waiting to trap and chew the boat to splinters. He heard Ann say: "I've got Drew's rope. Can you think of any use for it?"

The river was a foreign thing to a man who drew his life from land; a river was an enemy with unknown ways. The thought of the rope caught his attention at once and he looked at the rocks running by, calculating the possibility of shunting the boat near them and laying a loop over one of their sharp points. He made a guess as to the speed of the boat and his ability to snub it down and he said, "Pass it forward." He took it from her and laid it at his feet. It was a long chance, for once ashore they faced the complete isolation of the canyon, the walls giving them no hope of climbing out, the water permitting them no way of walking upstream toward the mine.

Meanwhile as he thought of these things, the small chance faded. The current rushed them on and the steady vibrating roar of other rapids grew greater. He said: "What are we coming to?"

"Bridal Veil. Broken water and rocks. A little worse than the last one."

He said: "How far have we come—how far on to Gateway?"

She delayed her answer, apparently making a thoughtful study of it. Over the stern of the boat Coleman saw the river rush downgrade straight at the base of the left canyon wall, swing from it and pass around a bend. The main current took them hard by the wall, so near to it that Coleman's left oar once touched the broken rock. It swung them around the bend and as they came into the straight stretch Coleman saw the river tilt and make its steep wild drop through a whitely jagged surface. Once there had apparently been a slide, scattering great rock chunks from bank to bank. Around and over and through these rock chunks, which made darkly awash shapes, the river broke and whirled and threw up its layers of spray. A half-mile of water poured over this ancient wreckage, straight on to another bend. At no place did he see a safe channel.

"We're four miles below the mine," said Ann. "Ten to Gateway."

"Quick four and a long ten."

She said: "I've watched Bridal Veil many times from the west rim. There's no main channel through it, but if you can hug the left-hand shore you won't have as many rocks to dodge. There's a little piece of beach below."

The current's smoothness broke into short, choppy ridges. He lowered his oars and pulled the stern square and he checked speed and side-slipped the boat to the left, and then was thrown at the shore faster than he had calculated, straight upon the rocks. He straightened and pulled hard, letting the boat bounce and sway toward the head of the rapids, toward one black finger against which the water struck and broke into spray.

"Tracy," she called, "I'll tell you one of old Tam's tricks. He drifts straight at those big rocks and lets the side current carry him around."

It was around nine or ten o'clock, the sun somewhere half up in the sky but not yet reaching to the bottom of Cloud River's narrow crack; everything down here was a pearl-gray shadowing against which the water made its white dance. He lifted his oars a moment and watched the half-drowned boulder leap at him; he dipped and rowed and checked the stern hard by the rock. He was on the crest of the water, and then he fell off and the current whipped him by the rock, around it and into the chop below; water poured aboard and the boat dropped as though the bottom of the river had vanished from it. It struck with a great jar, and immediately afterward lifted stern foremost high into the air. He had his feet stabbed against the floor cleats, but the drop and rise flung him forward. His knuckles, fixed around the oar handles, hit the floor and Ann, likewise unseated, fell against him. Her hands seized him at the shoulders and righted him on the seat.

The stern had yawed wide. The left-hand shore was quite near, all awash to the cliff face; and as he looked up at the cliff face he saw the dark flitter of spray on it and one small green bunch of ferns clinging high up. He hauled off from the shore's risk, pitched around other boulders and watched the stern fall far down, placing the boat half on its end. Somewhere behind him Ann sat high and lonely against the sky; he heard her short, startled cry as the stern struck a rock and swung end for end.

The bow was now downstream, placing Tracy's back to the lower river and thus ending his control. He could not back water against the swiftness of the stream. He poised the oars and turned on the seat and in that moment's glance noticed the white tongues of the river leaping. "Hang on!" he called.

He drove one oar into the river, holding it; he hauled full strength on the other and saw the stern slightly answer. He pulled the boat half about and felt the stream push roughly at it. Ann sang out: "Close to the shore rocks!" Now broadside to the current, he shoved hard with the right oar, still pulling with the left. The boat rose as though a hand had flung it and as it came down its bottom landed squarely on a rock; there it teetered and slowly slid off, and when it fell away his right oar's point hit the rock and flew from the oarlock. The handle sprang up and struck him under the chin, knocking him back on the seat. He let go to catch himself, straightened, and watched the oar whirl away in the water.

The river came through the floor boards in a steady gush; behind him was the quick clatter of Ann's bailing can. He used his single oar in a kind of sculling motion to hold the stern down. The roar which had been a solid booming all around them now was a great racket to the rear; he saw calmer water beyond and he saw the cliff face rise straight out of the river, below which one single patch of gravel beach lay half-touched by the sun. The stern would not hold to the single oar. It swung and smashed into the cliff, was caught at the bow by the current and flung around. Ann cried: "Watch out!" A moment afterwards the boat struck a rock and capsized.

Ann's warning had turned Coleman. He had reached out and seized her arm with his hand. The collision threw him free and the water coldness hit him like a board and he went down lower and lower into the black depths of the river. He touched bottom. He churned his legs steadily, he clung to the girl's hand and felt her whirl against him, and he rose and saw day and took in air—and went down again.

He fought the river with one hand; the other hand was fixed to Ann in a grip that would not relax. He remembered coming up again, and thought that he must have dropped and risen thus half a dozen times until images began to flicker and flash through his brain. Afterwards—so long afterwards that the day seemed to have rushed by—his feet hit solid bottom and he began to walk, with no knowledge of where he walked. He pulled Ann with him and saw day and breathed again. Ann fell against him, her eyes closed. He took her in both arms and pulled her to the beach. She was a weight that was hard to bear; he let her slide to his feet and then he dropped to his knees and slowly stretched full length on the rocks.

This was the first time in his life he had ever been so

punished as to be thoroughly humbled, the first time he had thus lain and felt himself at the last frayed ends of his vitality. He wanted only one thing, air to breathe, and he could not seem to get it. This water, so soft and yielding and smooth to the eye, had beaten him within a narrow margin of his life and it had left him as no other accident had left him—numbed and passive and powerless immediately to rise and fight back; he felt a new thing in his body—the terrible helplessness of being weak. The river had thoroughly scoured out of him the will to fight.

He watched Ann slowly stir on the gravel. She had been turned from him and when her face came around it had a blank expression; he saw how slowly her thoughts moved through the empty areas of the last few dizzying moments, filled them, and at last understood what had happened. He watched the gradual loosening of her face from its drab and gray preoccupation. Suddenly she reached out her hand and closed her fingers tightly around his arm. "For a moment, Tracy," she said, "I thought I was alone."

"Tough place to be without company."

"Yes," she said; and he saw the wake of terror in her eyes. Her fingers fell away and she put her shoulders on the gravel and stared at the sky.

The sun was overhead, breaking the rock-dull shadows in the depths of the gorge. The heat lying between these high walls began to reach into his marrow-deep chill; he looked at his hands and noticed that they were pale beneath the summer's tanned blackness, bleached and bony. Water slid through his clothes and along his skin and dripped down. The rocks under him grew cold; he moved to a dryer and warmer patch.

"I think," murmured Ann, "I must have lost consciousness for a minute. The last thing I felt was your hand. I knew you wouldn't let go."

"No," he said, "I wouldn't let go."

Some warmth came back to him, and some confidence. By the slowness of its return he knew he had been a long way on the road to a distant place. He let his mind move cautiously toward the thought of that place. The door stood a little way open and he had the feeling that maybe he had been near enough to look through. He shook the thought aside.

"Tracy," she said, "where's our boat?"

"Haven't looked."

"Have you thought of what's next?"

"No," he said, "not yet. Roll over to warmer rocks. Better get as dry as you can. It will be cold tonight. One thing it is not necessary to worry about. No way of going back upriver."

"And no way of climbing out."

High above them two stunted pines grew perilously on the lip of the rim, between five and seven hundred feet distant; between those pines and the beach on which they lay was a dark-gray wall without foothold. It came down from the rim in one perpendicular rush, worn smooth by a million years of the river's assault. Halfway to the top there was what appeared to be a ledge. He watched it for a long time, and cast it out of his mind. The wall on the other side of the river was equally sheer.

"No," he said. "Nothing there for us."

"That's why I wondered about the boat."

"The pieces of it are probably passing Gateway by now."

He sat up. He put his hands down to his wet boots and started to pull them off; he foresaw a tussle and he wasn't ready for a tussle. So he rose, feeling the thick and meaty aches in his body. Somewhere during the last hundred feet of the rapids he had taken a sharp beating from rocks although he had felt nothing at the time. His whole left side hurt him. The rapids lay behind, sunlight whitening the lacy brilliant leap of the water; and the sound of the water was a rush and a slash and a steady-echoing roar from wall to wall. The beach upon which they sat was not more than three yards wide and ran along the foot of the cliff for two hundred feet. The downstream end narrowed and pinched out against the bluff, the upstream end was a curving finger pointed into the stream, between that finger's end and the cliff was a pool of slack water in which a dozen or more logs, bleached by water and heat, lay jammed together.

Coleman said: "There's the boat."

The mention of it was enough to bring hope to her. She came to her feet, turning. The boat, striking the beach, had swung around in the current, had been lifted and thrown against the logs. It lay bottomside-up now on the gravel, one side caved in. "But not much use to us," he added.

She stared at it. She stood thoroughly motionless, her shoulders rounded, her features still; and then she turned her head to him and he saw hollow defeat in her eyes. Knowing her composure and her normal courage, he realized how violent a shock the sight of that wrecked boat had been; it shook her will. He moved to her and he put his arms around her and pulled her against him, her miseries hurting him as they hurt her. He said, rough and short: "What made you come with me?"

She lifted her arms and laid them on his sides. She held to him with the lightest touch. She put her head against his chest, her hair wetly and brightly shining against the overhead sun. She said noting; she held him and looked down.

"I know why you came," he added.

She lifted her head. "Do you?" she asked, and drew away. The fear had gone and the despair had been pushed back. Even when she was deeply serious her lips formed a slight upward slanting at their corners and this, with the usual light in her eyes, made it appear she was holding back a smile. As he saw it he felt small for the doubts he carried within himself; this girl was greater than anything he knew about.

She had turned to look again at the boat. She walked on to the edge of the pool and she reached down and lifted something and turned. It was Drew Trumbo's rope. "At least he tried, Tracy."

He took the rope and coiled it and built a loop and

slowly shook it out. This was a familiar thing, a well-understood tool whose weight was good in his hand; and he looked around, wanting some use for it. He considered the canyon walls again, yard by yard all the way to the top, seeking to break its impassable surface by the power of his wishes. He looked across the river, he swung on his heels and studied the small gravel bar upon which they stood. Below them was a long stretch of smooth water, bending at last out of sight. Down there—far down—was the murmur of other rapids.

"What's ahead? Better or worse?"

"No better. Remember how you climbed upgrade from Gateway, by the road? That's the way the river drops."

He quit shaking the rope. He let it lie idle in his hand. A rope was half a man's needs; a horse made the other half. But in the canyon there was no use for a horse. What took the place of a horse here? He swung about, again regarding the boat. "It could be patched up," he said aloud, "but it wouldn't last long."

He walked into the pool, knee deep, and climbed on the log jam. He tried his weight on one log and another. "A rope and a horse can do almost anything," he said. "On the river maybe it is rope and something that floats. I can roll three or four of these logs into the slack water and lash them together with the rope."

He was thinking aloud, piecing together a length of rope, a few logs and a smashed boat—and making some sort of a chance for them. He knew it was a small chance, but he was wrapping his stubbornness around those logs along with the rope. She still felt the quickness of his hands around her, he had seen her misery and it had gotten into him and made him reach out to comfort her. Then she asked herself: "Would he have done that to any woman?"

"But the logs," he said, "would rub the rope apart in about five minutes. Need something else to stiffen them. That brings us back to the boat. Take it apart. How many miles do we have to go?"

"The Punch Bowl is just below us. It is six miles on to Gateway."

"Well," he said, "it might work. If it doesn't, we can hope we hit another bar. If we hit another bar, then we can figure out what else to use."

He sat down and pulled off his boots and drained the water from them. He put them on and stepped into the water again and waggled his head at his own folly. "I'm not thinkin' too fast." He hauled the cracked boat ashore and tore off the broken sides. He used a rock to splinter the ends of the boards in order to get the nails free. It wrecked some of the boards, but the nails were more important than anything else. He made a pile of them on the ground; he had the boat knocked apart in an hour.

He took a look at the log jam. Some parts of it were too solid to stir, some gave beneath the pressure of his weight. He went all around the jam, sizing up the logs; he came ashore and sat down. Ann dropped beside him and watched him reach for his tobacco. It came out of his shirt pocket as a handful of brown pulp and when he looked at it he showed his first real distress. "Hell of a situation," he said.

"We've been very lucky," Ann told him.

"Written in the book when the luck runs out. I guess we haven't come to the end of the writin'."

"You just believe that, Tracy. You don't practice it. If you really felt that everything was arranged for us, regardless of how we struggled, you'd not be prying those nails out now. You'd not be fighting. What you really believe is that a man makes his own luck."

"Maybe the wish to live is the strongest thing of all."

"Not in you."

He looked at her with some doubt. "Nothin' much in me except to do the first thing at hand and sleep on it."

She smiled, long watching him, so that he saw in her eyes the shape, the color, the outline of something he could not name, but a thing that rushed powerfully upon him. This was strange—to live with his restless, vague wishes and yet not to know what those wishes were, and now to see in a woman the first form of them; as though, long dreaming of a picture and never able to bring it out of the misty background, he here watched it take shape. It had not happened before.

"If you only wished to live," she said, "you'd have left this country before now. If you only slept and never had hopes I would not have jumped into this boat." She abandoned the subject quickly. "Our luck may hold. We may land at Luke Wall's. Then the Basin will be at us again."

Habit made him reach a second time for his tobacco. "Damnation," he grumbled, and got up. "Well, one thing at a time." He waded into the pool and tackled the logs.

He worked for an hour before he found a log which would come free of the jam. He pushed it against the gravel and tried again; and the afternoon was half-gone when he had collected four logs of odd sizes and lengths in the slack water. He was tired in a way he had seldom been, still feeling the shock of the river, and steadily thinking of the journey ahead of them. Even as he labored he had not the confidence and the certainty which was always otherwise with him. His world was one of horses and land and of things done so many repeated times that the pattern was cut into him. This was another world, the power and the ways of water beyond his knowledge.

He laid the boards over the logs at intervals and nailed them down, using a flat rock for a hammer, thus creating a raft with an incomplete decking. The nails were not large and went only an inch into the logs, and he knew the hard beating of the rapids would pull them out. He laced the rope around and across the logs for greater strength. He battered a ten-foot length of the rope apart from the main rope and tied this as a life line around one log.

"You can slip your feet through that," he said.

The canyon was gray when he finished the chore. He pulled the end of the raft against the shallow gravel and he weighted the end with rocks to keep it from sliding back into the current; and he stood awhile watching it. Rope and nails made a flimsy job of it; nothing would hold it together except luck. Luck had been with them so far and it might stay with them or it might run out. The hope of it was all they had.

"We'll run it in the morning," he said. "Getting too dark now."

She sat down and as he crouched beside her he noticed the calm, close-seeing attention that went out from her to the sky. Trapped here, she would be thinking about freedom; cold, she would be thinking of warmth. Those things lay only a thousand feet away. As he watched her, he thought of Valencia Wilder. This other girl came into his head suddenly and stood before his inner vision, calling to him with her disturbing will. He said to himself: "Why am I thinkin' of her?" and tried to know the reason. She was nothing mild or meek; she was not innocence. She was a hungry, rebellious spirit speaking to him.

Ann spoke with a wistful amusement. "I should be thinking very serious thoughts. But I think of coffee hot enough to burn my tongue."

Wind came down the gorge, carrying away the heat; it went through his damp clothes and turned him cold. Ann would be chilled through in another hour. He had this in his mind but at the same time the memory of Valencia was keen and the impulses she lifted up in him were hard and blackly-colored so that he felt ashamed to be thinking them so near to Ann. Yet he let those thoughts work through him, knowing he had to find the roots of his own feelings. He drew a long breath, he stared into the gathered blackness down-river. A man was a mixture of things—and evil was in the mixture.

Ann's voice laid it soft touch on him. "You are far away."

He rose and walked to the edge of the pool. The raft still hung there; it had not shifted. He turned back to Ann and stood over her. He said: "You're getting cold."

"There's nothing to be done about that."

He sat down and turned and put his arms around her. He drew her against his chest; he spread the edges of his coat as far about her as they would reach. He said nothing; there was nothing he wanted to say. He wished only to hold her, to make her warm. She lay still, her head tipped upward and away from him. The warmth of her body was as great as the warmth of his own; the softness of her body came against him. The things that had been in his mind so short a time ago disturbed him and he was afraid that the stark wants which Valencia's memory had brought to him would reach over to touch Ann. It was an unpleasant thought; it held him still.

In a moment that fear left him, for the image of Valencia faded and the call she made upon him died and he felt a contentment wholly new. There was a difference and a change, like a sweet warm wind blowing. He thought: "Nothing's been like this."

The canyon grew black and the sound of the rapids pounded violently through this blackness; a moonlight glow diluted the sky's steel color and stars made a ragged pathway north and south. Ann stirred. She turned until he saw her face, round and soft in the shadows. Suddenly she murmured, "I am heavy on you," and drew upright. She had her back to him, square-pointed in the night. She sat in this manner, watching something, or listening, or caught in her own thoughts. Presently she turned and lay out on the gravel, half-curled. She said: "A little sleep is better than none, Tracy."

He stretched beside her, gouging holes in the gravel for his shoulders and his hips. He turned from her; she put her arm over his shoulder. Mist began to thicken in the canyon and became a wetness on the gravel and rolled against them and had the weight of a fine, thin rain. Long afterwards he heard her say: "Sleeping?"

"No."

"I have been thinking. Everything gets smaller and smaller until there's only one or two things left which are nportant."

"What things?"

She didn't answer and he didn't ask again. An hour of his cramped position was all a man could stand. He urned about, and this made her turn about; and so the ight dragged and the wet cold of the rocks got into him nd his bones began to ache. Somewhere beyond midight, as near as he could judge, he rose and walked the ull length of the gravel beach and back again, shaking he damp from his muscles. She had risen and when he ame close he saw the weariness on her face. He sat down nd pulled her into his lap; he held her cradled again and e knew, without understanding how he came to know it, hat she had been silently crying.

"The waitin' is about half-over," he said.

"I thought I was stronger."

"I've seen men give way for less reason."

"I wasn't afraid until you walked off. Being alone is what turns you inside out. I should do it better—I've always been alone."

"You've had your people."

"People have been around me and I have been around people. It isn't that kind of loneliness I mean."

"Everybody has to belong to somebody else."

"When did you learn that?"

He started to say, "A long time ago," but he didn't. For t occurred to him he would not have said this before. It was a new piece of wisdom, acquired during the last hours. A man grew, and never realized it; and a man died and was not aware of it. This was a law in the big book. 'Not long," he said.

She turned from him. He put his arms around her and drew close, to share with her the little heat left in them both.

He rose at the first break of light overhead. There had been no sleep for either of them, nor anything else than an uneasy resting that brought no rest. During the last small hours of the night he had risen with an actual shock, remembering the raft in the shallow water and remembering the river that reached for it with never still fingers. The river never left anything alone; it needed no sleep or rest, it was a power older than any living or moving thing upon the earth.

Ann rose with him and they walked the gravel bar in chilled silence, back and forth to whip the drugged weariness from them, to bring some warmth back and some vitality. The night before they had felt relief at being permitted to live; but now they were close again to the chance of the river and the sound and smell of it and the dank feeling of it.

Coleman said: "Six miles to go. How many rapids?"

"White water most of the way. The river drops fast from here to Luke Wall's."

"Any falls to go over?"

"No."

He stood at the water's edge, considering the flimsiness of the raft, and he went over every resource within his reach and found no other way by which to make the raft better. Then painfully careful, he searched the rims again with his glance, watching their black faces turn gray. Near the water a heavy dew laid its dull shine on the rocks. farther up daylight reached down so that he saw again the narrow ledge near the top of the eastern edge. He had abandoned this as a possibility the prior afternoon. Now he studied it, lowering his attention foot by foot, searching for a way of climbing; but as before he found none. He went over every possibility and thought of one new chance.

"Your father would make an attempt to get you," he said. "He might call in Tam Malarkey. If they could find another boat they might snub it downstream by rope around one bluff and another. Hand-line the rapids."

"There's no other boat on the river."

"Might make up a raft from the boards at the mine

dump."

"If they had thought of that they would have sent someone along the rim to find us and signal us. They said good-by to us when we dropped around the bend. We're dead to them."

Day had come, mealy within the canyon, bright-blue above. Coleman stepped on the raft; he walked over it, trying his weight on it. He cast off the stones anchoring it down and held out his hand to Ann. "Time to go."

She walked to it and she looked back with a disturbed glance at the gravel bar. She controlled her fear, but the shadow of it showed. She didn't want him to see it, and held her face away from him. But that sudden look she gave the gravel bar hit him in the heart.

"I know," he said. "This was good—but it isn't good any more."

"Most things are like that. We hang on, but we have to let go."

"Not everything," he said. "Lie down and hook your feet through the rope."

He needed an oar and had none; he needed a pole. He walked along the log jam but found nothing suitable, and so came back to the raft. He pushed the raft through the slack water and slowly around the curved finger of the sandbar. The current gave the raft one powerful blow, dragging Coleman deeper into the river. He was waist high before he pulled himself aboard. He crawled forward until he was beside Ann; he put his arms around one of the crossboards and jammed his feet against another crossboard. The smooth, swift water at the foot of the rapids began to turn the raft and to rush it forward.

"What stays the same, Tracy?"

The raft continued its clockwise turning all down the straight stretch of smooth water. The bluffs were sheer to either side, forming a long bend. In a little while, looking back, he saw that the gravel bar had dropped from sight; ahead of them was a growing grumble. He sat up, looking sharply downhill upon ragged layers of white and green flung up from the river's surface. The warning of that roughness began to reach them, the smooth current breaking into a chop which slapped aboard and laid its wetness upon them. He looked at the boards of the raft, watching them play and buckle as the logs shifted. He looked at the ropes.

Ann said: "I can understand now the queer way Luke Wall talks."

"You'll see him in a half hour," said Coleman.

"I wonder," she murmured, "if he'll welcome us. He won't be the only survivor any more. He's proud of that."

"Hold fast," said Coleman. He flattened and gripped the crossboards. The river shoved them along faster and the water ahead rolled up before them in high, broken curlers. The raft was at this moment running nose first; it lifted but it was too heavy and too slow to ride the crest of the curlers; it dove into them. Water rolled over the raft and these two people and weighted them down. Coleman flung one arm around Ann, hauling her tightly against him. The raft came up with a sluggish heave and the water poured away; the river was a steady thunder between the walls of a narrower gorge and for a moment, with the raft slowly tilting and falling downward, he saw the trough in which they traveled and the ragged white peaks of water flashing to either side. The raft sank a second time. Once more under water, he caught the dead cannonade of the gorge and he felt the water tear at the raft and fling it around. When they again rose they were faced upstream. The raft's bottom struck hard and was thrown aside and a board cracked like a pistol shot, quite near Coleman's head. Afterwards the logs seemed to have a looser play.

They had gotten through one bad patch; he turned his head and saw it recede behind him—and looked forward and viewed the onward explosions of spray and the teeth of black rocks bare above the surface. The raft was steadily swinging. It struck one end and hung against the force of the river and for a while the pressure of the current began to drive it down and drown it. Water threw Ann at

Coleman; it strained against him and wrenched one of his legs away from the cleat. The raft shivered and he thought it ready to break apart. Then the river boiled up, shook the raft free and hurled it on.

They plunged in wheeling, drunken lunges through the wildest stretch of the river. The raft's nose dipped and lodged and the back end rose until Coleman slid forward; it broke free and great layers of water rushed over it. Coleman tightened his grip around Ann. He braced his feet and felt the weariness of his straining go through him, softening his flesh. He had no clear idea of the time they had been running the river; the constant turning and the steady shock of dropping and being thrown up had dizzied him. He had only two fixed impressions—the nearness of Ann to him and the increasing looseness of the logs beneath. Some of the crossboards had worked free. He felt them slide beneath him, and he felt the playing of the board to which his hands clung. One hard jar would tear them all loose, after which nothing held the logs but the rope.

The raft ran momentarily in free water and he looked above him and saw the rims and thought they were lower than they had been. Light strengthened in the canyon; when he looked ahead he saw one streak of sunlight. "Ann" he said, "Ann."

The roar was stronger than the sound of her voice. He heard nothing from her; and after that he could not speak again. For the raft struck hard, slowly slid away and fell with a jar that knocked the wind from him. One of his feet slipped from the crossboard and his left leg dropped between logs and he felt a streak of pain as the logs slammed together. He yelled into the water's thunder and he saw the girl's face turn to him, white and solemn. He dragged his leg free and propped it against the crossboard at the same moment the river poured over them.

He was tired enough then to think the dull, fatal thoughts of surrender; he held his breath until his lungs, long punished, began to burn and his heart was a slugging sound in his ears. The raft came up and water boiled away. He breathed and found the air thin and insufficient. The crossboard at his feet had gone and he found himself straddling one log. He called to Ann: "Don't let your legs slip down!"

She said: "What?" He shook his head, sucking in wind. Strong light played on his eyes and water dripped into them so that he could not see. He felt the raft rock and run into easier water and he thought: "Smooth patch before the next rapids." He relaxed a little and then he stiffened himself, waiting for the rough water to seize them. But they ran on through smoothness, and through a strange quietness, and the raft grated against gravel and stopped. He heard a voice say:—

"You'll both live forever. Let go the rope, Miss Stuart. Let go and I'll lift you."

There was a little current lifting and rocking the logs, nothing more. Coleman cautiously released his grip on the cross slat and rubbed the water out of his eyes. He opened them and saw Luke Wall standing hip deep in the stream, Ann Stuart in his arms. Luke Wall gave him a close, thoughtful smile. "You see?" said Luke. "You see what I been through? Just the three of us know. Ain't a thing you can ever explain to anybody. Come off the raft before it breaks up and floats away—which it will do in a minute. A drink of whisky and a meal will fix it right. I heard yesterday you had started down the river. I been here sixteen hours, waitin' to haul you out and bury you."

Coleman said: "What time is it?"

Wall looked at him and laughed. "Now ain't it funny what a man will think of? You know what I asked when they fished me out? I wanted to know if it had been rainin'. It is six o'clock in the mornin'—but what is time to you now? Never will mean the same again. You got all the time there is."

"Stuart here, or any of Star Cross, or Drew Trumbo?"

"Trumbo rode through here last night. Nobody else."

"They'll come," said Coleman

"You'll be inside my house if they do," said Luke Wall. "And I am with you, son."

Another voice, a woman's voice, called from the bank. "Are you hurt, Tracy?" Looking up from the raft he saw Valencia standing at the edge of the bluff.

It seemed strange to him that she had gone out of his mind until this moment; now she was before him and he looked at her a long while, waiting for that hot, hard feeling to come back. Luke Wall had started up the bank. Suddenly Ann said: "Put me down, Luke." Luke Wall set her upon her feet and she walked slowly up the grade of the bank to its top, passing Valencia without looking at the girl.

16

AT LUKE WALL'S MEADOW

Returning from the bitter business in the mountains, Stuart passed through Horsehead during the early-morning hours and headed for the river crossing. "Tap," he said, "you move to Horsehead with a couple of the crew tomorrow."

"Drew Trumbo will be smellin' around the place."

Stuart let out a grating retort. "Trumbo will be hidin' in the hills with the fear of God in his heart. I am not concerned with him. Horsehead is part of our grass, and I am taking possession."

Tap said nothing, but his silence held dissent, causing Stuart to add a biting opinion. "Everybody in the Basin wanted Horsehead to be cleared off, but nobody had guts to go about it. I did the dirty chore. Now they'll want to share it. They'll get nothing—not one damned spear of grass. It is mine."

The storm signals were up in Stuart; they showed in the down-angled lines of his mouth corners, in the spotted flush on his face, in the jumpiness of his voice and in the stony way he stared before him. When that temper came upon the Star Cross owner there was nothing to do but be still, and Tap wisely did so. Still, certain unfinished pieces of this morning's business displeased him and when they reached the Star Cross yard he ventured to repeat his warning: "Trumbo will be smellin' around."

Stuart had a quick breakfast and went to his room to lie out on the bed. There were a good many things on his mind; one of them was the dully unpleasant knowledge that he was no longer young. The night's riding and the night's cold damp in the hills had taken the starch out of him; he felt the heaviness of his bones, he felt a gnawing exhaustion. He turned constantly on the bed and his heart made its heavy labor in his chest. Light came through the window and struck his eyes; he wanted to rise and pull down the shade, but felt too tired to do so, and laid a hand over his face.

The heavy crop of his years was in the threshing. His range stretched far out on the other side of Horsehead Crossing as he wished it and Pairvent and all those men were finished; but his daughter was dead and the Basin hated him and would never again accept him. He would drink alone and eat alone in town. The miserable business of Doña Gertrude had done that. These things went back and forth through his mind—the good and the bad, one upon another. Lying there, sleepless and exhausted, he reached out to possess the feeling of triumph he should have. It ran ahead of him, beyond his reach.

He raised to an elbow, intending to call to the cook to bring him a glass of water; but pride stilled the call. He looked through the open doorway at the room which was Ann's. He stared at the dresser within his line of vision, at the silver-plated jewel box on it, at the brush and comb, at her mother's picture. Both of those women had hated him, the hands of both had been raised against him. He had tried to smash that resistance down but there was a strange thing in women which could not be beaten—a shadow, a look, a feeling nothing could erase.

"I should have turned them both out years ago. But they stuck, and they've got the last word at last. They can both stand wherever they are and make me feel like it was my fault. Women are clever like that—mean and tricky and full of deceit when they smile." As for Ann, she had deliberately stepped into Coleman's boat. That was her doing; the decision was hers.

He absolved himself of her death, yet the misery of her act took possession of him. Except for the accident of Luke Wall, no human being had ever survived the river. She knew that and yet she had gone with the man, her body protecting him from the guns on shore. He lay long still, puzzling over it, and the gray ghosts of another philosophy moved vaguely before his mind, to increase his doubt. At last he fell into troubled sleep.

He awoke beyond noon with a dry throat and a numb weariness all through him. He rose with difficulty and sat on the bed's edge with his head in his hands, everything inside him burned out. But the terrible march of things kept on in his head. He thought of the other owners on the range, of Gunderson and Bill Yell and Frank DeLeon who had cut him in town. He owed none of these men anything and he needed nothing from them; men came to him, not the other way around. And still his growing isolation troubled him and he thought: "Maybe I just imagined it." The thing to do was to ride to town and try again.

He washed his face ate a cold dinner and struck out for War Bonnet, reaching there around four. He entered the saloon and stepped to the bar for his drink. Snass Moran pushed bottle and glass at him. He waited for Moran to speak, his own pride insisting that the other man make the first move, but Moran walked away, running his towel casually along the bar. Doc Fallon sat at a near-by table reading an old copy of *Harper's Weekly.* Doc Fallon didn't look up.

Stuart stared at the bottle, which was half-full; when he next thought to look, it was empty. He had no idea of how long he had been standing at the bar, neither speaking nor being spoken to, but when he turned away he noticed a lamp burning near the door. He walked into the warm twilight and got on his horse, making three tries before reaching the saddle. He drew a long breath, found his reins and started from town. He thought he saw Jack O'Boyle on the walk. He said, "Hello, Jack," and didn't hear an answer. If he had been sober he would have stopped and called O'Boyle to account at once. But he knew he was drunk and he wasn't sure it was O'Boyle.

Somewhere out on the prairie Tap caught up with him and led him home. The last thing he heard Tap say was: "Don't be too sure about Trumbo. You got to put him out of the way."

That was a planted seed which grew while he slept; when he woke the next morning it was a rooted purpose. He rose feeling fresh and hale again. "Big drunk is good for a man once in a while," he thought and ate a tremendous breakfast. He moved to the front room for his belt and gun and for a moment he paused at Ann's bedroom doorway. He went into the room and stood at her dresser. He remembered how close to red her hair had been and as he looked into the mirror above the dresser her face came before him with a realness that shocked him. It was so still at the moment that he felt her presence in the room. Suddenly he swept his hand across the dresser, caught up the brush and comb, the picture and the jewel box and carried them to the kitchen. He said to the cook: "Open the stove lid," and threw everything into the fire. The cook wheeled and put his back to Stuart.

Stuart walked from the house and called to Tap. "Get Niles Peck and come with me." The three men saddled and set out toward the hills westward.

Tap said: "If you're goin' to Trumbo's it would be better to circle south. He's apt to be watchin' us—he'll see us across the flat."

Stuart's brief flush of good feeling had soon worn out; and now he was in the worst possible humor. "Tap," he said, "you talk too much about the man. He got you buffaloed?"

"No," answered Tap with a breathlessness which revealed how badly the remark hit him.

The thought of his aloneness rode with Stuart. It haunted him, it grew as a fed fire, it unsteadied his mind. He had been cut by his neighbors, he who had the power to crush them individually. They looked at him across the distance of the Alma's dining room and the thing in their eyes went through him and turned like a knife. Because of that he had to strike back to restore his own pride, and the first man in his mind was Drew Trumbo.

They came to the ridge and bore southward through the trees until they reached the slope which fell toward Trumbo's house; and at this point the tumult in Stuart caused him to make a foolish move. "Tap," he said, "take Niles and circle Trumbo's. I'll come up from the back way."

Tap stared at him, trying to fathom the reason for doing so unnecessary a thing. He said quietly: "We're not surroundin' a camp, Mr. Stuart. It is just one man we want."

"Don't argue!" cried Stuart. "If you're workin' for Star Cross, do as I say."

Tap sighed and his thin face grew thinner from the strain of the insult. He spoke very quietly: "Star Cross is all I have got to live for, Mr. Stuart. You ought to know that."

"Go on, go on!" yelled Stuart.

"Just so," murmured Tap and rode on through the trees with Niles Peck.

The rashness grew. It was a poison irritating Stuart's nerves until they vibrated within him. He turned to the west, traveling a half-overgrown trail along the ridge, and came to the main road from Gateway. This he followed until he had gotten within a mile of Trumbo's place. Here he left the road and entered the trees. He had not gone fifty yards when a voice said coolly from some hidden spot before him: —"Now wait."

His horse heard the unexpected noise, and the horse stopped before Stuart thought of checking in, Stuart turned to stone in the saddle. He lifted his reins, ready to charge, and he swept the timber before him and saw nothing. The voice was Trumbo's—easy and insolent—but he could not find Trumbo.

"Come out," Stuart said, "come out and show yourself. You're big enough to face a man without hidin' in the bushes, ain't you?"

Trumbo said: "Your eyes are bad, Dan. Look this way."

He was on Stuart's sight flank, standing quietly beside a pine, his clothes blended with the gray-brown bark. He had a shoulder point against the tree and he gave Stuart a starved, bright smile. "Your mistake was in strayin' off from Tap and Niles."

"You been followin' us?"

"Had my eyes on you since you left the Star Cross yard."

"Like a damned Injun prowler. White men don't prowl."

Trumbo's narrowed smile was tight against his teeth. "Now, now, Dan. We know each other too well for that kind of hogwash. You are after me. I am after you. That is all there's to it."

"Is it?" said Stuart and slowly turned his horse's head on to Trumbo. He had not been too sure of Trumbo's motive; he was not entirely sure yet. But he saw very clearly the heartlessness of Trumbo's smile and he saw the mockery and the malice in Trumbo's eyes.

"You made a bad mistake," said Trumbo. "There never was a time when we trusted each other. But that was all right. Each man's entitled to watch his own cards. We could have gotten along. Your mistake was tryin' to turn on me and leave me dead with the Horsehead bunch. It was a pretty raw thing."

Stuart said: "You would have done it to me."

"Maybe. Still, there's a difference. I would have done the job. I would not have bungled it and left an enemy behind me. That was your mistake. I won't bungle it, Dan."

Stuart remembered that Tap and Peck were not far off. They would be at Trumbo's house now and they would wait a decent interval and then maybe start back to find him. He eased himself on the saddle slightly, made steady by his danger. "Drew," he said, "Hoby Spade is a weak sister, ready to tell the Basin what he knows. He'll crucify the both of us."

"I can manage that later," said Trumbo. "One thing at a time."

"If you're thinkin' of knockin' me out of the saddle, consider what happens next. Tap will hunt you like a dog, the crew with him. You'll run before him, which will be the end of you in the Basin."

"Maybe," agreed Trumbo and seemed to be impressed with the argument.

"I will make you this deal," said Stuart. "I will drive Spade out of the country. You take his range. I will add a piece from my old range. There's a big outfit you been wantin'."

"That's what I want," said Trumbo.

"Well, then," said Stuart, "it should be a deal."

He saw the frigid grin lengthen. "Like the last deal, Dan?" asked Trumbo.

"My word on it," said Stuart.

Trumbo stared at Stuart with the anger of a smart man who had been misjudged. "You damned old fool, do you think I can believe your word?" He came out from the tree, tall and poised, and he watched Stuart so steadily that the older man grunted a gruff question.

"What the hell's in your mind now?"

"I was thinkin'," said Trumbo, "how you tried to break Pairvent and make him crawl. You're the Indian, not me. I was thinkin' if I could string this out and make you die by inches. But it is not in me to kill a man for plain fun." He shrugged his shoulders, said conversationally, "Something to my credit, maybe," and drew and fired before Stuart was able to stir.

The older man gasped when the bullet hit him. He showed vague surprise and he dipped his head and he started to place a hand over his chest; before he completed the motion he rolled from the saddle, struck on his shoulder and sprawled face up in the shadowed dust. His hat rolled away and his face showed its red veins and its lines of age and unlovely character through a slow-growing pallor. Trumbo stepped forward to witness this, impersonal and without regret; this whole thing left him without any feeling and he recognized that fact and shook his head. "I'm goin' back to the kind of man I was before," he thought. "Or else I was always the same man, just foolin' myself I could be better."

He turned to the trees for his horse and got to the saddle; he listened into the late summer's stillness, not yet hearing the approach of Tap or Niles Peck. They would catch the echo of the shot and they would come. Maybe it would be best to stay here and finish up with those two. He debated the idea and rejected it. The better thing was to maneuver around and catch one man at a time, when the chance came. One man at a time until he had settled the argument for good. Horsehead was within his reach now if he did all this carefully. He cut across the road and paralleled it, moving south through timber.

Tap and Niles Peck got back to Stuart half an hour later and Tap sprang from his saddle and ran awkwardly forward, calling, "Mr. Stuart, Mr. Stuart!" Seated on his saddle, Niles Peck watched Tap crouch over the Star Cross owner and sway at the shoulders; presently Tap turned and Peck saw tears in the foreman's eyes.

"Dead?"

"He never drew his gun," said Tap drearily. "Trumbo did that. Trumbo never gave him a chance."

"Well," said Niles Peck, unmoved by it, "you told Stuart not to go it alone."

"He was powerful excited and he wouldn't listen."

"Never listened to nothin' anyhow," commented Peck. "Let's start home."

Tap thrust a hostile stare at Niles Peck. "You take it damned easy."

"I will not cry for the man. He didn't give a damn for any livin' soul—not even his daughter."

"She didn't know him," said Tap. "What's any woman know about a man? She had her heart set against him. I didn't like her either."

"You do your grievin'," said Peck. "I'm goin' back to the ranch, get my blanket and keep on movin'. You know what's goin' to happen to Star Cross now? Same thing that happened to Horsehead. Nobody loved Star Cross at all. Everybody hated the ground Stuart walked on. Then there was that Doña Gertrude business. I can smell it all over the Basin. If I rode into War Bonnet they'd point at me and say: 'There's one of the men that killed Doña Gertrude.' How long you think we're goin' to be let alone? I'm leavin' now."

Tap growled: "I ought to kill you for talkin' like that about Star Cross."

Niles Peck was a man with a record of his own; he gave Tap a stiff look. "I ain't fightin' a dead man's battle and I know when a deal is dead."

Tap said: "Get out of my sight. Don't let me see you again."

"You won't," said Peck. "Nor any of the crew. When I reach home with the news we'll all be on the road."

He made a gradual turn around Tap in order to keep his right flank to the foreman, and so faded in the timber. Tap swung, again toward Stuart, and he grew still and this stillness was upon him for a quarter hour and tears ran down his cheeks and his face was the face of a lost man; for Star Cross was his life and Stuart was Star Cross, and all that was now destroyed.

He drew Stuart's coat together, and rose. He said aloud: "I will be back to take care of you, Mr. Stuart. But I got to even this thing first." He went to his horse, climbed to the saddle and picked up Trumbo's tracks in the soft carpet of the forest; he followed them to where they reached and crossed the main road, and he continued with them.

Two miles or more from Stuart's location, the tracks curved back to the main road and went downgrade through the road's dust. Tap bridled at the thought of

Trumbo's brazen assurance and he said to himself: "I will watch him kick and I will watch him yell and I will spit in his face just before he dies!" His lips moved in relish of the thought; he dropped his head to study the pattern of Trumbo's tracks before him. The road at this point came near the rim of the canyon, so near that it reached the very margin of the great, long fall to the river, and made a quick bend away. A careful man in every respect, Tap looked behind him as he started around the bend to be sure he was not being followed; and thereafter looked ahead—and saw one rider come slowly into sight below.

The rider likewise had his head down and so was not aware of Tap; and the rider was Ben Solvay. Tap pulled in his horse and he held himself quiet, watching Solvay daydream forward. Between them lay two hundred yards of gray road dust glittering in the strong sunlight, so deep and soft that the sound of Solvay's traveling horse sank into it and died. Tap remembered one thing: Solvay had been with Horsehead; and even though the distance was too great for a good shot, his jealous loyalty sent his hand down to the gun.

The shout of the bullet was a first warning of Tap's presence to the idle-riding Solvay. He yanked up his head so quickly that his hat fell off, and for an instant he stared at Tap, pulling his mind back to the present moment from the far place it had been. There was a startled break of feeling on his face and then as he grasped the situation he whirled his horse into the trees. Tap's second bullet followed him.

Tap flung his horse around and likewise ran for the trees. Reaching this shelter he started in Solvay's direction. He heard Solvay's horse whip through the pine branches and he had one fugitive view of the man, low-bent, rushing deeper away. He tried a third shot and was disgusted with himself; he changed direction to meet Solvay's slanting course—and suddenly he lost the sound of the horse.

He listened for it as he smashed into the timber; he went a hundred feet or more before his caution stopped him. He heard the blowing of his own horse and, bent forward in his stirrups, he thought he caught the rasp of Solvay's mount. The sound came out of the forward left. Solvay, he decided, was over there playing 'possum. Thinking it, he rode straight on.

A bullet harked through the timber and smashed his arm, driving it up toward his face. This was his right arm. He stopped the horse and looked around him, toward his right, and found Solvay standing no more than twenty feet away. Solvay had tricked him, had left his horse in the thicket and had run back. Solvay said: "So long, Tap," and fired again. His aim was spoiled by Tap's side swing in the saddle, so that the bullet caught Tap high on the shoulder and keeled him against the saddle's horn. Tap fought himself upright, making no sound. He tried to reach over with his left hand to seize the gun hanging uselessly in his right fist. He did all this with a bitter, careful courage, never for a moment weakening in his hate or his single-minded intent. He tried and failed. Solvay's next shot hit him close to the heart.

There were these four around the table at the Gateway stage station—Luke Wall, Valencia, Ann and Tracy Coleman. Luke Wall said: "You need sleep. I remember that I came out of that water and never had my fill of bed for a week. Have no worry about it, Coleman. No enemy of yours will cross this doorsill whilst you're here. Just tell me one thing. Who are your enemies?"

"My father and my father's outfit," answered Ann, who had said almost nothing until now.

"I knew that already," said Luke Wall. "And who else?"

"Drew Trumbo," added Valencia.

"And I knew that, too. I just wanted to be sure. None of those will pass this door." He was a huge, flabby man with the face of an oriental god; and his half-hidden eyes made their bland search of these people. "The out-bound stage will be comin' down the hill in half an hour." He looked at Coleman. "If it is your intention to leave the country—" He let it ride and he sat gross and wholly comfortable in the chair.

Ann laid a quick glance on Coleman and brought it away; it was Valencia who continued to watch this man, Luke Wall observed, and as she watched him she betrayed herself.

"I'll go back to the Basin," said Coleman. He rose, clapping a hand to his tobacco pocket. He swung on Wall. "Give me something to smoke."

Luke handed him paper and sack and followed him out of the house. The two stood in the yard, under the strong sunshine, and now and then their voices came murmuring back. Ann put her hands on the table, her attention falling to them. Suddenly she lifted her eyes and found Valencia Wilder watching. The girl's anxiety and urgent wonder tumbled out of her.

"How did you happen to be with him?"

"I wanted to be," said Ann.

She read the tempest running through Valencia Wilder; the girl's hot spirit was roused, she was again fighting the world for what she wanted—the world from which she had never known kindness. "Does he want you?" she asked.

"I don't know."

"You should know when a man wants you. I would know."

"Does he?" asked Ann.

Valencia sighed. "I was not with him long enough," she murmured.

"You were in the Horsehead house with him," pointed out Ann, civil and distant. "You were near him. You made him aware of that, didn't you?"

"I made him see me," said Valencia and was pleased by knowing how that remark would hurt Ann. Then she added in a less lively tone: "I made him want me, which any woman can do to any man. I do not know if it is more than that." She looked long at Ann, unfriendly and yet reluctantly honest. "Want and love are not always the same."

Ann rose from the table. She started toward the stairs. On the first step she paused to look back. "You can try again, perhaps—and perhaps find out," she murmured and went up the stairs.

Valencia feared and hated the other's composure. "She's cold," Valencia thought, but that was only a reflex of her dislike; her realist's mind knew better. She rose from the table as Wall and Coleman came into the room. Wall went on into the kitchen, closing the door behind him. His heavy tread died away. Valencia turned and stepped to the fireplace, holding her back to Coleman, waiting for him to speak. She cried out silently to herself, "Let him come here, let him touch me!" She waited until she knew he wouldn't come to her; and then turned.

He had his eyes on her, he was thinking of her, and he seemed deliberately to be letting all of her into him. He wore a troubled expression, as though he struggled with himself; and thus he stood, a man caught in the contradictions of his own nature, heavy-whiskered and with the punishment of the river showing in him. He was very tired and his clothes were wet and the knuckles of his hands blood-raw.

She stepped toward him and she thought of him in the unashamed physical way of a woman who wants a man with all her heart. She hoped he would see it, she hoped it would sway him, she hoped he would seize her and end the growing agony of waiting. She never knew what changed him or when the change happened but when he looked down at the floor everything was over and she had lost. The light went out of the room and she stood heavy and helpless before him.

"I thought," he said quietly, "you might have taken the stage out."

"I couldn't go until I found out what had happened to you."

"Will you be goin' now?"

"Yes."

He said: "Solvay thinks a great deal of you."

She remembered Solvay for the first time this day. "Did he go back to you?"

"I didn't see him."

She said: "I sent him back, Tracy."

"He'll be somewhere in the hills. He's a good man."

She said: "I'll take the stage."

"That's goin' to be tough on him."

"People have to break their hearts once in a lifetime, Tracy." She thought steadily of Coleman, even as she tried to think of Solvay. "It will hurt him less to have me go than for me to marry him."

"I would not be surprised if he followed you."

The thought pleased her. "If he wishes me that much—" But she soberly put it aside. "If you see him and if he intends to follow me, try to stop him. He'd never be happy. Nor would I. He would remind me of too much."

He looked at her with a kindness that hurt her terribly. Wanting so much from him, she had only this. He said: "I wish you a better deal, Valencia."

She shrugged her shoulders. "I'll make my way."

He turned back to the yard, walking slowly beneath the sunshine. He stopped at the corral and laid his shoulders against it. He smoked out his cigarette and rolled four extra ones and laid them carefully on the top bar of the corral; he felt the sun go into him, he felt the water drip down along his body. He began to thaw and grow warm and as he grew warm his bruises increasingly ached; he shifted all weight from his bad leg.

Valencia was on his mind still but he saw her differently now and he was at peace with himself. Coming into the stage house he had faced her and he had deliberately let all the temptation and all the sweetness that she had make its way through him; he wanted to know about the dark, wayward side in him; he wanted to know if the unspoken offers of a woman could so ride and control him as to destroy the other things he felt. He had to know; and he knew now.

The echoes of a rider came down the narrow gorge of

the trail. Coleman turned and reached to the top corral bar for a fresh cigarette. He placed the cigarette in his mouth and swung back—to see Drew Trumbo stopped at the mouth of the road, watching him across the width of the yard.

Trumbo had stopped. He sat still and was in hard, deep thought as he looked upon Coleman, and presently shook his head and got off the horse and moved forward, steadily and flat of foot. Coleman watched him come; he had the unlighted cigarette in his mouth. It sagged from the corner of his lip and his eyelids came close together and made pucker lines at the edges, as though actual smoke curled around his eyes. He was half-turned and his head bent somewhat aside, so that he watched Trumbo from a slanted position.

His range of vision ran beyond Trumbo, straight at the house. Luke Wall and Valencia were blurred figures against the wall and he saw Ann looking from an upper window. It occurred to him then that he had thus first seen her, framed between the curtains of that window and with lamplight behind her. She had been smiling and that smile had changed the course of his life, although he had not known it then.

He held his slouched, off-balanced position, a heavy man with weariness in his bones. He knew what was coming and he knew Trumbo's character and his skill, and he was wondering how many other meetings like this were in the book for him, how much hard luck, how much evil and torment. There never had been any smoothness in his life, never a day of golden ease. It had always been a fight—with the wind or the range or the sun, with a man, or with himself. Where was the day of ease?

Trumbo had stopped several moments before, and Trumbo again seemed to be listening to his inner conscience. He seemed to be waiting out Coleman as well, to be trying to break the other's stillness. Behind him was a faint racket in the gorge road, rising above the rush of the river. He heard that—and that apparently pushed him. He had said nothing; he said nothing now. Coleman, closely watching, saw the man's shoulders lift one slightest moment before his hand dropped; on that signal Coleman drew and fired. He saw his bullet shake Trumbo and he watched Trumbo's gun drop, unused, to the full length of the man's arm, hold there a moment and then go sliding out of his fingers to the ground. Trumbo shook his head; an expression, dumb and dulling, showed on his face as he fell.

Wall ran forward, the lard fat on his body loosely shaking. The racket in the gorge grew and in another quarter minute the War Bonnet stage shot into the meadow, howled on its wheels and stopped before the station. The driver dropped from his seat and ran at Trumbo. Halfway over the meadow he halted, turned and went back toward the stage. He clapped his hands against his pockets, stopped and drew out his plug tobacco and bit off a chunk; he circled the stage and leaned against the front wall of the house. Then he slid down on his haunches and began to draw lines in the dust with his forefinger—still watching the shape of Trumbo dead in the yellow grass beyond him.

Wall slowed to a walk, looked down at Trumbo and came on. Great noises came out of his chest from his running and faint sweat glistened on his forehead; his big mouth hung open, sucking in air. His eyes, bedded back in their pouches, had a black and damp pleasure. He put an arm on the corral and thus supported himself.

"That man was tough before he came here," he said. "He had a record down the trail." He bent his head forward. "Where'd you get your trainin' at this business?"

"Down the trail," said Coleman and returned his gun to its holster. He stepped away from the corral and paused above Trumbo. "He wanted a lot of things. In due time he would have gotten them, but he couldn't wait. He thought the day was too short. Except for one thing. Luke, he was a good man."

"What thing?"

"He had no heart," said Coleman.

Wall said: "In my book a man is bad or he is good. He was no damned good at all."

Coleman shrugged his shoulders. "Nothin' in my book is that certain." He lifted his head, facing the mouth of the gorge and the great mountain tiers rising before him, black-covered even with the sun upon them; he stiffened and his chest arched and his eyelids pulled nearer and he looked upon the mountains with a bristling temper. "By God," he said, "I wish I did not have to sleep out half of this day."

Wall said dryly: "All that will keep. When you turn in you will not rise until mornin'. The river's been at you."

The two walked over the meadow. The stage driver rose up and said: "You goin' to change these horses?"

"Sure," said Wall. "Now."

The driver said: "That Trumbo there?"

"Trumbo," said Wall.

"Change the horses," said the driver. "I want to get down into the clear country. I see Niles Peck on the road up at the summit. He says Trumbo has just killed Stuart. I come down to Potter's Point and I pass Solvay who says he's just left Tap in the brush. Tap goes after him but is slow. Tap's dead. Change the horses, Luke."

Wall set about unhitching; he led the four horses away toward the barn. Valencia stood in the doorway and watched Coleman and stepped aside to let him pass in. He crossed to the stairs and turned back to look at her; she was still watching him.

"Good-by, Tracy."

"So long," he said and went up the stairs. He stopped at the head of the stairs for a moment and looked back at Valencia, and then went down the short hall and knocked at the door of the front room. He heard Ann's voice and opened the door and stepped in. She stood in the middle of the room. He went toward her; he saw nothing on her face and he felt afraid.

"You heard that driver?"

"Yes."

"Nothing for me to say about your father. But for you it is hard."

"I could cry very easily. Not for him but for everything nice he threw away." Some thought and some feeling ran behind her gravity. "You are out of trouble. Are you going back to the Basin?"

"Ann," he said, "one thing never changes. What is the need of my tellin' you? You know what it is. It was in your eyes when I saw you here one night, in the barn; it has been there ever since. You could love a man, if you found the man. If I am that man, then I have found what I want."

"You might have said that last night. You knew it then."

"I had to know somethin' about myself. There has been no woman before you and none will come after. That is what I had to know."

"You are a faithful man, Tracy."

"Faithful?" he said, and there came into his glance a smile and a warmth. He took her and kissed her and his heavy whiskers stung her and the hardness of his arms hurt her; and she lay in his arms and answered his need with her own. She was smiling with him, and heavy with the goodness that filled her.